Ruth was about to demand the gentleman's name when the person in question strolled boldly into the room, taking her completely by surprise in much the same way as she had done to him the previous day.

'Why, Colonel Prentiss! This is an unexpected pleasure!'

'A pleasure, I sincerely hope, Miss Harrington. But not unexpected, I trust? Surely you didn't imagine I would permit you to embark on your quest unaccompanied? What a very poor opinion you must hold of me if you did!'

Although nothing could have been further from the truth, Ruth could scarce own as much without seeming forward, or causing a deal of embarrassment to herself. Moreover, she wasn't altogether sure she had understood him correctly. So she merely asked, 'Did I understand you to say that it is your intention to accompany me to London, sir?'

A love of history, coupled with little desire to return to clerical work after raising two sons, prompted **Anne Ashley** to attempt writing romantic fiction. When not working on a new story she can more often than not be found— weather permitting!—pottering in her cottage garden. Other interests include reading, and a real passion for live theatre. She also very much enjoys relaxing on warm summer afternoons with her husband, watching the Somerset team playing cricket.

Previous novels by the same author:

A NOBLE MAN*
LORD EXMOUTH'S INTENTIONS*
THE RELUCTANT MARCHIONESS
TAVERN WENCH
BELOVED VIRAGO
LORD HAWKRIDGE'S SECRET
BETRAYED AND BETROTHED
A LADY OF RARE QUALITY
LADY GWENDOLEN INVESTIGATES
THE TRANSFORMATION OF
   MISS ASHWORTH
MISS IN A MAN'S WORLD
THE VISCOUNT'S SCANDALOUS RETURN
HIS MAKESHIFT WIFE

*part of the Regency mini-series
The Steepwood Scandal

**Did you know that some of these novels
are also available as eBooks?
Visit www.millsandboon.co.uk**

AN IDEAL COMPANION

Anne Ashley

MILLS & BOON

First published in Great Britain 2014
by Mills & Boon, an imprint of Harlequin (UK) Limited,
Large Print edition 2014
Harlequin (UK) Limited, Eton House, 18-24 Paradise Road,
Richmond, Surrey TW9 1SR

© 2014 Anne Ashley

ISBN: 978-0-263-23991-1

Harlequin (UK) Limited's policy is to use papers that are natural,
renewable and recyclable products and made from wood grown in
sustainable forests. The logging and manufacturing processes conform
to the legal environmental regulations of the country of origin.

Printed and bound in Great Britain
by CPI Antony Rowe, Chippenham, Wiltshire

AN IDEAL COMPANION

Chapter One

'Oh, my dear girl, you look positively frozen! Do come over and join me by the hearth!'

After reducing the contents of the decanter containing a fine Madeira, Miss Ruth Harrington accepted the invitation. Although not inclined to imbibe so early in the day, after her walk into the market town in unusually inclement weather for the time of year, she felt the need of a little something to revive her, and so decided to join Lady Beatrice in her customary before-luncheon tipple.

As she took the chair on the opposite side of the hearth and began to sample the contents of her glass, Ruth couldn't help reflecting, yet again, on the unusual relationship she enjoyed with the middle-aged widow seated opposite.

Seeing them together, anyone might be forgiven for imagining they were in some way related, that she was perhaps a favoured niece, or possibly some distant, much younger cousin. No one would suppose for a moment that she had come to Dunsterford Hall, almost a decade before, to take up the position of humble paid companion. Yet, not once in all the years that she had done her utmost to fulfil the duties for which she had been engaged had she felt like a servant, or, indeed, ever been treated as such.

In truth, her employer behaved to a certain extent like a thoughtful godmother, treating the girl she had rescued from a decidedly uncertain future with a kind consideration that some might have supposed bordered on love. In more recent years, though, Ruth had come to believe Lady Beatrice incapable of feeling that most tender emotion, not even to the smallest degree. Yes, she could be considerate when she chose to a favoured few. But she could also be thoughtless and intractable, thinking only of herself and her own comfort.

But little wonder, Ruth continued to reflect, when one considered her unfortunate marriage to Lord Charles Lindley, a cruel and unfeeling tyrant by any standard. No doubt any capacity she might once have had to give and receive love had long since withered.

'You look very thoughtful, my dear,' Lady Beatrice remarked, after raising her eyes to discover her young companion staring pensively down into the fire. 'I was surprised to discover from Whitton, earlier, that you'd taken your customary walk this morning. It's so uncommonly cold for the start of October. More like midwinter, I should have said.'

Only the fiercest elements had ever dissuaded Ruth from getting away from the Hall for an hour or so. It wasn't that she disliked the place, even though it couldn't be denied that the grey-stone house distinctly lacked any architectural merit to speak of and, worse still, always appeared to be shrouded in an atmosphere of impending doom. At least that was the impression most visitors held when turning into the driveway and catching their first glimpse of the building, surrounded as it was by tall trees that blocked out much of the natural light.

Not that Dunsterford Hall received many visitors, of course, Ruth reminded herself, at least not during the years she had dwelt beneath its slate roof. Its situation on the edge of the moor made it somewhat isolated, of course. Moreover, Lady Beatrice didn't encourage visitors as a rule. Apart from the parson and the doctor, and two or three favoured middle-aged ladies living in the locale, very few people ever called at the house.

And that was precisely why she herself would brave all but the most inclement weather to make an almost daily visit to the small market town situated within a mile or so of the Hall. Apart from her employer, and the servants, of course, she would never see a soul, else!

'You're right. It is unseasonably cold,' Ruth agreed. 'Dan Smethers predicts snow before evening.'

Above the rim of her glass one of Lady Beatrice's brows rose in a decidedly haughty arch. 'And who, pray, is Master Smethers, may I ask?'

Ruth was unequal to suppressing a smile. Without doubt there was a streak of quaint snobbery running through her employer's character, which had a tendency to surface from time to time. 'He's the blacksmith's son, ma'am.'

Lady Beatrice shuddered. 'I do wish, my dear girl, you might lose this propensity of yours for fraternising with tradespersons. It simply isn't the done thing for a young lady of your standing to be seen hobnobbing with those from the lower orders. I shall take leave to inform you that it creates a decidedly odd impression.'

'Ma'am, with respect, I do not think myself above anyone who works hard for a living. In truth, I feel distinctly inferior,' Ruth responded candidly. 'I do little enough for what I receive from you, not to mention enjoying a great many of those privileges reserved for those females much better placed in society,' she added, raising her glass of Madeira as a prime example of precisely what she had meant.

'There is absolutely nothing of which you need feel ashamed about your lineage,' the widow countered. 'Might I remind you that your paternal grandfather was none other than General Sir Mortimer Harrington, and your mother was a Worthing. No hereditary titles, of course, on either side,' she added, the snobbery rearing its head once again. 'Both old and worthy families, none the less. It's a great pity your maternal grandfather had no head for business. He brought his branch of the Worthing family to the brink of ruin with his ill-judged investments. Still, you'd know all about that, I'm sure.'

Shaking her head, Lady Beatrice released her breath in a long sigh. 'During my childhood your mother was one of my dearest friends, simply a lovely girl in both looks and nature. Had she ever been privileged to enjoy a London Season she could have had her pick of all the eligible bachelors and might have achieved a truly splendid alliance.'

Ruth acknowledged the truth of what had been said with a nod of her head. Her mother had, indeed, been quite breathtakingly lovely in her youth; the likeness painted by her own father, which took pride of place in her bedchamber, was testament enough to that.

'I don't recall ever hearing Mama bemoaning the fact that she was denied a Season in town, ma'am. She told me she fell in love with my father on first setting eyes upon him, as he did with her. It was so tragic he died within a year of their marriage. She never so much as looked at another man.'

'She showed sense in that, at least!' Lady Beatrice returned tartly, thereby strengthening Ruth's belief that her employer had scant regard for the male sex as a whole. 'Oh, I don't mean to denigrate your father, my dear,' she continued, appearing slightly shamefaced. 'I hardly knew the man, after all. I met him only twice and must own he was the most handsome fellow I ever clapped eyes on. That said, like most members of his sex, he was utterly selfish and thoroughly feckless. Why, the instant he discovered your mother was with child, he upped and left to go off and enjoy the sights and pleasures of Italy.'

Again she gave vent to a deep sigh. 'I do not deny he was a gifted artist—very gifted, in my humble opinion. Had he lived he might well have been recognised as such, and possibly would have made a real name for himself. And, I suppose, it was a blessing that he did leave your dear mama behind whilst he went abroad to paint, otherwise she might have succumbed to the same contagion that sadly cut short his life. But that doesn't alter the fact that he left your mother virtually destitute. Why, even his own father disowned him—cut him off without so much as the proverbial penny, when he refused to engage in what the General considered some useful occupation.'

'True,' Ruth acknowledged. 'But Grandpapa did attempt to make amends after learning of his son's death, even though he had been very much against the marriage in the first place. It wasn't that he disliked Mama. It was simply that he didn't think his son was in a position to support a wife.'

'Well, he wasn't wrong in that! And, to be fair to the General, it was your mother who refused his help. Why, she even flatly refused to come here and live with me when I was eventually in a position to assist you both.'

'Too proud, I suppose,' Ruth suggested, whilst at the same time understanding her mother's reasons for not accepting charity and being determined to support herself and her daughter. 'Besides, as the years passed Mama became very content living at the rectory, caring for Mr Stephens. And he was very good to us in return, as indeed was Grandpapa Harrington. Remember, he did leave me something in his will.'

'A sum that can only be attained upon marriage, or reaching the age of thirty, by which time he possibly considered you would be unlikely ever to find yourself a husband.' Lady Beatrice showed her contempt by waving one hand in a disparaging gesture, before looking thoughtfully across the distance that separated them. 'Well, my dear, I have seen to it that you need never marry. I didn't intend telling you this, at least not for a while, but now the subject has arisen, I think you should know that during my most recent meeting with Pearce, my lawyer, I made fundamental adjustments to my will. Apart from bequests to servants, I named your good self my main beneficiary.'

Ruth was genuinely taken aback to learn this. 'Ma'am, please do not think me ungrateful,' she said, finding her voice at last, 'but you have family. What about your sisters and their children?'

Again Lady Beatrice raised her hand in a dismissive gesture. 'They are comfortably circumstanced. Both my sisters contracted suitable marriages, so their children's futures are assured. Which yours is not. Besides, I have come to think of you as an adopted daughter. The money you receive from me is not a salary, but an allowance. I have never really looked upon you as merely a paid companion.'

'No, I know you haven't.' Ruth could not find it within herself to be angry, or even remotely annoyed. How could she, given the lady's most unexpected generosity? None the less, she couldn't resist adding, 'I shall take leave to tell you, ma'am, that you resorted to very devious means to persuade me to take up residence with you in the first place.'

'Cleverly cunning, I should say,' Lady Beatrice countered, appearing very well pleased with herself. 'I feared you might have inherited your mother's stubborn spirit and would not have agreed to reside here without being gainfully employed. And it must be said,' she added, taking a moment to study her well-kept surroundings, 'the house runs wonderfully smoothly nowadays and has for some few years. I'm well aware the servants all look to you for their orders, for which I'm exceedingly grateful. I've always found trifling domestic concerns quite wearisome. Why, I do not even need to concern myself over menus when we entertain! You see to everything so beautifully.'

Hardly taxing as they entertained so infrequently! Ruth mused, hiding a rueful smile behind the rim of her glass, before the seldom-heard sound of the door knocker being rigorously applied succeeded in capturing her attention. She rose at once to her feet. 'Now, who can that be, I wonder? Do you wish to receive visitors, ma'am?'

'I have little doubt it is the doctor. I shall receive him in here.'

Ruth betrayed her concern in a frown. 'You're not feeling unwell again, I trust?'

The bejewelled hand raising the glass to thin lips checked just for an instant. 'I do not enjoy robust health, Ruth, and haven't for some little time. I made that clear to you from the first,' she at last responded, replacing her glass on the table by her chair. 'If my heart permits, of course, I shall be here to bear you company for a good many years to come. But, who can say? If you would kindly show the doctor in, my dear.'

Ruth obeyed the command, escorting Dr Maddox into the drawing room personally, before taking herself upstairs to her bedchamber, where she discovered her most staunch supporter and ally busily returning newly laundered garments to the wardrobe.

Agatha Whitton turned as she detected the click of the door, her expression revealing anything but the friendly approval she'd always shown to the orphaned girl who had taken up residence in the house nine long years before. 'It's high time, Miss Ruth, you had some new clothes. Why, you've never so much as purchased new ribbon to trim a bonnet since I don't know when!'

As this was no less than the truth, Ruth didn't attempt to argue the point. It wasn't that she couldn't afford material for new dresses, either. Yet, she had always felt that, although not strictly speaking a servant, she ought to dress in accordance with her position in the household. After what she had learned earlier, though…

'Yes, you're right, Aggie. We'll go into town this afternoon and visit the haberdashery, if Lady Bea doesn't object.'

'Ha! You'll be lucky, miss! Take a look out of the window!'

Although she had received prior warning, the sight of white flakes fluttering down did take her somewhat by surprise. 'Great heavens! I've never known it come this early, not in all the years I've resided here at the Hall.'

'It's unusual, true enough, but not unknown,' Agatha revealed. 'I remember snow in September when I was a girl.'

Ruth turned away from the window, which offered a commanding view of the moor. She loved to walk out there, admiring the changing seasonal colours across the glorious landscape. There was no denying, though, that it could turn into a bleak, inhospitable place with frightening speed, quite merciless to any unwary traveller.

'I must confess it's a beautiful spot, Aggie. But don't you ever yearn to get away to visit other places in the country?'

'Ah, bless you, miss!' The maid's expression once again betrayed the affection in which she held the younger woman. 'That shows the difference between the likes of you and me. It's in your blood, I suppose. But with me it's different. I never expected to travel anywhere. My family has lived and died here on the edge of the moor for generations past, and most of 'em never journeyed above five miles from the place. If it hadn't been for Mistress's London-born abigail being unable to settle, I'd never have been offered the position of personal maid. You know as well as me, Mistress never travels far herself nowadays. It doesn't worry me none being stuck here all year round. It's all I've ever known, after all. But it's different for you, miss,' she went on, her voice hardening.

'Selfish, I calls it, the way Mistress keeps you tied here, never seeing a soul, hardly. A pretty young woman like yourself ought to have been wedded long afore now.'

'Had Mama been alive I possibly would have been,' Ruth felt obliged to acknowledge, knowing her mother would have somehow ensured that her daughter enjoyed some form of social life—attending the odd party and local assembly once in a while. Although obliged to earn a living, her mother had always been well respected in the local community. 'Lady Bea, of course, holds rather different views on the subject.'

Ruth wasn't aware she had spoken her last thoughts aloud, until she raised her eyes to discover the uncompromising mask the loyal maid all too often wore when her capacity to understand and sympathise had deserted her entirely.

'Oh, come now, Aggie, be fair!' Ruth urged. 'We might not have been there to witness, first-hand, what occurred, but we both have learned enough to be certain Lady Bea's marriage was anything but blissful. It's hardly surprising she was soured by her experiences, and avoids the company of men whenever possible. The wonder of it all is that she allows even kindly Dr Maddox anywhere near her.'

'She does so because she likes to quack herself,' Aggie returned, her compassion evidently very much in abeyance still. 'Between you and me, miss, I think there's a lot less wrong with Mistress than she'd have us all believe!'

Even though she clearly felt more sympathy towards her employer, Ruth was obliged silently to own that Lady Beatrice did call on the services of the good doctor very frequently. Seldom a week went by without seeing his battered gig turning into the driveway. All the same, she refrained from further comment and turned her attention to what was happening beyond the window, hoping that the unseasonable light flurries might remain so and be of short duration.

By mid-afternoon those hopes had been well and truly dashed, as had any chance of visiting the market town again that day. In stark contrast to the light dusting she'd observed from her bedchamber window earlier, the covering of snow was now inches thick, with drifts in places very much deeper.

As she continued to stare beyond the circle of trees in the general direction of the driveway, she was surprised to detect signs of movement just beyond the gateway. A moment later two figures on horseback, their faces well muffled against the driving snow, were slowly approaching the house, their intention clear.

Harbouring strong misgivings, Ruth turned to stare across at the hearth, where her mistress once again sat comfortably ensconced in her favourite chair, contentedly sewing before the substantial fire. The unexpected visitors were clearly male, so what reception might they receive from someone who abhorred their sex? Then, of course, there was always the distinct possibility they wouldn't be received at all!

'My lady, I very much suspect two unfortunate travellers are about to seek refuge under your roof.'

'Really?' Lady Beatrice betrayed mild surprise, but thankfully no sign of annoyance. 'Do you happen to recognise who they are?'

'No, ma'am. Their faces are well covered. Both are leading a separate mount, possibly carrying

their belongings. Which suggests they might have
travelled some distance, does it not?'

Lady Beatrice seemed to debate within herself
for a second or two. 'I suppose it is our Christian
duty at least to offer sanctuary until the worst is
over,' she reluctantly acknowledged. 'I know I
may rely on you to deal with the matter. Do go
and see what assistance we can render, my dear.
As they are travelling on horseback, and not in
a private carriage, I suspect they are persons engaged in trade. I dare say our groom could accommodate them both in his room above the stables
if they are obliged to put up for the night.'

Ruth didn't delay in going out into the hall and
opened the front door in time to see the far taller
traveller dismount from a sturdy bay. As he entered the relative shelter of the stone porch he almost filled the aperture, his voluminous cloak
brushing against both sides of the arched entrance.
A commanding figure he undeniably was, yet
when he removed his hat and lowered his muffler,
there was nothing remotely intimidating in the set
of his features. Apart from the slightly disfigur-
ing scar that ran from the corner of his right eye,

almost reaching the base of his nose, his expression suggested strongly an agreeable disposition.

Above the strong, straight nose, a pair of searching blue eyes surveyed her with equal interest, while a well-shaped mouth was set in a pleasant smile that seemed in no way forced. 'Forgive the intrusion, ma'am. But could my man and I beg the shelter of an outbuilding for a period for ourselves and our horses?'

His pleasantly deep and cultured voice revealed in an instant that he was an educated man. This and the fact that his clothes were of the finest quality suggested he was definitely not from the lower orders. Or engaged in trade, come to that! Ruth wasn't at all sure this made her position in any way easier. Had he been a tradesperson she would have agreed to his request without hesitation.

She delayed for a moment only before inviting him to step into the hall, then turned to the young maid who had come scampering through from the kitchen, instructing her to direct the gentleman's servant round to the stables.

'Our groom will see to his needs, sir,' she assured him, while relieving him of hat and cloak, and placing them down on a chair to be taken through to the kitchen to dry.

'It's uncommon kind of you to take pity on a stranger.' He held out his hand. 'Hugo Prentiss, ma'am.'

Although his large hand completely enveloped her slender fingers, there was nothing clumsy or remotely aggressive in his touch. If anything, his clasp was reassuringly protective. 'Ruth Harrington, sir. And it is not I who you must thank. If you would care to follow me?'

She then led the way into the drawing room, experiencing a moment's disquiet before Lady Beatrice's initial frown of annoyance at the intrusion was replaced by one betraying deep thought the instant her uninvited guest, bowing with surprising grace for a tall gentleman, made his identity known to her.

'Would you be one of the Hampshire Prentisses, by any chance, sir?'

All at once there was a disarming glint in masculine eyes. 'Cannot deny it, ma'am. Devilish rogues to a man! My brothers and I scandalised the county with our exploits in our youth.'

No one could ever have credited Lady Beatrice

with having a sense of humour, but this sally managed to elicit a surprising chuckle. 'As to that, I couldn't say,' she responded while bestowing a rare smile of approval on her unexpected visitor. 'But I do recall your sister causing something of a stir during her come out.' The softer expression then vanished completely. 'It was the year my husband passed away, so I remember it…particularly well.'

Although Lady Beatrice's tone had lacked any suggestion of emotion, the gentleman might have been forgiven for supposing she looked upon that year with deep regret. Ruth knew rather better, of course. If her employer had any regrets at all it was that her husband had not obliged her by meeting his maker a good many years earlier! Not wishing the amiable Mr Prentiss to waste his breath in words of condolence that would not be appreciated, Ruth quickly intervened by inviting him to take a seat.

'Would I be correct in thinking you were a colonel in the army, sir?' Lady Beatrice remarked, after Ruth had furnished both her and her unexpected guest with a glass of wine.

'You would indeed, ma'am,' he answered, while

nodding approval after sampling the burgundy. 'Unfortunately, I found serving in peace time not at all to my taste, and am now retired.'

'So what brings you to this part of the world?' Lady Beatrice enquired, surprising Ruth somewhat by this show of apparent interest.

'I'm having some major alterations made to a country house I've recently acquired in Dorsetshire and considered it the ideal time to catch up with some old friends of mine residing near Lynmouth. I left at first light to commence my return journey, carrying with me a detailed map of how to cross the moor, thereby saving myself several hours' travelling time by not following the coastal route. Needless to say we began the journey in fine conditions, otherwise we wouldn't have attempted such a course, I assure you.'

'I'm afraid the weather can close in remarkably quickly on the moor. But you're welcome to stay here, Colonel, for as long as you need.' She then turned to Ruth, who had remained standing in the hope of receiving further instructions. 'Would you be kind enough to see that a room is made ready for our guest. The blue bedchamber should serve very well. Don't you agree?'

Honoured, indeed! Ruth mused, successfully suppressing a smile until she had stepped into the hall, where she discovered her confidante and trusted ally emerging from the kitchen area.

'You look well pleased about something. Happy to have company for a change, I suppose,' Agatha suggested.

'Partly, yes,' Ruth acknowledged. 'Colonel Prentiss is a very personable gentleman from what I have seen thus far. Not only that, he seems to have succeeded in charming Lady Bea, would you believe? She certainly knows something of his family background and has proposed we make our unexpected visitor comfortable in the blue bedchamber.'

Agatha's eyes widened. 'Well, well, well! He must be a rare specimen to have won himself the best guest bedchamber!'

'Or the mistress is just being immensely practical,' Ruth countered, striving to bring a little common sense into the conversation. 'Colonel Prentiss is a tall gentleman—over six feet, I should say. Lady Bea possibly thought the four-poster in the blue chamber would best accommodate him. See to it, would you, Aggie, whilst I attempt to negotiate the yard.' She frowned slightly. 'You see, there is something about this Colonel Prentiss that suggests to me he wouldn't enjoy the comfort of the house if he supposed for a moment his manservant was suffering privation. So, I'd best go and check how things fare in the stable block.'

Ruth had the forethought to don a serviceable pair of outdoor boots and a thick woollen cloak before braving the elements. On opening the door she was pleasantly surprised to discover the weather had noticeably improved since the arrival of their unexpected guests. The men Lady Beatrice employed to tend the garden, take care of the livestock and generally keep the place well maintained had already begun to clear away some of the snow. There was now a negotiable path across to the stables, where she found the Colonel's manservant hard at work attending to his master's horses. After introducing herself, she asked if he had everything he required.

'Benjamin Finn,' he responded, touching his forelock politely. 'Thank you for the kindness of asking, miss. I'll do very nicely out 'ere. The Colonel and I 'ave sought shelter in far worse places than stables, I can tell 'ee.'

'I'm sure you have,' Ruth responded, instantly judging that the man standing before her enjoyed a somewhat closer association with his master than that of a mere servant. He was possibly held in the same regard as she held Agatha Whitton— a confidante and friend. 'But I'm equally certain your master wouldn't be content to enjoy the comforts of the house, if you hadn't everything you require.'

Ben Finn's weatherbeaten countenance all at once betrayed dawning wonder and a strong suggestion of respect. 'Well, I'll be dam—! Starting to get 'is measure already, are you, miss? Well, I can't say as you're wrong. Salt of the earth is Colonel Prentiss… One of the best. Could trust 'im with your life. There's many that 'as, I can tell 'ee.'

Ruth began to feel distinctly uncomfortable with the turn the conversation had taken. It had never been her intention to discover personal details about the Colonel, most especially not by quizzing his servant. Worse still, she didn't wish to appear to be showing undue interest in the unexpected guest. He was nothing to her, after all. And was never likely to be, come to that. Besides which, he wasn't even handsome!

Feeling quite unequal to returning the servant's gaze, she dropped her eyes to two serviceable cloak bags. 'Would those contain your master's personal belongings?'

'Aye, miss. I'll take 'em over to the 'ouse when I've finished tending to the 'orses.'

'I'll save you the trouble, Ben, I can easily carry them back with me,' she countered, taking a firm grasp of both handles, thereby putting an end to the matter. 'The kitchen maid will be along presently with a steaming bowl of nourishing broth to warm you up, which ought to keep you going until supper time, when I dare say, should you wish, you'll be invited to eat with the servants in the house.'

The bags turned out to be much heavier than she might have supposed and she felt quite out of breath, not to mention unbecomingly flushed through the exertion. Consequently, she wasn't best pleased to see none other than the Colonel himself emerging from the drawing room the instant she had deposited her burdens down on a chair in the hall.

His slight frown betrayed his disapproval even before he said, 'Miss Harrington, I very much appreciate you offering sanctuary beneath this roof, but I certainly don't expect you to dance attendance upon me. I'm not too proud to carry my own belongings. I've been doing so for years.'

She felt like a schoolgirl being scolded for some slight misdeed. With the possible exception of Agatha Whitton, and very occasionally Lady Beatrice herself, no one had ever attempted to criticise her actions for a good many years, not since her mother died. Perversely, she felt more amused than chastened by the mild rebuke, but even so, she had no intention of tamely accepting the reprimand like some cowed child, most especially not from a virtual stranger.

Although he towered above her, her head barely reaching his shoulder, she faced him squarely, resolute, but singularly lacking the least feeling of hostility towards him.

'And I'm not too proud to offer assistance where I can, sir,' she countered, her voice pleasantly level, with perhaps just the faintest trace of resolve. 'I do not think you perfectly understand my position in this household.'

'Perhaps not,' he conceded. 'But from what I've

gleaned thus far, I'm fairly certain you're not employed as a servant.'

Which instantly begged the question of just
what he'd discovered about her during her short
absence from the drawing room. Lady Beatrice
wasn't given to gossiping as a rule. After all, she
was rarely in company often enough to enjoy the
pastime, Ruth mused. Yet, something must have
encouraged her to talk reasonably freely in front
of her unexpected guest. Evidently, the Colonel
possessed a manner that inspired confidence and
induced even the most reticent of souls to reveal
information they might ordinarily keep to themselves.

Ruth regarded him with dawning respect, re-
alising all at once that much, much more lurked
behind the air of affability and that polished easy
manner of his; that behind the amused glint she'd
already observed in those masculine eyes dwelt
a character that was possibly both strong-willed
and unerringly astute. Yet another salutary lesson,
she mused, never to make snap judgements about
people. And never to go by appearances alone!

Doing her level best to suppress a wry smile,
though not altogether successfully if the Colonel's

faintly suspicious frown was anything to go by, Ruth sensibly turned away, while she attempted to school her features, and her eyes fell on the travelling bags once again.

'Rest assured, Colonel, I have no intention of taking your belongings any further than this. And I shouldn't attempt to do so either, if I were you,' she advised. 'I doubt very much your bedchamber is ready for you quite yet.'

'In that case, Miss Harrington, would you be good enough to direct me to the stable block so that I might consult with my manservant?'

She did so with alacrity and Hugo was very soon making his way steadily across the cobbled yard to find his henchman engaging in a sportive exchange with a kitchen wench.

By clearing his throat noisily he made his approach known, which resulted in the, now, furiously blushing maidservant scurrying away and his own servant wearing the most wickedly self-satisfied grin. 'You're an incorrigible flirt, Finn! Kindly remember we're not in Spain now.'

'Wenches are the same the world over, sir. Thems that are willing, and thems that ain't.'

'Well, so long as you keep it to flirting, I'll

not object,' Hugo told him bluntly, while staring out with some dissatisfaction at the amount of snow still surrounding the unappealing greystone house. 'After all, we don't know how long we'll be obliged to kick our heels here. I shouldn't wish to outstay our welcome by causing trouble among the staff.'

'I shan't do that, Colonel, 'ave no fear,' Ben assured him, staring up at his master thoughtfully. 'You don't seem too 'appy to be putting up 'ere, sir. That scatty wench let fall that they don't get too many callers to the 'ouse as a rule.'

'I'd already come to that conclusion myself,' Hugo admitted. 'Seemingly, Lady Beatrice Lindley has turned into something of a recluse since her husband's death. Through choice, I strongly suspect.'

'Do you know 'er then, sir?'

'I knew of her, yes. The seventh Duke of Chard was her brother-in-law. Married the duke's young brother. Seem to recall he was something of a rum cove. I never did much socialising when I was in the capital. Not my scene at all, so it's unlikely our paths ever did cross. But she knows my sister.'

Ben cast an eye over the rear aspect of the house.

'Grim sort of a place. Not like your new 'ouse in Dorset, Colonel. I'd not take kindly to being stuck out 'ere all year round.'

'No, and neither should I,' Hugo wholeheartedly agreed. 'From what I've seen of the place thus far, it distinctly lacks the Manor's comfortably friendly atmosphere.'

'Maybe so. But that Miss 'Arrington be a friendly sort,' Ben ventured.

There was no response.

'Very pretty…nice smile,' he suggested, but again received no response. 'Lovely big blue eyes.'

'They're brown,' Hugo corrected, staring fixedly at the gateway entrance to the property.

'Ah, so you did notice 'er then!' Ben announced triumphantly. 'I were beginning to wonder.'

'Of course I noticed her. A very personable young woman. Unlike you, though, I've no intention of setting up a flirtation with her.

'Besides which, I doubt very much she'd appreciate such overtures, as it very much appears she's going to be kept busy,' he added, gesturing towards the gateway, where a group of decidedly bedraggled and weary travellers were making their way towards the house.

Chapter Two

Ruth took one final look at her overall appearance in the full-length mirror. Vanity had never been one of her besetting sins; at least she sincerely hoped it had not. Notwithstanding, she had always taken pride in her appearance, and, yes, attempted to make the best of what nature had seen fit to bestow upon her.

Unlike her mother who had been breathtakingly lovely in her youth, Ruth had never considered herself in any way out of the ordinary. Oh, she was well enough, but certainly no ravishing beauty, she decided, taking a moment to glance at the portrait that had always taken pride of place in the bedchamber, before returning her critical gaze to her own reflection.

The large brown eyes, which had been acclaimed by more than one discerning soul as very fine, and the mass of glossy chestnut locks had most definitely been inherited from her father's family. Only the fairness of her skin and a gently curving mouth, which was neither too wide nor too small, could have been said to have come from her mother. Thankfully, she was neither overly tall nor too short and, although slender, her figure was accounted very good indeed. Yet, her reflection on this occasion brought scant satisfaction.

Although Agatha—bless her!—had arrived unexpectedly and had gone to the trouble of arranging her chestnut hair in a more elaborate style, nothing could detract from the fact that her best gown was sadly outmoded now and, worse still, made her look faintly dowdy. She resembled nothing so much as a well-mannered governess who might be asked to join the family for a special occasion, but who knew well enough how to appear insignificant and fade into the background.

But did it really matter how she looked? Who was she attempting to impress, anyway? Certainly not the middle-aged doctor who had arrived at the door with a decidedly bedraggled spinster sister in tow; nor was it the sharp-featured little lawyer or the attractive widow who had been among the group who had pooled their resources in order to hire an innkeeper and his conveyance to take them on the first leg of their journey. And as for the young sprig who had been stupid enough to attempt tooling a light sporting carriage in a snowstorm…? That beggared belief! Ruth decided. The only other male guest, of course, was the Colonel.

She had to own that she had attained a deal of pleasure in that tall gentleman's company. Perhaps it was because he possessed many of those qualities she admired. For instance, he had gone out of his way to be as obliging as possible, suggesting that one of his fellow stranded travellers share the blue bedchamber with him, thereby revealing he was anything but a selfish person. He had also proved himself a leader—a gentleman born to command. Moreover, there was an imperturbable quality about him that seemed to permeate others. Amazingly, he had even managed to reconcile Lady Beatrice to housing all the hapless wayfarers with a good grace.

Yes, she did rather like that tall gentleman, she reiterated silently. Given the opportunity, she would have very much enjoyed becoming better acquainted with him. That pleasure, she very much suspected now, would be denied her. It had ceased snowing completely late in the afternoon. If a substantial thaw set in overnight— and there was no reason to suppose it would not now the wind had changed course and was coming from the more usual south-westerly direction—the Colonel would undoubtedly wish to be on his way at daybreak and she would be unlikely ever to see him again. Not only that, there had been nothing in his demeanour to suggest he was interested in her in the least. He had been polite and friendly, offering what assistance he could in an attempt to minimise the extra work the household staff would be obliged to undertake. But by no word, look or gesture had he conveyed his interest in her personally was anything other than lukewarm, a casual meeting of strangers, destined to be brief and so easily forgotten. And maybe it was destined to be that way, she told herself.

The sound of a tinkling bell from the adjoining room obliged her not to dwell on the unsatisfactory conclusion of her reverie, and she went into Lady Beatrice's bedchamber to discover that lady seated before her dressing-table mirror, rummaging through her jewellery box, whilst Agatha stood behind, adding the finishing touches to her mistress's *coiffure*.

Although having received no professional training, Agatha Whitton had proved herself to be a most competent lady's maid, with an innate gift for arranging hair. She had even succeeded in teasing Lady Beatrice's somewhat lacklustre, greying locks into an attractive style.

'You wanted me, my lady?' Ruth enquired, thereby drawing the widow's attention to her presence.

'Yes, my dear. Do come over and help me choose something to wear this evening. I cannot decide between my pearls and the amethyst set.' She then turned to the maid. 'You may go, Whitton, and attend me later. No doubt I shall be retiring at a more advanced hour than usual. But, in the circumstances, it cannot be helped. I can hardly seek my bed, and leave my guests to their own devices, without attempting to entertain them for at least part of the evening, forced upon me though they all were.'

Ruth acknowledged Agatha's knowing look with one of her own, before the maid whisked herself from the room. She knew precisely what her confidante-cum-friend had been attempting to convey—that she, too, suspected that, although sounding slightly disgruntled at the unforeseen invasion of her home, Lady Beatrice Lindley was secretly enjoying the prospect of presiding over a dinner table with more company than had been under her roof at any one time for many a long year.

'I think either would go well with the lavender-coloured gown you've chosen to wear, ma'am,' Ruth responded, after staring, with a touch of envy, at the dazzling array of sparkling gems contained in the wooden casket. She herself had had no such difficulty in choosing her own adornment. The simple gold locket, once belonging to her mother, was the only necklace she possessed.

World-weary grey eyes regarded her through the dressing-table mirror, staring in particular at the gold chain encircling a slender throat. 'Perhaps you would care to choose something from my box yourself, child?'

Although moved by the offer, Ruth didn't hesitate to decline. 'It's kind of you, my lady, but this old gown would do no justice to any fine gem. My mama's simple trinket is more in keeping. Besides...' she shrugged '...I've no desire to make an impression on anyone.'

The response appeared momentarily to please the widow, before one thin brow was raised in a distinctly questioning arch. 'Do I infer correctly from that that there are no handsome young blades among our unlooked-for company?'

Ruth slanted a mocking glance. 'Well, you met the Colonel yourself, ma'am. One would scarce describe him as an Adonis, though at the same time it would do him a grave injustice to call him unappealing. I believe you are acquainted with another of the wayfarers—Lady Fitznorton's great-nephew, Mr Tristram Boothroyd. Apparently he's been sent down from Oxford for committing some misdemeanour or other. In disgrace, he's doing penance by suffering several weeks enforced rustication with his great-aunt.'

Lady Beatrice appeared to consider for a moment. 'Yes, I do seem to recall meeting him once, some years ago. He was little more than a boy at the time.'

'He isn't so very old now, ma'am, not yet two-and-twenty, I shouldn't have thought. He seems pleasant enough and handsome in a boyish sort of way. But one might question his intelligence. Somewhat irresponsible to take out a curricle and pair at the height of a snowstorm, wouldn't you agree? If he had no regard for himself, he might at least have considered his horses.'

'Sadly, not all are blessed with your sound judgement and thoughtfulness, my dear Ruth, especially not many of the male sex,' Lady Beatrice responded in her usual disparaging way. 'I understood from Whitton there are two other gentlemen beneath my roof?'

'Yes, ma'am. A doctor by name of Dent, Samuel Dent, who is travelling with his sister. She, so I understand, keeps house for him in London. I placed him with the lawyer, who was travelling with them, in the green bedchamber. The other member of their party is a Mrs Julia Adams. She's a handsome, pleasant woman…around the same age as the Colonel, I should have supposed, or perhaps a little older. She also resides in London, I believe.'

Lady Beatrice's brows again rose in two fine arches this time. 'My, my! So many travelling in our part of the world at this time of year. How unusual!'

'Not so strange, ma'am.' Ruth countered. 'One hardly expects snow so early. Besides which, they all seemed to have legitimate reasons for visiting the area. Colonel Prentiss, as you know, had been staying with friends, and Mr Boothroyd with his great-aunt. With the exception of Mrs Adams, who happened to be staying with her sister, the others were all putting up at the same hostelry in Lynmouth. Although I believe I'm right in thinking that it was Mrs Adams who arranged for the landlord at the inn to take them all as far as our local town in his somewhat antiquated carriage. There they hoped to travel by stages to Bristol and then on to London on the Mail.'

'That's all very reasonable, but what brought them all to the West Country in the first place?'

'Business brought Mr Blunt, the lawyer, here,' Ruth enlightened her. 'And as for the other three— apparently they were visiting dying relatives. In the circumstances I considered it thoughtless to question them too closely, as I gained the distinct impression that both Mrs Adams and the Dents have both suffered recent bereavements.'

'How very singular! It would seem I'm about to preside not over dinner but a wake!'

Although Lady Beatrice could never have been accused of indulging in frivolity, or of possessing a sense of humour, come to that, on occasions she did seem to derive a degree of morbid delight in other people's misfortunes.

'We must hope it will not turn out to be so solemn an occasion as that, ma'am,' Ruth responded, returning the jewellery box to its rightful place at the bottom of the wardrobe. 'We must trust to the Colonel and young Mr Boothroyd to lighten the evening with some lively conversation.'

Once again Ruth found herself the recipient of a long and considering look before Lady Beatrice said, 'Young Tristram might, indeed, bring a degree of levity to my table, but I very much doubt we can trust Colonel Prentiss to do likewise, given his turn of mind.'

Ruth was slightly taken aback by this declaration. 'What makes you say so, ma'am? I found the Colonel's manner not only polished and gracious, but also friendly and sincere. A most amiable gentleman, I would have described him.'

'I agree, my dear. On the surface he seems so.' She returned Ruth's puzzled gaze with a steely look. 'But how many times must I caution you against judging by appearances alone, especially where members of the male sex are concerned? A great many vicious defects can lurk beneath the outward trappings of masculine charm.' All at once her mouth was twisted by a decidedly sinister curl. 'I discovered the truth of that for myself.'

Lady Beatrice then seemed to return from some dark, haunted place in the depths of her memory and even managed a semblance of a smile. 'Oh, I'm not suggesting for a moment that Colonel Prentiss is some unfeeling monster beneath that outward show of affability. I do not know him well enough to judge. That said, I suspect he keeps a deal of himself well hidden. He doesn't wear his heart on his sleeve, that's for sure. To look at him no one would suppose for a moment that he suffered a tragic bereavement during his early manhood, from which, I strongly suspect, he has never fully recovered.'

In the pit of her stomach Ruth experienced an unpleasant tightening of muscles and was somewhat surprised by it given that she was barely acquainted with the gentleman. 'Do—do you mean he lost his wife, that he's now a widower?'

'Oh, no. He's never married, unless he's done so

recently, and quite secretly, for I have never read of any such occurrence in the newspapers. And he certainly doesn't give the impression of being a married gentleman. But he was once, I believe, engaged to be married many years ago, before he embarked upon his career in the army.'

For some reason that she failed to comprehend Ruth digested what she had been told with a distinct lack of pleasure. It ought not to have mattered a whit to her if Colonel Prentiss, a virtual stranger, had once given his heart to another; it ought not, but oddly it did.

'He must have been very young at the time,' she commented, feeling some response was expected of her.

'He was,' Lady Beatrice concurred. 'And his affianced bride, a Miss Alicia Thorndyke was a truly lovely girl. Tall and willowy, I seem to remember,' she went on, after pausing to study Ruth's much shorter stature through the dressing-table mirror, 'highly suited to a gentleman of the Colonel's size. They were childhood sweethearts by all accounts and quite constant in their affection for each other. I have always been blessed with a surprisingly acute memory, and recall Miss

Thorndyke's one and only Season clearly. She attracted several eligible suitors, but remained true to Hugo Prentiss.'

'What happened to her, ma'am?' Ruth felt sufficiently interested to ask.

All at once the widow frowned. 'Do you know, I'm not altogether sure I ever learned precisely how she died. It goes without saying that Hugo Prentiss, of course, has never found anyone to replace her. Rather sad, I suppose, but I dare say after all these years he's now resigned to his bachelor state.'

The sound of the gong announcing dinner put an end to any further possible revelations, for which Ruth was not entirely sorry. Conscious that her reactions had been studied closely, she could only hope she had not appeared overtly interested in the Colonel's past life. After all, she ought not to have been so. The trouble was she knew the opposite was nearer the truth.

By the time all the stranded wayfarers had gathered in the hall, just prior to filing into the large dining room, Ruth, thankfully, had her oddly disturbing feelings well under control again. In a determined effort not to betray a preference for any one person's company, she made no attempt to engage the Colonel in conversation. In fact, she went out of her way to appear more interested in the other unexpected guests, ensuring they had everything they needed to make their stay as comfortable as possible. Even when she seated herself at the dining table, she made a point of conversing mainly with the gentlemen seated on either side of her, while at the same time attempting to draw the two female guests into the conversation whenever possible.

The same could not have been said for their hostess, who betrayed a marked partiality for the Colonel's company. It could not be denied, either, that she showed an interest in Lady Fitznorton's great-nephew, whom she actively encouraged to regale them with examples of his less-than-commendable exploits up at Oxford. She did condescend as the meal wore on to direct the odd remark in the middle-aged practitioner's direction. Sadly, his sister received no such minor attention and, save for staring at them both fixedly from time to time, Lady Beatrice virtually ignored completely the hard-working lawyer, who had been obliged to travel on business, and the pleasant woman who had come to the West Country in the hope of seeing her father before he died.

Lady Beatrice's snobbery was clearly rearing its ugly head yet again. Although she had raised no objection whatsoever to all those seeking shelter under her roof being offered a seat at her table, she could not have made it more plain that she considered most of the company quite unworthy of the philanthropy she had shown towards them.

Yes, anyone might have been forgiven for supposing that Lady Beatrice was already heartily regretting her charitable actions towards so many strangers. Yet, as she cast a long, considering look at the head of the table, Ruth was amazed to detect a glint of what looked suspiciously like suppressed excitement in those world-weary eyes, which suggested nothing could have been further from the truth; that their hostess was, in fact, enjoying herself hugely for some very private reason of her own.

All the same, it came as something of a surprise, even to Ruth, when Lady Beatrice suddenly turned to the tall gentleman seated on her left to ask in a raised voice that instantly captured everyone's attention, 'No doubt you have seen much death during your illustrious career, Colonel…a great number of murders committed.'

The large, yet shapely, hand reaching for the glass of wine checked for an instant. 'When engaged in battle, ma'am, a soldier doesn't consider he's committing murder when destroying the enemies of his country,' he responded solemnly, after fortifying himself from the glass.

'Naturally not. Even so, I'm sure numerous instances of murder have been committed among the ranks.' Lady Beatrice, it seemed, was determined to develop the theme. 'After all, where better to conceal a murder than on a battlefield already strewn with corpses?'

She then again favoured Dr Dent with her undivided attention. 'And gentlemen engaged in your profession are equally well placed to rid themselves of those they do not wish to exist, without causing undue suspicion, don't you agree?'

The doctor visibly bridled at this accusation. 'I shall take leave to inform you, ma'am, that those engaged in my profession do their utmost to preserve life, not terminate it!'

Lady Beatrice's mouth twisted unpleasantly.

'That may also be so,' she acknowledged. 'But I am equally certain that some have hastened the deaths of patients, whether by accident...or design. Like the Colonel, here, practitioners are equally well placed to commit the undetectable murder.

'And the most unlikely people do commit murder, you know,' she continued, after pausing to stare almost accusingly at each of her listeners in turn. 'Why, anyone sitting here this evening might be quite capable of committing such an act... And might well have done so.'

'By heaven!' Tristram Boothroyd exclaimed in a jocular fashion. 'Best lock the bedchamber door tonight. What say you, Colonel?'

Unperturbed, and even smiling faintly, Hugo reached for his wine again. 'No need to take such precautions, lad. I'm a light sleeper.'

Ruth, for one, didn't doubt it for a moment. For all his appearance of relaxed affability, not much, she suspected, ever escaped his notice. In fact, Colonel Prentiss was not an easy man to judge at all. As Lady Beatrice had intimated earlier, he gave little of himself away. For instance, it was impossible to assess just what was passing through his mind at the present time: whether he had taken Lady Beatrice's remarks seriously or not. As for herself she didn't know what to think. For all that her ladyship didn't entertain frequently, she lacked none of the social graces. None the less, murder hardly seemed an appropriate topic for dinnertime conversation!

'You quite unnerve me, ma'am,' Ruth said, in an attempt to lighten the mood. 'If what you say is true, it must be nigh impossible to judge who is capable of committing such a crime. I, for one, could not point an accusing finger at any person here present. So, unless one happens to see or hear someone plotting, or committing the act itself, how on earth could one recognise a person capable of committing murder?'

With the contours of her mouth set in a thin smile, Lady Beatrice appeared supremely satisfied. 'There you have it, my dear! Disregarding the obvious exceptions—those who are observed actively engaged in acts of violence—it is extremely difficult to judge who might be capable of committing such a heinous crime... It is not always so straightforward, either, to assimilate what one has witnessed.'

'Oh, come now, ma'am!' Mr Blunt, the stooping-shouldered little lawyer, countered staunchly, thereby proving at a stroke that his appearance of timidity might not have been an altogether accurate assessment of his character. 'Surely one must know whether one has witnessed murder or not?'

'Do I infer correctly from what you've said,' Hugo put in calmly, 'that you believe you did witness such an event yourself, ma'am?'

'Not the act itself, Colonel, no,' Lady Beatrice responded, after once again staring at each and every person present. 'I witnessed the prelude and the aftermath.'

'I trust you reported what you did see to the appropriate authorities?' the lawyer enquired, thereby breaking the silence which followed the startling disclosure.

Raising her chin, Lady Beatrice regarded him down the length of her aristocratic nose, much as she might have done a menial. 'But what did I witness, after all, my good man? Two persons, standing close to a cliff edge, who happened to be exchanging high words. I was not raised to indulge in vulgar curiosity, so did not linger to discover what the altercation between the two might possibly have been about. Besides which, I had concerns of my own to occupy me at the time.

'But when I had walked some distance,' she continued, after a moment's reflection, 'and chanced to turn, I noticed just one of those I had glimpsed earlier walking back in the direction of the coastal town. At the time it never occurred to me to wonder what had become of the other. It was only a month or so later, after reading a report in the newspaper of a body being discovered amongst some rocks on a certain stretch of coastline, that I began to wonder, and realised, too, that I had been acquainted with the dead man.'

Tristram Boothroyd's suggestion that it might have been an accident was instantly challenged by Hugo. 'Were that the case, lad, I would have expected the incident to have been reported by the dead person's companion. You heard Lady Beatrice say this other person was seen walking back in the direction of the town. Had it been an accident, surely there would have been some urgency in getting help?'

'That is precisely the conclusion I eventually drew, Colonel,' Lady Beatrice revealed. 'As I mentioned before, at the time, I did not recognise the

victim. It was a blustery day and he had the col-
lar of his cloak turned right up, besides wearing
a hat and having his back towards me. The other
person's face I did see quite clearly. Although this
other was a complete stranger…justice might still
be served… The passage of time is kinder to some
and they change very little. What is more, I never
forget a face, you see…not ever,' and so saying
she rose to her feet, inviting the ladies to join her
in the drawing room.

Ruth, for one, was more than happy to oblige.
Although capturing the gentlemen's interest, the
conversation over dinner hadn't been quite the
norm, and she was pleased to be granted the opportunity to discuss less controversial topics with
the ladies in the drawing room.

Lady Beatrice, as was her wont, positioned herself by the hearth and, once tea had been dispensed, appeared quite content with her own
company and private thoughts, leaving it to Ruth
to entertain the ladies as best she could. She began
by remarking on the lucky chance that so many
were putting up at that particular inn at Lynmouth
and were able to share the cost of the innkeeper's

services. 'Not so lucky with the weather, though, sadly.'

'No, indeed,' the attractive widow agreed. 'Although Dr Dent, his sister and I were all born in the area, we never met until recently. My father was the vicar of a small parish near the town. My sister and I lived quite a solitary existence— my sister still does, come to that. It wasn't until I was obliged to seek employment and attained a post as a governess that I began to experience life.' She smiled wistfully. 'I suppose I must have seemed very naïve in those days… In fact, I know I was—a little country mouse. Most unworldly!'

'Oh, I do not think anyone would call you that, Mrs Adams,' the doctor's sister countered. 'If I may say so, you seem a very capable woman, quite able to take care of yourself.'

The widow smiled wryly. 'I suppose marriage and widowhood have added greatly to my experiences,' she responded in a quiet, reflective way, 'not to mention raising a child on my own and owning and running a profitable little enterprise.'

Ruth was impressed. Very few women went into business. There just weren't the opportunities. Marriage was the only option for most of her sex,

or engaging in one of the so-called genteel pro-
fessions, such as a governess or paid companion.

'How do you support yourself, if you do not
mind my asking, Mrs Adams?' she enquired, after
glancing in the direction of the hearth to discover
Lady Beatrice, eyes closed, looking very comfortable in her chair. Ruth might have supposed
her to have fallen asleep had not the lady of the
house been smiling faintly, seemingly at some
private thought.

'Oh, nothing in any way spectacular. After my
husband died I eventually returned to London
to live in the house that had been my late husband's home since boyhood. I was obliged to live
quite frugally for a time, as my late husband had
invested most of his money—wisely, as things
turned out. After a few years I was able to buy a
much larger property and turned it into a board-
ing house. I have two permanent lodgers with me
now and others who stay on a regular basis during the Season. I'm hoping to persuade my sister
to come and reside with me. I've plenty of room
and I could do with the extra help. And, of course,
she'll not be able to remain at the vicarage now
that Papa has been taken from us.'

'My dear,' Lady Beatrice unexpectedly inter-jected into the proceedings, thereby corroborat-ing Ruth's suspicions that she had possibly been attending to everything that had been said, 'would you be good enough to arrange for a couple of tables to be set up before the gentlemen rejoin us. I'm sure they would enjoy a game or two of cards before finally retiring.'

Surprisingly enough Lady Beatrice's prediction turned out to be accurate. Despite the fact that all the guests, with the possible exception of young Tristram Boothroyd, had been up and about since first light, they all seemed more than happy to make up pairs for whist—even both female trav-ellers were content to join in proceedings.

It surprised Ruth not at all when Lady Beatrice commandeered Colonel Prentiss as her partner. After all, she had more in common with him than with any of the others. What did give her pause for thought was the invitation directly afterwards issued to the good doctor and his sister to sit at the hostess's table and make up the four, thereby obliging Ruth to take a seat at the other.

She wasn't offended by the deliberate exclusion.

She didn't even object to having Mr Boothroyd as her partner. Although he was not a particularly skilful player, he provided her and their opponents with some lively conversation. Even the strait-laced little lawyer uttered a wheezy chuckle a time or two. What had initially escaped her entirely, however, was the reason behind her deliberate exclusion. It wasn't until Colonel Prentiss suddenly suggested a change of partners and turned directly to Ruth, issuing the invitation to join him, that the truth suddenly dawned on her. Seemingly Lady Beatrice had no intention of allowing her companion to become better acquainted with at least one of the guests.

Lady Beatrice wasted no time rising to her feet. 'I'm afraid, Colonel, I must deny you that pleasure. Miss Harrington's presence is required elsewhere.' She then turned to the others, encompassing them all in a brief glance and the faintest of smiles. 'I shall bid you all goodnight…and better fortune for the morrow.'

She moved slowly across to the door, bidding Ruth accompany her as she did so. 'It is my custom to break my fast in bed,' she added, her back firmly turned towards the assembled company, 'so I doubt we shall meet again. Do feel free to ask my servants should you require anything further in the morning', and with that she left the room, without so much as a backward glance, and leaving Ruth to close the door behind them.

Candles a-plenty had been placed on the table in the hall, enough for everyone to see themselves safely to the upper floor. Lady Beatrice lit her own before speaking again. 'I feel unusually fatigued this evening, but suspect with all the disturbances of the day I shall find it difficult to sleep. Be kind enough to indulge me by making that beneficial nightcap I reserve for just such occasions as this. You do it so much better than anyone else. And send Whitton to me.'

There was sufficient light in the hall to guide Ruth safely through to the kitchen, where she discovered Agatha sitting alone by the range. 'Lady Bea's ready for you now, Aggie. Have all the other servants retired…? I cannot say I'm surprised,' she went on, after receiving a nod in response. 'Cook must be absolutely exhausted. And she'll need to be up bright and early tomorrow.'

'That she will,' Agatha agreed, rising wearily to her feet. 'The snow will mostly be gone by then.

At least the roads will be passable, so I expect they'll all be wanting to be on their way.'

'Yes, I suppose so,' Ruth agreed hollowly, contemplating with a distinct lack of enthusiasm taking leave of at least one of the unexpected company. 'I've enjoyed today. It has made such a pleasant change. You'd best go up, Aggie,' she added, while going about the kitchen collecting the various ingredients she required to make the requested nightcap. 'Don't worry about extinguishing the candles, I'll see to that.'

Soon after the maid had departed the door leading to the passageway swung open again, catching Ruth completely unawares. 'Why, Colonel, you did give me a fright!'

The warmth of his natural smile as he strolled into the room had an even more alarming effect on her pulse-rate than his unexpected appearance had done. 'I'm sorry if I startled you. I sometimes forget that certain ladies can find my size a trifle alarming.'

'I don't,' she assured him promptly, then could only be grateful for the dim light in the kitchen, which she hoped concealed the sudden heat in her cheeks from that all-too-perceptive blue-eyed gaze. What on earth had possessed her to say such a thing? Why, her response had been tantamount to flirting, for heaven's sake!

Thankful that the necessity of plunging a poker into red-hot embers enabled her to turn her back on him for a few moments, she attempted to regain at least a modicum of her natural poise. 'Have you everything you need, sir, or is there something I can get for you?'

'I thought to have a last word with my servant about our departure tomorrow, but I rather fancy I've left it too late. He'll have sought his bed long since.'

Receiving no response, Hugo watched her going about the task of making a hot toddy, her tread so light, as she moved about the kitchen, that she hardly made a sound on the stone floor. 'I also came to tell you that everyone has decided to retire and that I've extinguished the candles in the drawing room.'

Her expression revealed her gratitude, even before she voiced it. 'Why, that was considerate of you, sir. Thank you.'

'Not at all!' Hugo countered, dismissing the thanks with a wave of his hand. 'Very least I could do, Miss Harrington, most especially after…after unwittingly upsetting you earlier in the day.'

'Upsetting me…?' Ruth's puzzlement could not have been clearer. 'But you haven't upset me, sir. Whatever made you suppose you had?'

His gaze betrayed a suggestion of amusement. 'Because I could only suppose it was the mild scold I administered for carrying my bags that induced you to virtually ignore me for most of the evening.'

The bluntness of the response left Ruth almost reeling for a moment. That he'd been fully cognisant of her deliberate avoidance came as no very real surprise. After all, hadn't she already decided there was absolutely nothing wrong with the tall man's understanding? But now he was proving himself to be so confoundedly astute, too astute to be fobbed off with a deliberate lie! Yet, how on earth could she admit to having avoided him without offering some explanation for her actions. And the truth of the matter was she didn't know the reason for it herself!

Deciding the best form of defence was attack, she said, 'I shall take leave to inform you, sir, that it would take a deal more than a mild verbal chastisement from a virtual stranger to overset me. I'm not such a poor creature.'

Behind the amused glint lurked a growing respect. 'I'm pleased to hear it. Here, let me take that,' he added, reaching for the tray, after she had completed her task. He sniffed appreciatively. 'Smells delicious. I'm almost tempted to have one myself.'

'Have that one. I can easily make another,' she obligingly offered, but Hugo shook his head.

'No, it's time you were abed.' He slanted a look that was gently teasing and yet at the same time touchingly earnest. 'I should feel aggrieved if I'm obliged to set out on the morrow without being granted the opportunity to say a final farewell.'

Had he but realised it, Ruth herself was continuing to experience scant pleasure at the prospect and yet sensibly accepted there was precious little she could do to delay his departure. Moreover, although he lived in an adjoining county, he might just as well have resided on the other side of the world, so slim were their chances of ever meeting again, at least by accident.

Sensible though she might have been to have accepted this already, as she accompanied him up the staircase, she racked her brain for something, anything that might delay him seeking his bed immediately. Sadly, any hope of doing so was thwarted by surprisingly discovering Julia Adams lurking in the passageway at the top of the stairs.

She appeared momentarily startled by their appearance, then seemed to collect herself. 'Oh, I was hoping you hadn't retired, Miss Harrington. I was just attempting to locate your room. There must be a split in my valise. I'm afraid everything has become so very damp. Could you possibly oblige me by lending me a nightgown?'

'Of course,' Ruth responded before masterfully suppressing a resigned sigh as she turned to the Colonel. 'Just put the tray down on that table outside Lady Beatrice's room, sir, and I shall bid you goodnight.'

After taking a minute or so to locate the required garment, Ruth emerged from her bedchamber in the hope of seeing the Colonel still lingering there, only to discover Mrs Adams awaiting her.

After handing over the freshly laundered nightgown, Ruth didn't delay in whisking herself into Lady Beatrice's room to find the lady sitting up in bed, supported by a mound of pillows, and not, as expected, appearing in the least fatigued.

'Was that Colonel Prentiss I heard you conversing with a few moments ago?'

'Yes, and Mrs Adams. She wished to borrow a nightgown,' Ruth enlightened her before placing the small tray containing the nightcap within easy reach on the bedside table. 'If there's nothing else I can get for you, ma'am, I shall retire myself.'

She was subjected to a piercing stare. 'Yes, you do look tired. A pity, I was hoping to have a private talk with you. There was something I wished to explain,' Lady Beatrice revealed, then shrugged. 'No matter, it can wait until morning. Just lock my door before you leave. I don't feel safe with so many…strangers in the house. And you would do well to do likewise.'

Although she happily did as bidden, Ruth flatly refused to be influenced by such foolish flights of fancy. Who was likely to visit her at the dead of night, for heaven's sake? Certainly neither Dr Dent or Mr Blunt, she mused, changing into her nightwear. They were far too strait-laced for such capers; not to mention too sensible to risk their respective livelihoods if rumours of such scandalous goings-on were ever spread abroad. As for Tristram Boothroyd…? Well, he possibly viewed her in the light of some dull maiden aunt, she decided, somewhat dispirited at the thought. And as for the Colonel…?

For a few deliciously frivolous moments she allowed herself to ponder on just such an occurrence, and what her possible reaction might be, before common sense prevailed and she took herself roundly to task for even contemplating such a scandalous situation. The Colonel was a gentleman, kind and considerate, but certainly not interested in conducting a dalliance with her. He'd be the very last person to pay her a midnight visit!

Yet, later, something did succeed in rousing her briefly from slumber. The fire in the grate had long since ceased to send flickering darts of light about the bedchamber and the room was in total darkness, save for the suggestion of candlelight beneath the communicating door. There was not so much as a sound except that of her own breathing and there was no shadowy movement from any corner. Even so, Ruth couldn't shake off the eerie feeling that she wasn't alone, until sleep finally reclaimed her.

Chapter Three

The hand gently shaking her shoulder eventually succeeded in rousing Ruth from slumber; she opened her eyes to discover Agatha surprisingly standing by the bed. Only on those rare occasions when she had been unwell had she received the attentions of Lady Beatrice's personal maid, so quite naturally Ruth's first instinct was to suppose something must surely be wrong.

'The mistress's door to the passageway be locked,' Agatha reminded her. 'And as I was obliged to come this way I thought you might like to know some of the visitors be already enjoying breakfast.' All at once a glint of mischief was clearly discernible in the maid's dark eyes. 'And—er—Colonel Prentiss be among them.'

'And why, pray, should you suppose I might be interested to discover that?' Ruth responded, striving for that air of sheer indifference she was definitely not experiencing.

'Because, when I was about to go up to tend the mistress last night, he came out of the drawing room and asked particular-like if you were still about,' Agatha revealed, much to Ruth's surprise, though she was determined not to read too much into the startling disclosure. After all, hadn't he made a point of saying his original intention had been to have a last word with his servant?

Aware that she was being regarded closely, she again strived for that air of detachment. 'Colonel Prentiss is a well-mannered gentleman, Aggie. He sought me out to express his thanks, in person, for all the extra work he and his fellow travellers had obliged the servants to do. And so, too, did Mrs Adams, as it happens,' she added in the hope of vanquishing any foolish notions the maid might be harbouring with regard to her and the Colonel. Because after today, she silently reminded herself, echoing her thoughts of the night before, she would be unlikely ever to see him again.

'You'd best take that hot chocolate in to your mistress before it gets cold,' she advised in a valiant attempt to gain a respite from those all-too-perceptive dark eyes.

Mercifully, it worked. Ruth was then able to swing her feet to the floor in order to get herself ready for the day ahead. She had just reached the washstand when the sound of breaking china, accompanied by a half-stifled scream, reached her ears. Naturally curious, she slewed round to discover Agatha already standing in the communicating doorway, her face ashen.

'Oh, do come quick! It's the mistress...I can't wake her...I think she's...'

Ruth didn't wait for the explanation Agatha seemed unable to give. Sweeping up her dressing gown, she brushed past the maid to discover Lady Beatrice lying in bed, eyes closed, head lolling on one side. For all the world she appeared sound asleep, yet Ruth sensed something was very wrong. The curtains at the windows had already been thrown back and she could see quite clearly, even before she had reached the bedside, that the occupant looked deathly pale.

A shiver of revulsion trickled through her as she forced herself to reach for one of the hands lying limply on the bedcover. The flesh felt cold, lifeless, as she raised the wrist, then let it fall.

'Yes, I think she is…dead,' she managed to utter, before a kind of creeping numbness threatened to overcome her, and it was a moment or two before she was able to combat the shock sufficiently to concentrate her thoughts again. 'If Dr Dent is not among those at present in the breakfast parlour, then go to his room, and inform him his presence is required here urgently.'

Ruth watched Agatha unlock the bedchamber door and disappear into the passageway before returning to her own room in order to change out of her nightwear. Surprisingly, her nimble fingers, though shaking slightly, worked speedily, but even so, she wasn't granted the time to sweep her long tresses into the simple chignon she normally sported, before she surprisingly detected the sound of voices in the adjoining room.

Disregarding her irregular appearance, she returned to Dunsterford Hall's most impressive bedchamber to discover not only Dr Dent, but also Colonel Prentiss, standing by the bedside. The sight of that tall figure had a surprisingly beneficial effect, instantly soothing Ruth's troubled spirits. Yet, when he turned to look at her, there wasn't so much as a trace of that warmth she'd so often glimpsed in his eyes. He appeared unusually grave, his gaze for once frighteningly piercing, as though he were attempting to discover her innermost thought.

It took a stupendous effort, but somehow she succeeded in breaking the hold of that intense gaze and transferred her attention to the much-less-impressive figure who had already begun his examination. She waited a moment or two, then somehow managed to demand the answer to the question she very much feared she already knew only too well.

'Yes, of course she's dead,' the doctor responded almost testily, as though he felt his time had been wasted by being asked such an obvious thing. 'Been dead for several hours, I should say.' He turned at last to look at her. 'I recall she left the drawing room quite abruptly last night. Did she make mention of feeling unwell before finally retiring?'

'Quite the contrary,' Ruth assured him. 'I brought her the hot toddy she'd requested. She was sat up in bed, looking remarkably bright and cheerful in the circumstances.' Ruth frowned, as she recalled something else. 'In fact, she gave me the distinct impression there was something she wished to discuss with me. But I was feeling weary myself, so sought my own bed quickly. The only thing I can tell you, Dr Dent, is that Lady Beatrice did suffer indifferent health and had done so for some few years. Her own doctor visited frequently. In fact, almost weekly. She admitted to me herself, quite recently as it happens, that her heart was not strong.'

He nodded, as though he had expected something of the sort. 'It has been my experience that it is much the same with many of these highly strung middle-aged ladies, prone to nervous conditions and weaknesses. Died in her sleep, as most of us would choose to do, given the choice,' he continued, matter of factly, as he wandered back over to the door. 'There's nothing more I can do here, Miss Harrington, so I'll continue preparing for my departure. We all wish to be away as soon as may be. Apparently your groomsman is taking the cart into the local town this morning to pick up supplies, and my sister and I, together with our fellow travellers, have begged a ride. I trust you don't object?'

It was only then that Ruth appreciated fully for the very first time the significance of the sad and totally unforeseen event. It was only natural the good doctor would seek her approval. He must have supposed that she would automatically take command of the household until such time as Lady Beatrice's heir took overall control. He wasn't to know, of course, that she was Lady Beatrice's chief beneficiary and that Dunsterford Hall, together with the majority of Lady Beatrice's private wealth, would come to her.

For a moment or two she toyed with the idea of offering him the use of the comfortable, if somewhat antiquated, carriage that seldom left the shelter of the coach house, then thought better of it. For the time being she felt it might be wise to keep her good fortune to herself, at least from the vast majority.

'Of course I don't object,' she assured him. 'Sadly, the groom will have several extra errands to run in town this morning. I shall pen some necessary letters without delay so that I do not keep you kicking your heels here for longer than necessary.'

To her intense surprise she won a look of approval from the normally taciturn Dr Dent before he left the room. Unfortunately, she glimpsed no such expression on the Colonel's face as he continued to bend over the cold, lifeless figure between the sheets, seeming to examine far more thoroughly than the doctor had done.

As she approached the bed she saw him slip a hand into the pocket of his jacket, before he moved over to the cupboard by the bedside and picked up the vessel that had contained the hot toddy. He raised it to his nose and appeared, if anything, grimmer than before.

'Is something amiss, sir?'

When he turned to look directly at her again it was with the same fierce intensity, which made her feel hopelessly unprotected, as though she could conceal absolutely nothing from those eyes of his.

'Was Lady Beatrice in the habit of taking strong opiates?'

Hugo could see at a glance that his question had taken her somewhat by surprise. All the same, she

answered promptly enough. 'Her own doctor pre-
scribes a draught, I believe. She keeps it in the top
drawer, there by the bedside. But I cannot imagine she would have needed it last night, not after
the hot toddy I made her. It was very strong. Although she sometimes had trouble sleeping,' she
added after a moment's thought, 'so she might
have added a few drops.'

Hugo continued to study her as intently as before. 'And her sudden demise doesn't come as a
shock to you at all, Miss Harrington?'

'I wouldn't go as far as to say that, sir,' she confessed, appearing distinctly troubled herself now.
'Lady Beatrice admitted to me only quite recently
that her constitution had never been strong. She
frequently requested her own doctor to visit her
here. As I mentioned before, she suffered a weakness of the heart and felt she might go at any time.
Nevertheless I...'

'You're still shocked by the turn of events,' he
finished for her and she nodded. 'In that case,
Miss Harrington, it might be wise to permit Lady
Beatrice's own practitioner to examine her. After
all, he would have been more familiar with the
state of her health than anyone else.'

'Yes, yes of course,' she agreed after a moment, and then went directly over to the corner of the room to seat herself before the escritoire. 'I shall send a letter with the groom. I need also to make arrangements for the funeral and get in touch with Lady Beatrice's man of business.'

Hugo, who had been heading back across to the door, checked at this. 'Yes, of course, you must,' he agreed. 'It might also be wise, as the lady was a person of some standing in the locale, to apprise the local Justice of the Peace of the unforeseen turn of events.'

The hand moving smoothly back and forth across the page stilled and a pair of soft brown eyes, clear and questioning, not to mention surprisingly trusting, surveyed him again. 'If you consider that necessary, Colonel, then of course I shall.'

It was at that moment Hugo found to his surprise that he was not proof against that innocent, trusting look. 'If it will help, Miss Harrington, I can visit the worthy myself and apprise him of what has taken place here. He will perhaps require the names and directions of those strangers residing under this roof last night. I see no reason why they cannot leave, however.'

'Indeed, not, sir. After all, not one of you was ever really acquainted with Lady Beatrice, and none of you benefits by her death.' A sigh, clear and carrying, floated across to the door. 'Only I can be accused of being guilty of that, as will be revealed when Lady Beatrice's lawyer is consulted.'

She was silent for a moment, then seemed to shake herself out of a brown study, and even managed a semblance of a smile as she looked in his direction again. 'Thank you, Colonel. I have more than enough to concern me at the present time, without having to call on the Justice of the Peace. Sir Cedric Walsh lives in a large, stone-built house a mile or so out of town. I should be very grateful if you could visit him on my behalf and explain.'

Once again Hugo studied her for a long moment before finally leaving the room and returning downstairs to the breakfast parlour. One glance at the congealed mounds on the plate was sufficient to convince him that his breakfast was now cold, but he wasn't unduly troubled. His appetite had deserted him completely, so he merely reached for the coffeepot as he resumed his seat.

'Devilish thing to have happened,' Tristram Boothroyd announced, thereby breaking the subdued silence. 'Didn't know the lady very well, of course... Well, hardly at all, really. But it just don't seem right sitting here, eating her fare, while she's—'

'Oh, please don't, Mr Boothroyd!' Miss Dent implored. 'It's such a dreadful thing to have happened. And Lady Beatrice so kind to open her home to us all, too!'

Hugo refrained from remarking that, in his opinion, it was quite a different person altogether who was deserving of their gratitude. Instead, he drew their attention to the fact that, given the circumstances, they ought not to depart the house without at least leaving their directions in the event that contact with any one of them again became necessary.

'But why should it, sir?' The lawyer seemed all at once a little put out. 'Dr Dent has given us every reason to suppose Lady Lindley died of natural causes.'

'That might, indeed, be the case,' Hugo con-

ceded. 'None the less, given the—er—suddenness of the lady's demise, I think it might be
wise to obtain a second opinion and suggested to
Miss Harrington that she make contact with Lady
Beatrice's own practitioner without delay.'

'Oh, that poor girl!' Appearing genuinely dis-
tressed, Julia Adams rose from her chair. 'I feel
so wretchedly guilty having to leave her to deal
with all this by herself. I shall go to her now and
see if there's anything I can do before we depart.
And,' she added on reaching the door, 'I, for one,
have no objection to leaving a note with my direction, if it's of any help.'

Detecting the light knock on the bedchamber
door, Ruth paused to bid enter, before sealing the
missive she had been writing with a wafer. She
then turned to see Mrs Adams slip almost tentatively into the room.

By her own admission the widow was no
stranger to death. She had witnessed her father
being placed in the ground only a few short days
before and had buried a husband tragically not
many weeks after their marriage had taken place.
So it came as something of a surprise to see the

look of almost stunned disbelief flickering over the attractive widow's features, as though she was having the utmost difficulty in coming to terms with the sight that met her gaze.

A short time before Agatha had returned to the room and had respectfully drawn the sheet over Lady Beatrice's face. Which was perhaps just as well in the circumstances, Ruth decided, studying her visitor intently, for a female closer to swooning she had yet to see!

'Was there something you required of me, Mrs Adams, before your departure?'

The gently voiced enquiry, thankfully, seemed to break the trancelike state the widow had appeared to be under. She finally drew her eyes away from the direction of the bed only to place a hand momentarily across her forehead.

'Oh, what must you think of me, Miss Harrington? I'm not usually so easily overset.' She not only looked, but also sounded, now, deeply ashamed of herself. 'It must have been the shock that perturbed me so much. The last time I saw Lady Beatrice she was so very much alive and well. I would never have supposed such a thing could happen. And without any prior warning, too!'

'It was unexpected, certainly,' Ruth agreed, feeling slightly uncomfortable herself now. Whilst her mind had been fully occupied writing those various urgent letters, she'd hardly been conscious of Lady Beatrice's body lying just a few short feet away. She could appreciate Mrs Adams's reaction now. It did give one a distinctly uncomfortable feeling sharing a room with a corpse.

'Dr Dent informed us all that—that it was her heart,' the visitor revealed hesitantly.

Having been imbued by Colonel Prentiss's obvious scepticism, Ruth wasn't altogether sure herself now. 'Or some kind of seizure, we can only suppose. No doubt we shall learn more when her own practitioner conducts a second and more thorough examination.'

Having sealed the last of her letters, she rose to her feet. Time was pressing and she didn't wish to be the cause of delaying anyone's departure, though it had to be said this particular visitor seemed in no great hurry to leave. 'If there's nothing particular I can help you with, Mrs Adams, I must go down to the stables to ensure our groom has these before he sets forth.'

'Oh, Julia, please.' She spread her hands in a

helpless gesture. 'This has disturbed me more than I can say. And it is somewhat foolish of me as I never met Lady Lindley before yesterday! And unforgivable, too,' she added, 'because I came, specifically, to see if there's anything I can do to help. I feel so guilty leaving you with all this to deal with. You only have to say the word and I shall be more than happy to remain for a few days.'

Ruth felt moved by the offer, because she didn't doubt it had been sincerely meant. 'That is most kind of you, but I'm sure you must be longing to return to your daughter. Lady Beatrice was no blood kin of mine, though naturally I'm saddened by her unexpected demise. The servants here at the Hall are all very loyal and shall provide all the assistance I need, I feel sure.'

'Well, at least allow me to take those letters down to your groom. My bags are packed and I believe everyone is keen to leave as early as possible, so I'll take this opportunity to bid you farewell, Miss Harrington. I intend leaving my direction with Colonel Prentiss. London might seem a long way away. But should you feel the need to make contact with me in the future, I should be only too happy to assist in any way I can.'

Thankfully, this sentiment had eventually been echoed by everyone, and an hour later, armed with the necessary information he required, Hugo was making the final preparations for his own departure.

After securing his overnight bags to the packhorse himself, he was on the point of mounting his sturdy bay, when he caught sight of a slender figure emerging from the kitchen doorway.

Dressed respectfully now in sombre black and with her hair appropriately confined at the nape of her neck, she glided across the cobbled yard towards him. As she drew close he could see there was little colour in what otherwise would have been a flawless complexion. Thankfully, apart from the unusual pallor, there were no other telltale signs of grief. The large brown eyes were bright and free from any suggestion of redness, and the perfect contours of a lovely feminine mouth were even curled in a semblance of a smile.

'I'm glad I've managed to catch you, Colonel, before you leave,' she said, while handing him a folded sheet of paper. 'I've written down Sir Cedric Walsh's precise direction for you, though his house isn't at all difficult to locate. Simply stay on the main coastal road and you'll see it, standing by itself on a slight rise. Julia Adams informed me that you asked for everyone's direction,' she added, when he made no attempt to speak.

He continued not to do so for a further moment or two while he studied the openness of a sweet face; a face that for all the world betrayed only two things to his searching gaze—trust and honesty.

Not for the first time during his short stay did he experience something deep within him stir, only this time it seemed stronger, reminding him of a feeling he had not experienced in many a long year.

'Believe me when I tell you I'm more than willing to remain if you imagine I might be of service to you, Miss Harrington, should the local Justice of the Peace consider a further investigation into the death of Lady Beatrice is required.'

For a moment he thought he detected a glint of what might have been hopeful expectation in those lovely eyes, only for it to disappear a moment later as a distinctly wry smile this time touched her lips.

'That is kind of you, sir,' she uttered softly in a kind of resigned sigh. 'But you must be longing to return to the comfort of your own home...and family. Should Sir Cedric choose to bestir himself and look into the matter of Lady Beatrice's death, though I'm not altogether certain he will given his reputation for indolence, then I'm sure Dr Maddox and Lady Beatrice's lawyer will offer me all the assistance I require.' She held out her hand. 'Goodbye, sir. It has been a sincere pleasure making your acquaintance, and...and safe journey.'

Releasing the slender fingers the moment he felt the first sign of withdrawal, Hugo then watched her until she had disappeared into the house. Not once did she attempt to look back over her shoulder, but as he reached the front gate and chanced to glance back over his, he saw that slender form staring out at him from the drawing-room window.

Unwillingly urging his mount onwards, he headed down the lane that led to the market town. Throughout his adult life he had been a man given to decisive action, someone continually admired for his clarity of thought and discernment, yet he felt anything but resolute now. Torn between a strong sense of righteousness and a surprising feeling of protectiveness towards a female he scarcely knew his thoughts were in turmoil.

Plagued by such drastically contrasting feelings, he rode on in stony silence until he had reached a pair of impressive wrought-iron gates, flanked by two hideous gargoyles mounted on tall, brick pillars. Beyond stood an impressive stone-built mansion, undoubtedly the property of Sir Cedric Walsh. Hugo was only too aware of what he ought to do, what was demanded of any man of honour. Yet he made no attempt to gain access to the sweeping driveway. Instead, he took out several folded sheets of paper from his pocket and stared at them with an expression of intense loathing.

'Is something amiss, Colonel?' his manservant asked tentatively, wondering if he had done something to put his master into such an obviously unsociable mood. Raising a hand, he thoughtfully scratched the grizzled hair beneath the edge of his misshapen hat. 'Not done something wrong, 'ave I, sir?'

'No…but I'm about to do just that,' Hugo announced, before resolutely thrusting the several sheets of paper back into his pocket, and urging his mount to move off down the road once more. 'Come on, Ben. Let's away from here. How I wish I'd never come to this place... And the sooner I forget I ever did the better for my peace of mind!'

Ruth gazed out of the drawing-room window, experiencing a distinct feeling of pleasure at the clear signs of spring to be seen everywhere. Although not particularly hard, the winter had seemed interminably long, starting as it had on that never-to-be-forgotten day at the beginning of October. On numerous occasions in recent months she had recalled that particular day. Not only had it brought into her life, for a brief period, one of the most personable gentlemen she'd ever encountered, but it had also been, of course, the prelude to a drastic change in her lifestyle and personal circumstances.

As a mark of respect for her late benefactress, Ruth had continued to observe strict mourning for very many weeks, only recently donning more cheerful hues, though still avoiding anything that might be considered unbecomingly bright.

Although she had avoided socialising on a vast scale, she had been determined not to live like a virtual hermit, as the previous owner of Dunsterford Hall had done. She had made several new friends and acquaintances in recent months and, as a consequence, the house saw many more visitors crossing its portals. One frequent visitor was the late Lady Beatrice Lindley's man of business. He had worked tirelessly on Ruth's behalf, most especially during those early weeks, when Lady Beatrice's two sisters had attempted to contest the will. They had been unsuccessful and now Dunsterford Hall was legally hers to do with as she chose.

As yet she had made no firm plans about her future. The house was large, far too large for her needs, and although she had done her best to make the place more cheerful, by ordering the cutting down of several trees closest to the property, the building stubbornly clung to its gloomy atmosphere.

The door opening interrupted her musings and she turned to see Dr Maddox entering the room. It was the first time he had called at the house since the demise of its previous owner. Although she had attempted to call on his services in order to attain a second opinion about Lady Beatrice's death, Ruth had subsequently discovered he had departed for Bath early that very same morning to visit his ailing sister, leaving his young apothecary to deal with less urgent cases. He had remained away for almost six weeks, by which time Lady Beatrice had long since been occupying a spot in the local churchyard.

After supplying them both with a glass of Madeira, Ruth invited him to sit down. 'How is the patient, Doctor?'

'Your cook has sustained a severe sprain and she'll need to keep off that left ankle for a few days.' The middle-aged practitioner regarded her with a hint of approval. 'Clearly you take the well-being of your servants seriously, Miss Harrington. Too many in your position consider the attentions of the local farrier more than adequate for the lower orders. Yet, when it comes to their own mild disorders…well, it's quite a different matter.'

Ruth half-suspected him of alluding to the previous owner of Dunsterford Hall. Silently she was obliged to own that the doctor had spoken no less than the truth. Not once could she recall Lady

Beatrice requesting the practitioner's services for any one of the servants. All the same, she couldn't bring herself to say anything disloyal about her late benefactress. How could she? She owed that particular lady so much.

'It has been quite some little time since you were last under this roof, sir,' she reminded him. 'It was a great pity Lady Beatrice suffered such indifferent health for so many years. Had she not done so she might have got out and about a deal more, and not been a virtual recluse.'

'That was entirely of her own choosing,' Dr Maddox returned bluntly. 'There was never much wrong with her from what I ever discovered.'

It was a moment or two before Ruth was able to assimilate what the doctor had unwittingly revealed. 'But, surely she suffered from a weakness of the heart? I distinctly remember her telling me so.'

His bark of laughter was derisory. 'She might have told you so, m'dear. But you may take it from me she was as sound as a bell. Absolutely nothing wrong with her, save for an excess of nerves. Like most females of her station in life, she was wont to quack herself. She did have some trouble sleeping, I own. But in my opinion that was the sum of her ills. I had my young apothecary make up a draught containing a mild quantity of laudanum. That seemed to do the trick.'

This disclosure, unsurprisingly, disturbed Ruth. 'But—but if it wasn't her heart that killed her... then what could it have been?'

The doctor shrugged, appearing unconcerned. 'Who can say? I distinctly remember that lawyer fellow of hers telling me, not long after I'd returned from Bath, that a doctor had been staying here at the time and had examined her. Evidently he didn't consider there was anything suspicious about the death. And it must be said that fatal heart attacks and seizures can strike without any prior warning whatsoever.' He took a moment to lower the level in his glass. 'Had I not been visiting my sister at the time, I should have wished to examine Lady Beatrice myself. But there's no reason to suppose anything untoward occurred, now is there?'

Dr Maddox tossed the remaining contents of his glass down his throat, before taking the time to study the troubled expression clearly visible on Ruth's delicately featured face. Then he rose to his feet and laid a fatherly hand on one slender, drooping shoulder. 'Don't concern yourself, m'dear,' he advised. 'Unforeseen occurrences do happen. There's no reason why you should be troubled and not enjoy the good fortune that has come your way.'

Wasn't there a very good reason for her to be plagued, now, by doubts and guilt? Ruth asked herself later, as she entered the bedchamber that had taken her weeks to make her own. Although she'd had the large four-poster bed in which Lady Beatrice had died removed to another bedchamber and replaced by the very one she had slept in for years, the room remained much the same as it had in its former occupant's time.

Sighing, she seated herself at the escritoire in the corner of the room, and drew out a certain letter from one of the drawers, a letter she had received several months before, and one which she had retained as a keepsake.

My dear Miss Harrington, she read anew. *I trust this missive finds you well and more accustomed to your new position at Dunsterford Hall. I read Lady Beatrice's obituary in the newspaper and hoped you were not too burdened by reactions to her death from her relatives.*

Raising her eyes, Ruth stared blindly at a spot on the wall opposite, wondering whether he was perhaps acquainted with Lady Beatrice's two sisters and had suspected they might not take too kindly to the contents of their sister's will.

Ruth could well understand their disappointment and their resentment, too, come to that—that she, no blood relation, had inherited most everything their sister had owned. She could appreciate fully why they had attempted to contest the will. What she found hard to forgive was that neither sister had attended the funeral, nor had they sent a representative. Moreover, neither had had the common courtesy to respond to the letters she had written, informing them of their sister's demise.

Returning her attention to the missive in her hand, she read yet again the amusing account of the Colonel's return journey to Dorset, before fixing her eyes on his short closing paragraph.

The unfortunate event that took place during my brief stay at Dunsterford Hall in no way diminished the pleasure of having made your acquaintance and I sincerely hope that if, for any reason in the future, you should feel the need to consult someone over the tragedy that so unexpectedly occurred, you will not hesitate to make contact with me. In the meantime I remain, Your obedient servant...

Narrow eyed, Ruth once again studied the wall opposite. When first she had received the Colonel's letter she had not considered its contents in any way odd, merely the gracious offer of assistance from a kindly gentleman. But now she began to suspect there was more to those final few sentences than she had first supposed.

Rising to her feet, she went across to the bell pull and gave it a sharp tug, while at the same time casting her mind back over the sequence of events on that unforgettable October morning.

She recalled vividly her first glimpse of Lady Beatrice. Naturally, she had been shocked. But she hadn't been in any way suspicious, simply because she had believed Lady Beatrice had suffered from a weak heart. Dr Dent had accepted this explanation readily enough, though it had to be said his examination had been brief in the extreme. Colonel Prentiss, on the other hand, had spent far more time by the bedside, she reminded herself, seeing again that strange, almost accusing, expression on his face, as though he had been sceptical about something... But what? At the time she'd imagined he had suspected some kind of seizure. It had never occurred to her to suppose that he might have considered the death had not been due to natural causes. If this had been the case, what on earth had aroused the kindly Colonel's suspicions?

Ruth shook her head, completely baffled. But suspicious the Colonel most definitely had been; she felt certain of it now. After all, it was he who had suggested contacting the Justice of the Peace, and attaining a second doctor's opinion. It was just sheer ill luck that Dr Maddox had been away at the time. And as for not receiving a visit from the local Justice of the Peace...? In truth, given his reputation for indolence, she hadn't been unduly surprised. Maybe, though, she ought to have called upon him herself when she had failed to receive a visit from him.

Those uncomfortable feelings of guilt returned with a vengeance. At the very least she ought to have gone out of her way to ensure a second doctor examined Lady Beatrice. Knowing now what she did, she was forced to own she had been grossly at fault not to have done so. But at the time…

The door opening interrupted her guilt-ridden reverie, and she turned to see her maid entering the room. 'Ah! Aggie, come in and close the door. There's something I wish to discuss with you.'

Striving to gather her thoughts in some semblance of order, Ruth went over to the window. 'Dr Maddox gave me some very disturbing information this morning.'

'Oh, it isn't as bad as that, miss,' Agatha assured her. 'Cook will be up and about in a day or two and we can manage well enough in the meantime.'

'I wasn't referring to Cook's unfortunate accident, but to your late mistress's state of health during her final years. According to Dr Maddox there was nothing wrong with Lady Beatrice's heart.'

'Ha!' Agatha scoffed. 'Well, that comes as no surprise to me!' She tapped her temple significantly with one finger. 'All in the mind, it were. Wasn't I forever telling you so?'

'But don't you see, Aggie…if Lady Beatrice didn't die of a heart attack, then what did kill her?'

'Who's to say it wasn't her heart?' Agatha returned, betraying supreme unconcern. 'People do go off just like that—one minute fine, the next...'

'That's just what Dr Maddox said, but I'm not so sure now.' Ruth regarded the maid in frowning silence for a moment. 'You assisted with the laying out,' she reminded her. 'Did you notice anything suspicious on her body—any marks of any kind?'

Agatha shook her head. 'There was nothing, miss, not so much as a scratch on her anywhere, except... Now you come to mention it, I did notice a spot of dried blood round the nose, but that was nothing, surely?'

'I hope you're right,' Ruth responded, sounding anything but convinced.

'But what are you suggesting, miss? That Lady Bea was murdered?'

Agatha might make light of it, but Ruth wasn't amused, for the suggestion had struck a chord of memory, and all at once there was a clamorous warning bell chiming in her head.

'Good heavens! I'd forgotten all about that. I thought she was in jest,' Ruth announced, much to her maid's further puzzlement. 'I never for a moment supposed she might have been in earnest over dinner that night!

'I wonder...?'

Chapter Four

'All packed and ready to go, no doubt,' Hugo remarked as his good friend, dressed in fashionable travelling attire, came strolling into the library.

'Yes, just waiting for the last of my belongings to be taken out to the post-chaise.'

There was a hint of a sportive smile tugging at Hugo's lips. 'Must be somewhat demeaning for someone of your vaulted stature, my lord, to be obliged to travel by hired carriage, though travelling post-chaise is beyond the means of the majority of common mortals, it must be said. All the same, it's strongly rumoured the cattle and carriages kept at Kingsley Hall are second to none.'

A suggestion of a challenging gleam suddenly sprang into the Viscount's eyes. 'You might be an inch or two taller than me, Hugo, old friend, but I fancy I could still slip a flush hit beneath your guard. I might now be the head of the Kingsley family, but I hope I never become so high in the instep that I fail to enjoy the simple pleasures in life.'

'I'm sure you won't, Luke. Seriously, though, how are you coping with the extra responsibilities now you've succeeded to the title? You haven't raised the subject once since your arrival,' Hugo reminded him.

His lordship sighed. 'I shan't pretend that adjusting to life as a viscount has been easy. That is why I've very much enjoyed this short, relaxing stay with you. All in all, though, I'm content enough. Briony, bless her, took it all in her stride.' His lordship stared about him for a moment. 'I'm glad we spent the first years of our life together, here, in this house. It will always hold so many happy memories for me. After all, our two sons were born here.'

His lordship again took a moment to study the room. 'I must say I approve the changes you've made since purchasing the Manor. Adding this library wing was nothing short of inspirational, Hugo!'

'Well, I always said, after I'd retired from the

army, I would need to find a permanent place for all my books. I've been collecting them for years, remember. Not only that, adding the two wings has provided me with four extra bedchambers, not to mention another two new reception rooms. The extra space will prove most useful when I've a number of guests staying at any one time, most especially my sister's family.'

Viscount Kingsley surveyed his long-time friend with a trace of pathos in his expression now. Hugo had seemed to alter very little in appearance during the fifteen or so years they'd been acquainted. He was as tall and straight-limbed as he had been in his youth, and what changes had taken place all seemed to be for the better. The faint scar he had won during his last year in Spain and the lines now visible about his mouth and eyes only added more character to a wholly masculine face. The bushy side-whiskers he'd sported throughout the Peninsular Campaign were now gone, but the red-brown hair was as thick and shining with health as it had always been.

'Do you never envisage a future visitor to this house taking up permanent residence one day?'

Hugo didn't pretend to misunderstand and considered carefully before answering. 'There was a time, and not so very long ago as it happens, when I would have answered that question with an emphatic no. But now...well, now, I'm not so very certain.' He shrugged. 'I must be honest and admit, though, that at five-and-thirty I've become somewhat set in my ways and content with my own company for the most part.'

He took a moment to consider further before adding, 'Contrary to popular conceptions, I do not believe I've been guilty of actively seeking a replacement for Alicia, a replica, if you like. That said, I've always betrayed a distinct preference for statuesque, blue-eyed blondes. So I suppose I must hold up my hand and say, yes, I have been guilty of making comparisons down the years. Sadly, I've found most all unattached young women wanting...with perhaps just one exception. And that was because she resembled Alicia not at all, so there were no comparisons I could possibly have drawn.'

'Oh, so someone has at last succeeded in igniting a spark of warmth in that great barrel of a chest of yours after all this time,' his lordship ventured when Hugo all at once turned his head to stare silently out of the window.

'Perhaps,' he conceded, before his well-muscled shoulders shook in silent laughter. 'But maybe it was fortuitous we were destined to part company after the briefest of associations…as I might well have discovered, had I stayed, that she was, in all probability, a murderess.'

'You jest, of course!'

'Not at all,' Hugo assured him. 'She was undoubtedly the most likely suspect, and yet…'

'You find me positively agog with curiosity!' His lordship looked it, too, as he made himself comfortable in one of the chairs. 'What the devil have you been about since leaving the army?'

'Absolutely nothing at all!' Hugo assured him. 'Pure chance, old fellow, that I happened to be putting up overnight at a place where a decidedly suspicious death occurred.'

Seeing at a glance his guest wasn't going to be satisfied with that sketchy explanation, Hugo relented. 'Oh, very well, but without revealing any names, I'll tell you this much—last autumn, while work was being carried out here, I decided to get away for a few weeks. Having an army of workmen invading the house almost daily was tedious to say the least, so I accepted a long-standing invitation and went to stay with some friends of mine in north Devon. You know my partiality for travelling in the open. So when Finn and I set back to Dorset on horseback, I decided not to take the coast road, but to cross Exmoor, as I'd never seen that part of the country before. Without warning the weather set in. Before we knew it we'd been caught in an unseasonably early snowstorm and were forced eventually to seek shelter.'

Hugo paused briefly to shake his head, wondering at himself. 'You might have supposed by now I would have learned to trust my instincts. The moment I caught my first glimpse of that unprepossessing pile I felt a distinct shudder run through me. Being a practical sort of fellow, of course, I put it down to the biting wind.' He smiled ruefully. 'To be fair, though, inside the house was far more—how shall I phrase it?—pleasing on the eye—at least in one particular quarter it most definitely was.'

There was a return of that glimmer in Lord Kingsley's eyes. 'Handsome filly, was she?'

Smiling faintly at the clear memory, Hugo shook

his head again. 'No, pretty—sweet face, lovely large, trusting brown eyes.' All at once he was no longer smiling. 'That's what made it all so damnably hard to comprehend, Luke! She appeared so honest…and so astonished by the demise of the widow who owned the property. Yet, apart from myself, and a young cub who'd got himself stranded through his own crass stupidity, the other sheltering travellers were all complete strangers to the area and, more importantly, unacquainted with the owner of the house.'

'And the young woman…? Was she related to the owner?' his lordship asked, after digesting what he had been told, and received an immediate shake of the head in response.

'No, she was… Well, it's difficult to explain exactly her position in that household. She wasn't a servant, nor, strictly speaking, a companion either, I wouldn't have said. All the same, she seemed at the owner's beck and call much of the time. She certainly ran the household. That said, the widow must have had some regard for her.' Hugo frowned as a further damning recollection returned. 'It transpired the young woman was destined to inherit the bulk of the widow's estate.'

'A strong motive for murder,' his lordship suggested, and Hugo acknowledged the truth of it.

'Even so, I just couldn't bring myself to believe her capable of such an act.'

'But, then, you hardly knew her well enough to be sure what she was capable of doing,' his lordship pointed out and again Hugo was obliged to agree.

He released his breath in a sigh, wondering at himself. 'For a man who has always prided himself on doing the right thing, even if it meant going against inclination, for once I behaved quite out of character.'

'In what way, old friend?' his lordship prompted, once again breaking the silence that followed the startling admission.

'I felt suspicious enough about the death to believe the local Justice of the Peace ought to be informed. Although the widow's demise was put down to natural causes by the doctor who happened to be taking shelter in the house at the time, I suggested a second practitioner's opinion ought to be sought. Whether this ever happened I have no way of knowing. Somehow I doubt it. And as for the local Justice of the Peace...' Hugo smiled ruefully. 'When it came to it, I simply couldn't bring myself to make contact with the fellow, simply because I knew I would be placing that young woman, guilty or not, in the most precarious position. And I just couldn't do that to her, especially as...'

'Although perhaps not already struck by Cupid's dart, you were very much attracted to her and simply couldn't bring yourself to believe that such a damnably lovely girl might be guilty of such a despicable act,' his friend finished perceptively.

'That's it exactly!' Hugo acknowledged. 'I'm still not entirely sure in my own mind one way or the other... And I doubt now I shall ever know the truth for certain. Soon after my return here, I did write a letter, offering my services should she ever feel the need of help. Her reply, courteous and brief, gave me no reason to suppose she'd suffered any difficulties with regard to the sudden demise of the widow. Which strongly suggested that no second doctor's opinion had ever been sought. And just why was that? I asked myself. Was it a genuine oversight on her part...or was she merely ensuring that no further inquiries into the widow's death would ever take place?'

'A mystery, as you say, old friend,' his lord-ship responded, after the housekeeper had entered briefly in order to inform him that all his luggage had now been safely stowed away on the carriage. He then rose to his feet, smiling faintly. 'For my part I'm deriving a deal of satisfaction from the knowledge that you're as human as the rest of us poor males and, as such, susceptible to a pretty face. You're not the first to fall victim to a clever female's cunning and I doubt you'll be the last. My advice is best forget the whole business. After all, there's not much you can do to unearth the truth after all this time.'

Half an hour later, still ensconced in his library, Hugo was attempting to deal with several urgent matters requiring his attention when he detected the sound of a carriage pulling up before the front entrance. Although it was not unusual for him to receive visitors so late in the morning, he'd given instructions that he didn't wish to be disturbed. So when his housekeeper appeared a few minutes later, he felt the conscientious servant would never have dreamt of ignoring his expressed wishes un-less there was a very sound reason for doing so.

'There's a young lady wishful to see you, sir.'

As this hardly seemed an adequate enough reason for the interruption, Hugo experienced a stab of irritation. 'Is there, indeed!' He scowled as he placed his pen in the standish and gave the servant his full attention. 'And does this young woman have a name, Mrs Bailey?'

'Indeed, she does,' a pleasingly light and refined voice announced, before a trim figure, clad in a fetching pearl-grey carriage dress and matching pelisse swept gracefully past the housekeeper. 'But was reluctant to make it known for fear of being thought to importune a gentleman on so short an acquaintance.'

Although he automatically rose to his feet in order to clasp the gloved hand held out to him, it was several moments before Hugo fully appreciated that the unexpected visitor was none other than the female who'd returned to his thoughts all too often for his peace of mind during the past months.

'Good gad!' he muttered, staring in dawning wonder at the pretty face framed in a bonnet fetchingly trimmed with pink ribbon. 'Why, Miss Harrington! What an…unexpected pleasure!'

The sportive gleam that instantly sprang into her brown eyes was just as he remembered. 'That is kind of you to say so, sir. But I suspect you're more stunned than anything else. I'm much changed, I know, since last we met. That is the result of now having more than enough money for my needs, not to mention receiving the attentions of my late employer's personal maid.'

Hugo found his smile coming effortlessly to his lips. He'd forgotten how unashamedly honest she could be. Truthfulness seemed to shine out of those unforgettable brown eyes of hers like a beacon!

Suddenly conscious that he was in the gravest danger of devouring her every wholly feminine feature with his gaze, he turned to his house-keeper. 'Be good enough to pour wine, Mrs Bailey. I'm sure Miss Harrington will join me in a glass of Madeira.'

'I should be delighted, sir,' she assured him, while accepting his offer of a seat by the fire. 'Although Somerset is a neighbouring county, I feel as if I've been travelling for weeks. The post roads are well enough, but some of the others are little more than dirt tracks.'

'And that is why I frequently travel on horseback, most especially round these parts,' he responded, before a disturbing thought occurred to him. 'I trust you're not travelling alone, Miss Harrington?'

He was obliged to wait for the assurance he sought until after his guest had been handed a filled glass. 'And I should be very much obliged to you, sir,' she added, 'if you could ensure my maid receives refreshment. Poor Aggie has even less experience of travelling about the land than I do.'

'See to it, Mrs Bailey,' he said, then waited for the housekeeper to leave them alone before favouring his visitor with his undivided attention again.

Although his fiercest critics would scarce describe him as a libertine, he had enjoyed a number of pleasurable relationships with females throughout his life thus far. Some women he had admired for their intellect and some for their beauty, grace and charm, while with others he had enjoyed more intimate relations. Not for a very long time, though, could he recall a female who had left him with such a lasting impression on so brief an acquaintance as the young woman now sharing his hearth had done. She was certainly not the loveliest creature he had ever clapped eyes on and, although not slow-witted, he would hardly describe her as a bluestocking. Yet there was something distinctly enchanting about her, unforgettable; something that had instantly roused his interest, and had aroused, too, his every masculine protective instinct.

Disturbingly, he experienced those same reactions stirring within him anew and sustained some difficulty before he could concentrate his thoughts. 'So, what brings you to my part of the world, Miss Harrington?'

Ruth didn't attempt to hide her surprise. 'Why, I came for the sole purpose of seeking you out, sir,' she admitted and then saw his hand check, before finally raising the glass to his lips. The reason for the reaction seemed obvious, so she didn't hesitate to reassure him. 'Believe me, Colonel, I have no intention of attempting to put you, or myself for that matter, in a compromising situation by remaining here longer than necessary, so I shall come straight to the point of my visit. Were you completely satisfied that Lady Beatrice Lindley's demise was due to natural causes?'

Although a gentleman of no little experience, Hugo was somewhat taken aback by the bold directness of the question. Yet, he ought not to have been, he told himself. Her frankness was something he'd admired from the first—had made him doubt her guilt when everything else only served to confirm it. That same doubt at her guilt stirred again and rapidly welled.

'Since you've taken the trouble to travel all this way to hear the answer from my own lips, I'll tell you plainly…no, I was not.'

Despite the seriousness of the response, and its worrying implications, Ruth couldn't help experiencing a degree of satisfaction knowing she had been right. 'I knew it! Knew I couldn't have misjudged you so!' The spark of gratification quickly faded from her eyes. 'I could have wished I had realised at the time, but I'm ashamed to say I did not.'

After releasing her breath in an audible sigh, she added, 'My only excuse for not suspecting anything untoward was, I suppose, the suddenness of the death and the fact that Lady Beatrice had told me herself that she suffered from a weak heart, a condition that might shorten her existence at any time… And I had no reason, then, to disbelieve it.'

'But you do now,' Hugo suggested, after studying her intently over the rim of his glass.

Ruth nodded, returning his gaze unblinkingly. 'I recall quite clearly you advising me to seek a second opinion. Sadly, it will be to my everlasting regret…my everlasting shame, that I didn't act on that good advice. You see, I discovered Lady Beatrice's own practitioner, Dr Maddox, had left the county early that very same morning to visit a sick relative and was not expected to return before the end of the month. But that's no excuse,' she continued in a voice clearly edged now with bitter regret. 'I should have called on the services of another practitioner…but I didn't. Mr Pearce, Lady Beatrice's man of business, betrayed no surprise either at her death. In fact, no one betrayed the least surprise—not the vicar, nor any of her acquaintance. The doctor was a frequent visitor to Dunsterford Hall, perhaps the most frequent, and I can only imagine, like me, everyone assumed she suffered indifferent health.'

Again Ruth shook her head as the memories

came flooding back to taunt her. 'I had so much to organise at the time…so many people to contact… And, I suppose, when I didn't receive a visit from Sir Cedric Walsh, I automatically assumed he wasn't sufficiently concerned, or wasn't prepared to bestir himse—'

'Ah!' Hugo interjected, instantly claiming her full attention. He had the grace to look a little shamefaced. Although he might have acted from the purest of motives, there was no denying the fact that he, too, was guilty of concealing a possible crime. 'The reason you received no visit from Sir Cedric is because I failed to enlighten him as to what had taken place at Dunsterford Hall.'

Ruth was puzzled and it clearly showed. 'But why, sir? Something made you suspicious at the time, I know it did. I myself only began to feel uneasy quite recently.'

'May I be permitted to know why?' Hugo enquired, thereby neatly avoiding answering her own query.

Ruth shrugged. 'Oh, there's no mystery there. It was simply because I had reason to call on Dr Maddox's services. It was the first time he'd set foot in the house since his return from Bath the previous autumn. Naturally, we fell into talking and he mentioned he'd been surprised to discover Lady Beatrice had died whilst he'd been away. He went on to reveal that, for her age, she was in reasonable health and that there was nothing wrong with her heart. He did add that seizures and heart problems can strike at any time and without any prior warning. All the same, he had succeeded in placing a seed of doubt in my mind. If she hadn't died of a heart attack…then, what had killed her?'

Raising her eyes from their contemplation of the liquid in her glass, Ruth looked directly across at him once more. 'Then I remembered you, sir… the expression on your face when you had stood by the bedside, and I knew—knew you hadn't been wholly satisfied with Dr Dent's judgement.'

Hugo's smile was distinctly crooked. 'You were there at the time, Miss Harrington,' he reminded her. 'The examination was brief in the extreme. Why, the incompetent fellow hardly looked at her. He was more interested in getting away from the house at the earliest opportunity.'

'You thought him incompetent?'

'I certainly wouldn't entertain him as my own practitioner,' Hugo responded bluntly. 'For one thing, he quite failed to notice there were traces of dried blood round the nose.' He observed her surprised start. 'Would I be correct in thinking you noted that, too?'

'No, I didn't. But Aggie did. She mentioned it when I questioned her quite recently. She helped with the laying out, you see. She also confirmed there were no marks on Lady Bea's body at all, not so much as a scratch.'

Hugo nodded. 'Well, she certainly hadn't been strangled. There was no sign of bruising round the throat. There was, however, a deal of laudanum in that hot toddy you made her.'

Ruth frowned. 'I recall you saying something of the sort at the time. And it is true Dr Maddox prescribed a draught containing laudanum. I asked him particularly about that. But he assured me the dose wasn't strong, just sufficient to help her sleep when the need arose.'

'But what had been contained in that nightcap had been strong,' he assured her. 'It was quite discernible in the dregs that remained.'

Perplexed, Ruth frowned. 'Why should she have taken laudanum? That toddy would have been sufficient to send her to sleep. You saw me make it yourself,' she reminded him. 'I wasn't exactly sparing with the brandy, which she always preferred in preference to rum.

'You assisted me by carrying it upstairs,' she further recalled, when he continued to stare at her searchingly, much as he had done at the time of the death. 'She must have added the laudanum herself, except...'

'Except what, Miss Harrington?' he prompted, when she turned her head to stare resolutely down at the hearth in silence.

'Except, if she did add anything to that nightcap herself, I cannot imagine she added too much by accident. She did suffer periods of disturbed sleep, haunted by recurring nightmares. At such times she would make use of the draught kept in her bedside cupboard. But she knew precisely how many drops to add to her nightcap.'

The deepening frown betrayed her growing concern. 'Something else about that night has been troubling me, too, of late. Lady Bea wasn't prone to vastly contrasting mood swings, at least not during the decade I lived under her roof. To a certain extent she was an indolent creature, fiercely protective of her peace and quiet, rarely bestirring herself unless necessary. I never knew her to betray the least enthusiasm for anything. Yet, that night she was strangely animated, like an excited child who had been presented with a new toy. I recall I put the change I perceived in her down to presiding over a table with more guests than had been under her roof in many years. But in recent days I have thought long and hard about that particular evening.'

At last Ruth raised her eyes from the contemplation of the logs in the hearth and looked directly at the gentleman with whom she had always felt so surprisingly at ease. 'Do you recall what she spoke about that night, sir? I thought at the time it was a most inappropriate topic of conversation for the dining table.'

'I'm afraid, Miss Harrington, you must put my appalling recollection down to my declining years,' Hugo responded, after having cast his mind back unproductively. 'I must beg you to refresh my memory.'

She obliged without hesitation. 'Lady Beatrice raised the alarming subject of committing murder, remarking, among other things, how easy it would be for someone to conceal such a crime.'

'Ah!' Hugo raised one finger triumphantly. 'It's such a relief to know I'm not quite yet in my dotage. Yes, I do now recall. She remarked about concealing a corpse on a battlefield, if I remember correctly.' His gaze once again grew searching. 'And you now suppose that that conversation ultimately resulted in the lady's demise?'

'Well, don't you, if she didn't die of natural causes?' she returned in a flash. 'Remember, she declared that any one of us seated round that table could be a murderer and that no one else would know—that it was impossible just by looking at someone to know whether he or she was capable of committing such an act.'

Tossing what was left in his glass down his throat, Hugo went across to his desk and began to rummage through a particular drawer for a certain something he'd placed there for safekeeping several months before. It was a moment or two before he was successful. He then rejoined his guest by the hearth, placing the fruits of his search in the palm of her hand.

'A piece of lace...?' Ruth continued to study the remnant in frowning silence, all the time realising that it must be in some way significant. 'Where did it come from, sir?'

'I extracted it from Lady Beatrice's clenched left hand,' he finally revealed, after resuming his seat. 'And it was torn from the left side of the pillow directly beneath her head. I should add that I discovered all this whilst you and the doctor were speaking over by the door.'

For safety's sake, Ruth placed her glass on the table by her chair. Although it would have been true to say that, increasingly, she had begun to suspect her benefactress's death had not been all that it had seemed, to have her worst fears confirmed did come as something of a shock.

Still not quite wanting to believe it, she forced herself to say what she felt sure her companion had suspected all along. 'You believe then that, some time during that night, someone entered Lady Beatrice's room, and smothered her with her own pillow…after first having attempted to drug her with laudanum so that she would put up no struggle, or cry out?'

Without waiting for the answer, Ruth went over to one of the tall sash windows and stared out on to a sizeable patch of well-maintained garden that was showing even more evidence of spring than her own back at Dunsterford Hall.

'Had she been strangled then I would instinctively have suspected a man. But a woman could quite easily smother someone, most especially if the victim had been drugged first. Did you ever suspect anyone in particular?'

When again he didn't attempt to respond, she turned to look directly at him. Although he continued to stare steadfastly down at the carpet near his feet, his seeming reluctance to meet her gaze she felt was answer enough.

The wry smile that touched her lips was in no way forced, simply because she couldn't find it within herself to feel in the least resentful. 'I see,' she said softly. 'And quite understandable, if I may say so. After all, I had most to gain by the lady's demise. Moreover, I of course had easy access to her bedchamber.'

After contemplating the patch of carpet by his feet for a few more moments, Hugo at last met her gaze; a gaze so level, so earnest, that it told him all he needed to know. 'I will not insult your intelligence, Miss Harrington, by suggesting I never considered such a possibility for a moment. That said, even at the time, I couldn't quite bring myself to believe you capable of such a thing... And now I'm convinced of it.

'Which means, of course,' he continued after wandering across to the decanters, 'that if a murder was committed—and I strongly suspect if not murder, then something untoward definitely occurred in that bedchamber—then one of those putting up at the house that night must surely be the guilty party, as I don't for a moment suspect it was one of the servants.'

Declining the offer of a second glass of Madeira, Ruth resumed her seat by the hearth, then waited until he had rejoined her. 'No, I don't believe it was one of the servants, either. Apart from anything else, why on earth should any one of them wish to dispose of the person who provided him or her with a livelihood? It just doesn't make sense. But then, I cannot imagine any one of those taking shelter that night calmly entering Lady Beatrice's bedchamber, with malice aforethought, and placing a pillow over her—

'Oh, good Lord!'

Her expression, somewhere between comical dismay and mortification, amused Hugo. 'What is it now, Miss Harrington? Don't tell me you've already solved the mystery and have hit upon the guilty party?'

'No, sir... But whoever it was didn't gain entry to Lady Beatrice's bedchamber from the passage-way. The door was locked. I locked it myself.'

'May I be permitted to know why you locked it?'

'Because I was asked to do so by Lady Beatrice herself. She said she felt somewhat nervous with so many strangers in the house.'

'With good reason, as things turned out,' Hugo commented drily. Then he grew serious again, concentrating his thoughts. 'Which means access was gained via your bedchamber, I imagine.'

'There was no other way,' she confirmed.

'And you heard and saw nothing?'

'I'm not certain,' she answered, scrupulously truthful. 'I do recall being disturbed by some-thing that night. I did wake, as it happens, if only briefly. But I heard and saw nothing, except the flicker of candlelight beneath the communicating door. As I've already mentioned, Lady Beatrice was sometimes an indifferent sleeper and would often read well into the night. So I thought nothing of it and went straight back to sleep, little re-alising…' All at once an involuntary shudder ran through her. 'It's a wonder I wasn't murdered as well.'

Hugo smiled reassuringly. 'I doubt you were ever in any real danger, Miss Harrington. No, Lady Beatrice Lindley was the intended victim. Her death, I strongly suspect, was, indeed, the direct result of what had been uttered at the dinner table. And I also strongly suspect that the reason for it lies somewhere in her past…quite distant past.'

'Yes, I rather think you're right, sir,' Ruth agreed, before rising to her feet. 'So, I shall not uncover the truth back at Dunsterford Hall, shall I?'

Hugo automatically rose also, but stared down at her suspiciously as a rather disturbing possibility was at that precise moment crossing his mind. 'You're not thinking of attempting to take the matter further, I trust, Miss Harrington? If you take my advice you'll return to Somerset and forget about the whole thing. The world believes Lady Beatrice died of natural causes. This might yet turn out to be the case. It might be best all round if things are left as they are.'

Ruth couldn't mistake the genuine concern in his eyes, in his deep, attractively masculine voice also, and was moved by it. None the less, it quite failed to weaken her resolve.

'Sir, thanks to the generosity of Lady Beatrice I shall live a very comfortable existence for the rest of my life. It's the least I can do to attempt to discover the truth about the happenings of that night. I hold myself entirely to blame for not securing the services of a second doctor at the time. Had I done so the authorities might have decided to look into the matter. I doubt very much they would be interested in doing so now, with so little evidence to go on—a piece of torn lace and the sketchy memories of a dinnertime conversation.' She spread her hands in a helpless gesture. 'The whole thing seems so implausible. I don't even know whether I quite believe it myself, entirely... But, as I've mentioned before, I owe it to Lady Beatrice to do my utmost to uncover the truth if I can.'

Hugo ran impatient fingers through his thick and slightly waving hair. 'So, what do you intend to do now?' he demanded somewhat testily.

'Why, travel on to London, of course, and discover all I can about Lady Bea's past,' she answered, surprised that he felt the need to ask, especially as he had suggested that course of action in the first place. Honest to the last, she added, 'I don't quite know how I'm to set about it, as I'm not of Lady Beatrice's world. But I dare say something will have occurred to me before I reach my journey's end.'

Hugo stared down at her, now, in exasperation. Had she been a raw recruit under his command during his years in the army he would have known exactly how to deal with the situation. As it was, he felt powerless to prevent her from doing precisely as she wished. Which, of course, only fuelled his frustration still further and, amazingly, gave rise yet again to that overwhelming desire to protect her.

Unfortunately, before he could attempt to reason with her further, she disarmed him completely by boldly reaching for his right hand and holding it, oh, so gently captive between both her own.

'Sir, I cannot express my thanks adequately enough for your assistance in this matter,' she said, releasing her clasp far too soon for his liking. 'I shall not importune you further by taking up any more of your time. But I should very much like to write to you to let you know how I progress, if you do not object?'

Hugo declined to answer. Instead, he saw her safely to her hired carriage, where he made his final farewells. Then, he wasted no time in returning to his library, where he once again rummaged through a certain drawer in his desk, until he had succeeded in locating several folded sheets of paper. Just why he had retained them, he didn't know. Yet, now, he felt he had been destined to do so, just as he had been destined to stay in that certain house on the edge of a moor for one unforgettable night all those months ago.

Half-smiling, he went over to the bell pull situated by the hearth, and gave it a sharp tug.

'Send Finn to me, Mrs Bailey,' he ordered when she entered in answer to the summons. 'Then arrange for the two large trunks to be brought down from the attic. I have decided upon a protracted stay in the capital. If all goes to plan, I shall be leaving early in the morning.'

Chapter Five

'London!' Still somewhat awestruck, Agatha gazed dreamily above the breakfast table at a spot somewhere behind her young mistress's head. 'Whoever would have thought it, eh, miss? You wait till I tell them all back at Dunsterford Hall that I've been to London. They'll scarce believe me!'

'Oh, I expect they will, Aggie,' Ruth countered, nowhere near as excited as her maid at the prospect of visiting the metropolis for the very first time in her life. 'As soon as Mr Pearce receives the letter I sent him yesterday, he'll visit the Hall and deal with everything there on my behalf.' Her frown betrayed her concern even before she added, 'I can only hope he manages to arrange the transfer of ample funds, enough for our needs, fairly swiftly. I've sufficient, I hope, for the time being at least.'

She refused to be unduly concerned over financial matters at this early stage, even though she was sensible enough to appreciate that residing in the capital for any length of time was likely to put a severe strain on her purse. 'I dare say we'll have time enough to do plenty of sightseeing whilst we're there,' she continued, attempting to generate some of her maid's enthusiasm. 'But we mustn't lose sight of the real reason for our visit.'

At this reminder, the maid's smile faded. 'Do you know, miss, I just can't believe any one of those people *did* for Lady Bea.' Having been taken fully into her young mistress's confidence during supper the evening before, Agatha shook her head, genuinely perplexed. 'They all seemed so…ordinary, somehow, not the murdering kind at all.'

'I know what you mean,' Ruth agreed. 'Yet I'm more convinced than ever now, after talking things over with Colonel Prentiss, that Lady Beatrice's death, if not murder, was distinctly suspicious. Something untoward happened that night. I sense it in every fibre of my being, just as the Colonel did all those months ago.'

'Well, all I can say is if it does turn out to be

true, then I expect the mistress deserved it. And it's no good you looking at me like that, miss!' Agatha continued, after receiving a reproachful look. 'You're bound to think the best of her. It's only natural you should, after what she did for you in the end. But there's no getting away from the fact that there was a spiteful, selfish streak in Lady Bea's nature, so there was. The only person she ever really cared about was herself.

'And another thing,' she went on, seemingly determined to have her full say in the matter, 'you can bet your sweet life she had a good reason for leaving you her money. And I don't believe for a moment it had anything to do with loving you like a daughter. Why, she had no such nice feelings! If you asks me, she left you all her money to spite her family and for no other reason!'

Ruth would dearly have liked to say something in Lady Beatrice's defence, but was too honest a person to make the attempt. The simple truth was, of course, she didn't know why Lady Beatrice Lindley had seen fit to be so generous towards her. Oh, there was no denying they'd rubbed along very well together, had from the first. They had enjoyed each other's company for the most part.

Yet, there had been no strong bond of affection between them. As Agatha had so clearly pointed out—her late mistress hadn't been a female given to displays of strong emotion.

She sighed. 'You might be right, Aggie. But I cannot help feeling rather ashamed that, in all the years I lived at Dunsterford Hall, I never really tried to get to know Lady Bea, not really; never tried to discover precisely why she chose to live the life of a virtual recluse. I just went along, year in, year out, accepting the situation as it was, never once attempting to change things. Had I done so, I just might have succeeded in bringing a little happiness into her life. She did live such a joyless existence, you know.'

Before Agatha could even attempt to utter a response, the door behind unexpectedly opened and the young serving maid who had brought them their breakfast earlier entered the private parlour to say that a gentleman had called, wishful to speak to Miss Harrington.

Curious to know who might wish to see her, as she was a stranger to the area, Ruth was about to demand the gentleman's name, when the person in question strolled boldly into the room, taking her completely by surprise, in much the same way as she had done to him the previous day.

'Why, Colonel Prentiss! This is an unexpected pleasure!'

'A pleasure, I sincerely hope, Miss Harrington. But not unexpected, I trust. Surely you didn't imagine I would permit you to embark on your quest unaccompanied? What a very poor opinion you must hold of me if you did!'

Although nothing could have been further from the truth, Ruth could scarce own as much without seeming forward, or causing a deal of embarrassment to herself. Moreover, she wasn't altogether sure she had understood him correctly, so she merely asked, 'Did I understand you to say that it is your intention to accompany me to London, sir?'

'You did,' Hugo confirmed, eyeing the coffee-pot with distinct pleasure, as he had been obliged to break his fast that morning in something of a hurry so as to ensure his timely arrival at the inn. 'But first, I should be exceedingly grateful if you would share the contents of your coffeepot with me before we set out on this adventure together.'

Once the inn servant had been dispatched to

collect a further cup and her unexpected visitor had himself comfortably seated at the table, Ruth didn't hesitate to assure him that he was most welcome to share her carriage. Which resulted in not the expected words of gratitude, only the severest look of masculine disapproval she'd ever received in her life.

'I suspected almost from the first that your experience of the world was severely limited, Miss Harrington, but I never realised until now just how green a girl you are!'

More amused than chastened by the rebuke, it took every ounce of control Ruth possessed not to laugh. 'Hardly a girl, sir,' she pointed out, after regaining sufficient control. 'I shall take leave to inform you that I've now turned six-and-tw—'

'It matters not a whit how many years you have in your dish, Miss Harrington,' Hugo interrupted, having easily detected the slight twitching of that sweetly shaped feminine mouth. 'You're still an unmarried woman and, as such, are considered by the polite world to be totally ill equipped to go jaunting about the country on your own.

'And it's no earthly good you pointing out the fact that you're travelling with your maid,' he continued, when she was about to do just that. 'Admirable creature though she undoubtedly is, your abigail would be insufficient to protect you from the vicious spite of our censorious world should it become known that you travelled in a closed carriage all the way to London with a gentleman who was not a near relative. You would need a respectable duenna for such a purpose. And as there's no time to engage the services of such a creature, it is better by far that we travel separately.'

Ruth wasn't at all sure whose reputation he was attempting to protect—hers, or his own. Although she would certainly appreciate his escort for the duration of the journey, the last thing in the world she would ever wish to do was place him in a position whereby he felt honour-bound to offer her the protection of his name. No—unthinkable!

'Sir, please do not imagine I'm ungrateful, but—but unless you have personal business of your own to conduct, I do not perfectly understand the need for you to travel to London. It isn't my intention to place myself in any danger, I assure you. Moreover, I've the protection of the post-boys, and shall put up at the very best inns for the duration of the journey.'

Hugo favoured her with a half-mocking, half-sceptical look. 'Life can hold many pitfalls for the seasoned traveller, let alone the innocently unwary, Miss Harrington. That apart, I'm not merely making the journey for your benefit, but for mine also. We are now of one mind and believe that something untoward occurred at Dunsterford Hall during the early hours of that fateful October day. And I, let me remind you, was among those temporarily residing there. I'm convinced, now, that you're not the guilty party. And I've every intention of proving, beyond doubt, my own innocence.'

Ruth was about to assure him that she had never supposed it could be otherwise, when Agatha's surprising squeal of indignation not only checked the assertion before it had reached her lips, but also succeeded in capturing Hugo's wholehearted attention.

'I'll take leave to tell you, sir, that Miss Ruth isn't capable of doing such a wicked thing!' The maid resembled nothing so much as a ruffled hen determined to protect her young. 'A sweeter, more kinder-hearted young woman you could never meet, nor work for, neither!'

'Aggie...please!' Ruth begged, touched by the display of staunch loyalty, while feeling highly embarrassed about it as well.

'Your devotion to your mistress does you great credit,' Hugo assured her, the sincerity in his voice belied somewhat by his expression of comical dismay.

Although he was not accustomed to being spoken to in such a fashion, at least not by a servant, he could not find it within him to be offended, or even remotely angry. If anything, he was reassured by the outburst, because it only went to substantiate what his instincts had already begun to tell him—that, in this unsophisticated country wench, he just might have found himself a surprising ally.

Consequently, he decided then and there to attempt to build a mutually beneficial relationship with the maid. 'However, at the risk of causing further offence,' he went on, after deciding she would appreciate honesty more than tact, 'it must be pointed out that your mistress had most to gain by Lady Beatrice's demise.'

'It's true, Aggie,' Ruth hurriedly concurred, before she could be embarrassed further by her maid's unguarded tongue. 'Colonel Prentiss is only giving voice to what most everyone would believe if—er—certain details about Lady Beatrice's death ever came to light.'

'But I now firmly believe,' Hugo continued, just as though Ruth hadn't spoken, 'that your present mistress is completely innocent of any wrongdoing and that someone in the house that night had a far greater motive for putting a period to Lady Beatrice's life—and that motive lies somewhere hidden in your late mistress's past. Just how far back we'll be obliged to search, of course, remains to be seen. But I think we can safely assume that the incident she witnessed involving two persons on a cliff walk didn't occur during those years she spent in Somerset.

'Ha! Fresh coffee!' Hugo added as the inn servant re-entered, thereby putting an end to further discussion for the present.

Surprisingly enough, during the following days, as they made the journey in separate carriages towards the capital, the subject was seldom touched upon again, not even when they ate alone together in private parlours. The journey took longer than expected, with instances of horses losing shoes, and even a broken trace, delaying their arrival.

Ruth didn't care a jot that they were obliged to enjoy each other's company for longer than expected. Quite the opposite! Travelling about the country was a novel experience for her—exciting and educational. Moreover, that wonderful, easy camaraderie they had enjoyed from the first had so rapidly intensified that when Hugo had suggested they cease unnecessary formality, at least when in private, she found it the most natural thing in the world to call him by his given name, just as though they had known each other for years.

For his part Hugo, too, had found himself enjoying the trip. He supposed he'd grown so accustomed to travelling long distances during his adult life that the exercise of journeying to one's own capital had long since lost the charm of novelty. Surprisingly enough, though, seasoned campaigner that he'd become during his army career, even he had found himself easily imbued by his sweet companion's natural enthusiasm for life.

Seeing his country through new eyes had somehow rejuvenated him, had succeeded in sweeping aside the cynical, world-weary mantle that had increasingly threatened to shroud him at certain times in recent years. Not since the heady, irresponsible days of his youth had he felt so carefree, had he derived so much enjoyment from the simple pleasures in life. And it hadn't been too difficult to pinpoint the precise source of this reinvigoration.

No, there wasn't a shadow of doubt in his mind now—the arrival of Miss Ruth Harrington in his life had been nothing short of a godsend. Not for a very long time had he felt so at ease in the company of a young woman who was not a member of his immediate family. Not only was she very pleasing on the eye, she was also quick-witted, charming and thoroughly unspoilt; all in all, an absolute joy to be with. Rational gentleman that he was, though, he appreciated they hadn't known each other for very long and the sensible course would be to rectify this before attempting to further his suit.

Not only that, it was imperative at this stage not to lose sight of the reason for making this trip to the metropolis, he told himself, as he attempted to tie his neckcloth with the aid of the inadequate and badly mottled mirror in his bedchamber. Perhaps when the mystery surrounding Lady Beatrice's demise had been solved, or a certain captivating young lady was satisfied that nothing further could be done to uncover the truth, then that was the time to embark on a more meaningful relationship.

Hugo released his breath in a heavy sigh. Ever the realist, he was forced to own that he wasn't every woman's idea of the ardent lover, or husband, come to that. Momentarily he allowed his mind to wander back to the distant past. He and Alicia Thorndyke had grown up together, had been childhood friends. She had always accepted him for precisely who he was, faults and all. This wasn't the case with Ruth, of course.

Alarming though it was, her ideals might well run to handsome knights in shining armour; gentlemen who would sweep her off her feet with heroic deeds, and shower her with romantic compliments, deserved or otherwise. Sadly, he was not of their number, and he doubted he could ever bring himself to indulge in insincere flattery to win a lady's affection, least of all Ruth's.

He was aware, also, that he was far too large for

some women's tastes, and although his features were regular, there was nothing outstanding about any one of them. More disheartening, still, was the fact that his charming travelling companion had not once given him any reason to hope that she looked upon him in any other light than that of some surrogate elder brother— trustworthy and dependable. He had designated himself the role of protector, and in so doing had succeeded in winning her complete trust. And sadly, for the present, he was going to be obliged to be content with that state of affairs alone!

Just as he was going to be forced to settle with the arrangement of his cravat, he decided, feeling distinctly dissatisfied with both outcomes, as he shrugged himself into his coat and left the bed-chamber.

Like most inns at which they had put up throughout the journey, this hostelry was noisy, with arrivals taking place sometimes very late in the evenings, and recommencing again early in the mornings. The clattering sounds in the coffee room reached his ears long before he had descended the narrow staircase to discover not only his own manservant, but also the personal maid who had steadily grown in his estimation as their journey to the capital had progressed.

'Ah, Aggie, well met!' Hugo declared, having quickly adopted the pet name used by the maid's own mistress. 'No, you needn't scurry away, Finn,' he continued, thereby thwarting his own servant's attempt at a tactful withdrawal. 'This concerns you, too.'

Having quickly gained their full attention, Hugo didn't waste time in issuing orders. 'You both know the reason for making this trip. And it's imperative we keep this to ourselves as much as possible. Notwithstanding, this doesn't mean you won't be in a position to discover a great deal. Below-stairs gossip, not to mention that which takes place in and around stables, can sometimes prove invaluable.'

Agatha looked doubtful. 'Well, I'll do my best, sir. But I doubt I'll discover much. I don't know London ways.'

'You'll soon grow accustomed,' Hugo assured her. 'And so must your mistress. You'll find yourself accompanying her about a good deal.'

If possible Agatha betrayed more doubt. 'Ooh, Mistress won't like that,' she warned. 'Used to going about on her own is Miss Ruth. Values her freedom, so she does.'

Totally unmoved, Hugo flicked a speck of fluff from his jacket sleeve. 'Then I'm afraid she's going to have to accustom herself to your company very quickly. She cannot continue her country ways in London, as I shall take great delight in making perfectly clear to her.' He glanced briefly in the direction of a certain door leading off the coffee room. 'Already ensconced in the private parlour, is she?'

Without waiting for an answer, Hugo sauntered across the room in the direction of the private parlour. For a tall man he walked with a lithe elegance, something which had struck Ruth at their very first meeting, as had the natural charm of his personality, a characteristic she valued more highly than a handsome face.

As he entered the parlour she received the full warmth of his pleasant smile, and returned it, unashamedly, with one of her own, before setting aside the journal she'd been reading. Her smile then faded as a distinctly unpleasant thought crossed her mind.

'This will be our last supper together,' she reminded him, while valiantly attempting to prevent her voice from betraying the sadness she was increasingly feeling at the prospect.

From the very start of their journey she had experienced the most wonderful secure feeling that comes from knowing one is wholly protected by another human being. It was a totally new experience and one which she was silently obliged to acknowledge she very much resented having to forgo once their journey's end was reached.

Somehow, though, she managed to keep the despondency she was experiencing from revealing itself in her voice as she said, 'Long before this time tomorrow, barring further mishap, we should have arrived in the capital. Which reminds me, Hugo,' she added as he took the seat opposite at the table, 'you couldn't, by any chance, put me in the way of a decent hotel that isn't too shockingly expensive?'

Apart from that first day, when she had insisted on paying her full share of all costs incurred at the various inns, she had never once alluded to money. Now Hugo came to consider the matter, it stood to reason that she would have set out with limited funds, as her intention had been to travel only as far as Dorsetshire.

'Do not concern yourself. I shall stand your banker until such time as you're able to draw funds from a London bank.

'Now, don't waste your breath in futile argument, Ruth,' he continued, when she opened her mouth to do just that. 'What are…friends for, if not to help in times of trouble?

'Besides which, we oughtn't to waste time on unimportant financial matters when there are more pressing issues to discuss. And I shall begin by suggesting you don't put up at a hotel. I've been giving the matter some thought and have come to the conclusion that it would be better by far if you stayed with my sister Sarah.'

'Oh, sir, no!' Ruth was appalled at the mere idea and didn't attempt to conceal the fact. 'It would be too much of an imposition. I wouldn't have the brass-faced nerve even to propose such a thing!'

'You're not going to do so. I'll do the asking. She'll love to have you to stay,' he assured her. 'She's a dizzy wench at times, but has a great fondness for me. In fact, I'd go so far as to say

I'm her favourite brother, possibly because I'm closest to her in age.'

Ruth was swiftly warming to the notion. She'd discovered a little about his family already and the idea of discovering a deal more was tempting. She was aware that his upbringing had been, compared to her own, very conventional. The second son of a wealthy landowner, Hugo had continued with tradition and had sought a career in the army. His older brother, Harry, had inherited the family home and lands, and his younger brother Percy had gone in to the church.

She found herself sighing as a thought suddenly occurred to her. 'I cannot help feeling that my life might have been vastly different had my own father adhered to his sire's wishes and sought a career in the army.'

The wistful note in her voice was unmistakable. 'You cannot blame him for following his own inclinations. By your own admission he was a gifted artist.'

'Oh, several people have remarked upon that,' she assured him, 'and that he might one day have been recognised as such had he lived. Even Lady Beatrice acknowledged that much!' Again she found herself involuntarily sighing. 'He died so young—younger than I am now. He was barely four-and-twenty. Sadly, I was destined never to know him, but at least Mama adhered to his wish as far as I was concerned…well, almost. If the child Mama was carrying turned out to be a girl, he wanted her named Angelica, after Angelica Kauffmann, the artist,' she explained. 'Mama did as he asked, having me christened Angelica Ruth. But she always called me Ruth. It was my maternal grandmother's given name.'

'Angelica, eh? Pretty name.' He smiled. 'Must start calling you that.'

'I shouldn't bother, if I were you,' she told him bluntly. 'I shouldn't answer to it if you did. I never have.'

Hugo considered her in silence for a moment. He now knew something of her formative years—of how she had been raised in a rectory and how she had received a far broader education than most of her sex, thanks mainly to the attentions of the kindly rector.

'And when you lost your mother, you were obliged to leave the home where you'd been so happy?'

'It was for the best, really,' she responded, betraying little emotion, except perhaps for a touch of sadness behind the eyes. 'By that time the Reverend Mr Henry Stephens was a very elderly gentleman. He hadn't enjoyed particularly good health for a number of years. Sadly, he has since died. It was, in fact, he who persuaded me to accept Lady Beatrice's offer to live with her. I couldn't possibly have remained at the rectory with him, as young as I was. And, as I had no close relatives then living, he thought, for a gently reared young woman, the position of paid companion was the ideal solution. Except,' she added reflectively, 'I was never really employed, precisely.'

Nor treated like a surrogate daughter either, come to that, he thought to himself, but said, 'So, you were then obliged to adjust to a completely different lifestyle, I should imagine.'

'Heavens, yes!' Ruth concurred. 'The rectory was always a hive of activity, with people coming and going at most times of day, whereas Dunsterford Hall...'

'Was the antithesis—a mausoleum,' he finished for her, and she chuckled at the candour, a warm infectious gurgling sound that never failed to win a response from him. 'Oh, very well, if it wasn't quite that bad, one would hardly describe it as a place flowing with warmth and friendship.'

'That's true enough,' Ruth's innate honesty obliged her to concede. 'Though, I must say, it has improved immeasurably in recent months. Many more people now visit, you see.'

Hugo considered the simple admission for a moment, then asked, 'Why do you suppose it was that Lady Beatrice chose to live like a virtual recluse? Now, I would be the first to admit I didn't know her well…hardly at all, really. But my one hazy recollection is of a woman who was quite active in London society. What made her change, do you suppose?'

Ruth shook her head. 'I don't know. She rarely spoke of her past life. She seldom spoke about any member of her family, either. And I can never once, in the decade I lived with her, recall her mentioning her husband by name. In fact, I gained the distinct impression some years ago that she had scant regard for men. I'd even go as far as to suggest that she loathed the male sex as a whole.'

One masculine brow rose sharply. 'Now that might prove interesting.'

'That was one of the reasons she gave for leaving me her money,' Ruth revealed, hardly aware she was speaking aloud, 'said I should then be independent, should never need to marry.'

An inn servant entering to set cloths on the table for dinner instantly captured her attention. Consequently, she quite failed to see a trace of annoyance flicker over Hugo's features for one unguarded moment.

'I still maintain that it's in Lady Beatrice's past that we might discover the key to the mystery of her demise,' he said, when they were once again alone. 'And it's for that reason staying with my sister could prove highly beneficial. Sally's a sociable creature. Nothing she loves more than a good gossip. What she doesn't know about London society isn't worth knowing. She'll know something about Lady Beatrice's past life, I'm sure, or at the very least she'll know of someone who does.

'Furthermore,' he went on, when the openness of her expression revealed that she was rapidly assimilating the benefits of staying with his sibling and was no longer prepared to dismiss the notion out of hand, 'Sarah, madcap creature though she is on occasions, will be an ideal chaperon for you.'

Amenable though she always attempted to be, Ruth found herself bridling at this. 'How many times must I remind you, sir, that I'm hardly a chit out of the schoolroom? I have no need of a chaperon.'

'And how many times must I be forced to re-mind you, Miss Harrington,' he countered with equal formality, 'that country manners will not serve in the metropolis, where strict codes of conduct must be adhered to at all times if you're to stand the remotest chance of being accepted into the polite world. And it's imperative you do move in polite circles if you're to stand the remot-est chance of solving the mystery of Lady Bea's death. I can do my bit to help, of course, but let me tell you it would create a very odd impression if I were to be seen squiring you about all the time. And the last thing I wish to do is draw undue at-tention to ourselves.'

Or perhaps give rise to the wrongful impres-sion—that your feelings are engaged, Ruth couldn't help supposing, experiencing a distinctly hollow feeling inside, but said, doing her level best to sound enthusiastic, 'Yes, your sister would prove more suitable, I agree. But would she be willing to do so, do you suppose? The last thing in the world I should wish is to become any kind of burden to—to anyone.'

'You could never be that,' he assured her softly. 'Besides which, in my sister's last letter she vowed she was fatigued to death of her humdrum existence in the country and the catalogue of children's ailments she'd been obliged to deal with during the past months. She assured me she was staying in the capital by herself for the first few weeks in order to recoup her strength and to bring a little excitement back into her life, after months of trifling domestic concerns.'

Hugo's expression betrayed his own slight misgivings, even before he added, 'As I've said before, Sal can be a scatty wench, but she's not altogether indiscreet. We have little choice but to confide in her.'

Chapter Six

Although Hugo had given his assurance that his sister would be only too happy to house a total stranger, Ruth wasn't so sure he was telling the absolute truth when she saw him exchanging a private word with both sets of post-boys the following morning, just prior to setting off on the last leg of the journey. She became increasingly certain that he was perhaps taking too much for granted where his sibling was concerned when her own carriage began to fall further and further behind, thereby allowing Hugo to arrive at the Lansdowns' town house well in advance of her, in order, Ruth strongly suspected, to prepare his sister for the unexpected, and perhaps unwelcome, guest.

Up to a point the assumption had been correct—Hugo had every intention of having a word with his sister in private, but not for any of the reasons Ruth might have supposed. He knew his sibling well enough to be sure that she'd be only too willing to put someone up at his behest, providing, of course, the house wasn't brimful to the attic with guests already. What he knew he couldn't wholly rely upon was his sister's discretion, for on rare occasions she had been known to speak without thinking.

Since her marriage to Lord Lansdown, some fifteen years before, her one burning ambition, apart from providing her husband with several healthy pledges of her affection, had been to see her favourite brother, too, enjoying a life of connubial bliss. Tirelessly she had striven to find him the ideal mate, parading a succession of what she had deemed suitable candidates for his inspection at every available opportunity.

With commendable patience Hugo had borne with his sister's folly down the years, mainly because he had known that her interference had stemmed from the very best of motives. It had come as no very real surprise to him that Sarah had singularly failed to introduce him to a female with whom he could happily spend the rest of his life. What had come as a monstrous jolt to his equilibrium was perhaps having discovered his ideal life's companion for himself, when he might least have expected to do so, on that bitterly cold early October afternoon, in such a remote spot!

As the carriage drew to a halt before a fashionable residence in a most sought-after part of town, Hugo was obliged to cease his musings and alighted before the post-boy could even draw down the steps. The servant who answered the front door promptly in response to his summons delivered the welcome tidings that the mistress of the house was, indeed, at home and happy to receive visitors. Then, without further ado, Hugo was shown into the sunny front parlour, where the lady of the house lounged on a chaise longue, absently flicking through the pages of the latest edition of the *Ladies' Journal*, and wearing a garment he considered more suitable for the privacy of the boudoir.

'Good gad, Sal! What the deuce are you about, donned in little more than your shift at this time of day!'

The response to this disparaging remark was an unladylike squeal of delighted surprise. The

Ladies' Journal went flying into the air a moment before Hugo found himself holding yards and yards of some bright-yellow flimsy material, while receiving his sister's customary show of affection.

'Oh, Hugo, darling! What on earth brings you here? Not that I care a jot! I was feeling quite *ennui* and was wondering how best to brighten the day. And here you are—the answer to all my prayers!' Finely arched brows rose all at once to meet above the bridge of a decidedly tip-tilted nose. 'And what do you mean, you wretch...in my shift? I shall have you know this is a lounging gown. All the fashionable hostesses are sporting them this Season.'

'In that case, Sal, I should strive for a little more originality, if I were you,' he advised with brotherly candour, while removing his arms from a waist that had sadly thickened in recent years. 'You're far too tall to don such fripperies. You resemble nothing so much as an oversized canary. Now, come and sit down, because I have something of importance to say to you and there isn't much time.'

Garrulous creature that she was known to be,

Sarah, Lady Lansdown, loved nothing more than unearthing a piece of salacious behaviour. Although it had to be said that her favourite brother was not wont to conduct himself in a fashion that ultimately gave rise to gossip, it was unusual for him to turn up on the doorstep without advance warning. She sensed a mystery and so dutifully remained silent while she drew him towards the chaise longue and sat down beside him.

'Oh, do tell, you infuriating creature!' she urged, unable to curb her insatiable curiosity a moment longer, when all he did was to remain, annoyingly, staring at a spot somewhere on the floor. 'What devilry have you been about? Not put a period to someone's existence, have you?'

Hugo couldn't help but smile at this. For all that she could be a scatty wench on occasions, his sister wasn't altogether lacking perception. 'I've not, Sal,' he assured her, 'but I very much fear someone might possibly have done just that. And I'm here to uncover who that certain someone might have been, with the help of a—er—friend.' He reached for one of her hands and held it in his own. 'And I want you to do me the very great kindness of putting this very special friend up here and taking every care to make this first visit to London extra special.'

'But of course I shall! I wonder you need ask!' Something then seemed to occur to her and she regarded him frowningly. 'But I do not perfectly understand, Hugo. Why cannot you take care of him yourself. You'll stay here together, surely?'

'For the present, yes, providing you can manage to put me up as well. But it's more important you house my...friend.' Hugo paused for a moment while the footman who had admitted him to the house returned with refreshments, then waited until they were alone again. 'Is Lansdown with you?'

Sarah shook her head. 'You know how he dislikes town life. He's in the country with the children, but has promised to join me here in time for my party at the end of the month.'

'Better and better!' Hugo announced, well pleased. 'That means you can devote most of your time to your house guest, without too many distractions.'

'Well, of course I shall! But, Hugo...' She was still clearly perplexed. 'I do not perfectly understand. Surely your friend would much prefer your companionship to mine. After all, there are numerous places where females are not permitted to go.'

'Precisely!' Hugo concurred, if anything, confounding her even more. 'And that is where your help will be invaluable. Although she isn't lacking intelligence or any of the social skills, she isn't quite up to snuff when it comes to the strict codes of conduct demanded of any unmarried female residing here in the capital.'

It took a moment or two for her to digest fully what had been said, but Hugo was left in no doubt the instant she had succeeded in doing precisely that, for his hand was tossed aside, almost in disgust.

'How—how dare you ask me—me, your own sister—to look after your...your...'

Words seemed to fail her and Hugo watched, totally unimpressed by the display of feminine outrage, as she whipped out a flimsy square of lace and proceeded to dab at her eyes. Nor was he amused by it, either. He had been given the nickname 'The Gentle Giant' by those who knew him well, for no one would argue that, for the most part, his disposition was amiable. Yet there was a darker side to his nature that could surface if sufficiently provoked, a side his sister had witnessed occasionally in their youth and had never forgotten.

Instinctively she edged a little away. 'It—it's no earthly good you glowering at me in that odious fashion, Hugo. You've never brought a female to my home before…well, at least not one who wasn't less than perfectly respectable… Oh, dear,' she finished lamely, when his steely expression, if anything, hardened.

'And I shouldn't dream of doing so now. Miss Harrington is a lady in every sense of the word. But if you feel yourself unable to treat her with the respect her gentility merits, then I shall find more suitable accommodation for the duration of her stay,' and so saying Hugo rose to his feet, only to have his hand clutched once again by urgent fingers.

'Oh, Hugo, you are quite abominable! You do misunderstand one so!'

'I misunderstand nothing,' he assured her. 'And, so that you do not, I shall make it clear that Ruth is no lightskirt. She isn't my mistress. Nor has she been any other man's, come to that. At the risk of offending further your delicate sensibilities, I shall tell you plainly that I have experience enough to recognise a virtuous young woman when I meet one.'

'Oh, how you do take on so!' Sarah exclaimed, seeming all at once unequal to meeting his gaze. 'But you must own you've never brought a female to my home before… Well, not one that wasn't related to the family in some way, besides having at least five-and-fifty years in her dish.'

'Had Ruth been such a one, I shouldn't be seeking your assistance now.' He gazed down at her from his towering height, his expression betraying anything but brotherly affection. 'However, as I've mentioned already, if you feel yourself unequal to the task of chaperoning a gently reared female, albeit one that was obliged to make her own way in the world during the last decade, then I shall take myself off and make arrangements elsewhere.'

Throughout their childhood Sarah had never been able to withstand her favourite brother's look of staunch disapproval. She discovered she couldn't even do so now. 'Oh, do sit down, Hugo, and stop glowering at me in that hateful way! I'm sure I don't deserve it. It's only what any respectable matron might suppose, after all,' she went on lamely, while nervously pleating at the folds of her fashionable attire. 'You know I shall take every care of your—your friend, if it will please you… And, of course, if I like her.'

'Believe me, Sal, you couldn't fail to do otherwise,' he assured her with certainty and then re-seated himself. 'I have much to tell you, and there isn't much time. So do not interrupt!'

Before she had mounted the steps, the green-painted door of the fashionable town house had been thrown wide, thereby allowing Ruth and her maid prompt access to a chequered hall. As her arrival had clearly been expected, she could only suppose Hugo had achieved his objective. Think highly of him though she still did, she now knew him a good deal better, after their many days spent on the road, and could only hope he hadn't resorted to devious stratagems where his sister was concerned in order to get his way. She didn't doubt that he was more than capable of doing so!

For several moments, after she had been shown into a small and elegantly furnished salon over-looking the street, she very much feared that that was precisely what had occurred. Hugo rose at once to his feet and came smilingly forward to grasp her hand. Sadly, the lady who had been left seated alone on the chaise longue offered no such warm welcome. In fact, if anything, she appeared rather stunned, her jaw having dropped percep- tively, as though she were having difficulty be- lieving the evidence of her own eyes.

'Ruth, allow me to make known to you my sis- ter, Lady Lansdown,' Hugo said, grasping her hand, and leading her inexorably forward, thereby allowing her little alternative. 'Sarah, my very good friend Miss Ruth Harrington.'

The instant Hugo released his hold, Ruth tenta- tively held out her hand. 'It is a pleasure to make your acquaintance, my lady.'

It seemed an age before her fingers were finally grasped, albeit briefly. Even so, the response gave her the courage to say what was at the forefront of her mind. 'It is most kind of you to welcome me into your home. But please do not feel obliged to house a complete stranger. I am sensible of the fact that it is a great imposition, even if your brother is not.'

The simple assurance seemed to act as a miraculous restorative, immediately breaking the trance the mistress of the house appeared to have been under. 'Oh, no…not at all! No imposition, I assure you! It's just that you—you are not quite what I was expecting… Oh dear, I've said the completely wrong thing again, haven't I, Hugo?'

Ruth looked from the sister's look of comical dismay to the brother's expression of exasperation and drew her own conclusions. A glint of amusement added an extra sparkle to her eyes as they remained staring up at Hugo. 'Would I be correct in thinking your sister assumed that our association went rather deeper than—er—mere friendship? Well, I suppose it was a mistake anyone might be forgiven for making.'

She returned her gaze briefly to the lady of the house to discover features now set in a rather thoughtful expression. 'You see, my lady, it would never have occurred to me to suppose it might be considered improper to travel to London with a gentleman who was not a close relative. Even though we did travel in separate carriages some might still consider it grossly improper. You're right, Hugo. I do have much to learn.'

For answer he threw back his head and barked

with laughter, unsure of what had amused him more—Ruth's candidness, or his sister's further expression of stunned disbelief.

'I think I could do no better than to leave you two ladies alone to become better acquainted. There are one or two matters requiring my immediate attention, so do not delay luncheon on my account. I shall have something at my club and shall see you both again later.'

All at once Ruth's amusement gave way to a surge of uncertainty and she instinctively reached out to place a gently restraining hand on the arm of the being whom she had rapidly come to trust above any other. 'You will come back, though, won't you, sir?'

The note of anguish was clear for anyone to hear; clear as the look of tenderness that appeared in Hugo's eyes as he placed his hand over hers in gentle reassurance. 'Of course I shall, and be here for as long as you have need of me.'

Sarah, who had studied the affectionate little exchange with dawning wonder, waited only until her brother had left the room before giving voice to her incredulity, 'Well, I never would have believed it! And after all this time, too!'

She then stared again at her unexpected house-guest for several long, thoughtful moments, before declaring further, 'Well, I must say you're nothing like I might have expected... No, nothing like at all! But then tastes do change as one matures, I suppose.'

'Beg pardon, ma'am?' Ruth responded, quite naturally puzzled by the pronouncement.

'What...? Oh, nothing, my dear. Merely thinking aloud. Do remove that charming bonnet of yours and come and make yourself comfortable next to me on the sofa,' she added, patting the richly coloured upholstery beside her invitingly. 'I'm sure we shall become the very best of good friends! In fact, I'm determined on it!'

Although she felt she would need to get to know the lady a good deal better before committing herself to any sort of friendship, Ruth was somewhat encouraged by the warmth of the smile she finally received, most especially as it closely resembled that of a certain special gentleman's.

'Oh, and dark chestnut hair, too!' Sarah acknowledged, when Ruth had done as requested and removed her bonnet, just prior to seating herself. She frowned. 'I wonder if that is where I have been going wrong all these years?'

'I'm sorry, my lady, I do not perfectly understand,' Ruth responded, wondering whether the journey to the capital had fatigued her more than she might have supposed. Her companion seemed to talk in riddles. Quite unfathomable!

'Oh, you mustn't mind me,' Sarah advised, reaching for one slender white hand and retaining it companionably. 'I do have a tendency to say what I'm thinking, making absolutely no sense whatsoever.

'Now, Hugo did tell me something about why you're here,' she continued, 'but I'd much rather hear it all again from you. We have plenty of time before luncheon for a long, comfortable coze, so, you may begin by telling me all about yourself.'

When Hugo returned to the house later that same afternoon, he was immediately struck by his sister's altered demeanour the instant he entered again that small salon overlooking the street to discover Sarah humming a ditty, while gazing dreamily into space.

Long before he had left the house earlier, his

sister's outraged modesty had given way to interest, and then, unless he had very much misunderstood the matter, utter amazement. Why she should have been quite so surprised by Ruth's appearance he could only speculate, of course. All the same, he strongly suspected that Miss Ruth Harrington hadn't turned out to be anything like the female his sister's ever-fertile imagination had conjured up as his ideal mate.

On first making Ruth's acquaintance, no one with a ha'p'orth of intelligence could mistake the fact that she was a young lady of quality, both gently bred and virtuous; moreover, one blessed with an abundance of natural charm, and a quick mind. What she lacked in worldly experience she more than made up for in a ready wit and a willingness to learn. As a connoisseur of feminine attributes, he rated her well above the norm, if not strictly speaking a beauty. Consequently, Hugo doubted his sister's stunned disbelief had arisen from any serious flaw Sarah had immediately perceived in her unexpected houseguest's overall appearance. Oh, no, it was much more likely, he mused, that her amazement had stemmed from the fact that Ruth resembled not at all that tall, willowy female, with flowing blonde locks and bright blue eyes, whom she had imagined would suit her brother perfectly.

He didn't doubt, either, that his sister had already begun, mentally at least, to matchmake in a very big way. He had appreciated from the first that this might prove a very real hindrance to furthering his relationship with Ruth, but had been obliged to weigh this possible danger against the many benefits in placing Ruth in Sarah's care. This did not mean, of course, that he would tamely brook interference in his private concerns, a fact that he had every intention of making perfectly plain. He fully intended to do his own wooing in his own good time!

'Where's Ruth…?' He was not unduly alarmed to discover she wasn't there. In fact, he had every intention of putting her absence to good use. 'Resting, I suppose?'

'Yes, poor girl. Clearly she's not accustomed to travelling great distances… Well, hardly at all, from what I can gather. And the exertion has finally caught up with her. But it won't do her a mite of harm to rest. She must accustom herself to town hours quickly, if she wishes to move in polite circles. Which I'm reliably informed is her objective.'

After helping himself to a glass of wine, Hugo seated himself in the chair opposite. 'And you do not envisage any bar to this, I trust?'

'Good heavens, no!' Sarah appeared amazed that he felt the need to ask. 'You must be aware yourself that her birth is perfectly respectable— the Cambridge Worthings on the distaff side, and a general for a grandfather on the other. I should say not!'

Sarah gazed thoughtfully down at the hearth for a moment, before adding, 'The life she led in her formative years might, quite naturally, result in a few raised eyebrows if it were to become common knowledge. But I'm sure we can avoid too many references to her childhood.' She frowned as she stared across at her brother. 'It might be as well, too, not to mention her recent—er—good fortune.'

Hugo shrugged, thereby betraying his complete unconcern at the prospect of this being spread abroad. 'I should imagine that if either of Lady Beatrice Lindley's sisters are intending to spend the Season in town this year, then downright spite might come into play. Besides which, being comfortably circumstanced will prove no handicap. Quite the contrary, I would have thought.'

Sarah almost gaped. 'But, do consider, Hugo… she'll have every dastardly fortune-hunter in town after her!'

Hugo smiled. 'You underestimate her if you suppose she's incapable of piercing the insincerity of money-seeking wastrels. And then, of course, I shall do my utmost to protect her from unwanted attention.'

'That's all very well, Brother, but just supposing that not all those who are attracted to her are merely bent on improving the state of their finances? She's a fine-looking young woman, after all.'

'I'm well aware of it. And would be amazed if she didn't attract a following from discerning members of my sex,' he returned, not altogether happy at the prospect, but having already accepted the likelihood of it happening. 'After the life she's been obliged to lead during the past decade, she richly deserves to find a gentleman with whom she could happily spend the rest of her life. And I, for one, sincerely hope she does.'

If Sarah had been perplexed by his attitude a short time before, she appeared positively astounded by it now. 'Oh, I see,' she murmured. 'Well…at least…I think I do.' She regarded him in silence before asking, 'So it is your wish that I take her to some fashionable parties and…and introduce her to some eligible gentlemen?'

'I don't see how you could possibly avoid doing so, as it is her desire to mix with the fashionable world. But don't forget, Sarah, she has a reason for wishing to do so and it has nothing whatsoever to do with finding a husband.'

'N-no, I quite appreciate that,' she assured him. 'And it just so happens that I discovered quite recently that Lady Constance Styne is overseeing her eldest granddaughter's come-out this Season. If my memory serves me correctly she was a close friend of Lady Beatrice for many years. I shall make it my business to ensure our paths cross in the near future. But in the meantime, Hugo…'

Experiencing a surge of unease, not to mention perplexity at her brother's attitude to various matters, Sarah began to gnaw at her bottom lip, wondering how best to approach what might be termed a delicate subject, then quickly deciding only bluntness would serve. 'Hugo, if you wish me to chaperon Ruth to some fashionable parties, I'm afraid certain necessary additions must be made to her wardrobe.'

One masculine brow rose, clearly betraying surprise. 'Oh, why so? I've observed nothing amiss with her attire.'

'Well, that's absolutely no commendation!' Sarah returned tartly. 'As you've spent so little time in the capital in recent years, you're hardly in a position to say what is fashionable and what isn't. And I tell you plainly, her attire is sadly provincial. Well made, I will own,' she conceded. 'I saw that for myself when I helped her and her maid unpack earlier.

'Furthermore, she knows precisely what suits her,' she continued, pleased to be discussing a subject on which she was far more knowledgeable than her brother. 'Her day dresses will do very well, with perhaps one or two additions, and a few accessories. But I'm afraid she has brought nothing suitable for evening wear. She's going to need several new gowns.'

'So wherein lies the problem?' he asked, smiling to himself as he had a fairly shrewd notion of what his sister was about to demand of him next.

She didn't disappoint when she spread her hands in a helpless gesture and said, 'Well, I hardly know her, Hugo. And the last thing I should wish is to cause offence.'

'And you think the suggestion would be better coming from me, is that it? Well, perhaps you're right,' he conceded. 'But should it slip my memory to broach the subject at an appropriate time, then just take her about and buy whatever she needs and have the bills sent to me.'

It would have been a rare female who wasn't both dazzled and delighted by the sheer choice and wide variety of female attire offered for sale in the capital, and Ruth, very much conforming to type, enjoyed immensely visiting various bazaars and warehouses during the following days. It wasn't until her first week in London was drawing to a close and the Lansdowns' fine town carriage had conveyed them to the premises of one of the city's most select modiste's, that she felt she must call a halt to what she considered a rather extravagant spending spree.

Any formality having ceased between them almost from the first, she didn't think twice about grasping Sarah by the elbow in an attempt to edge her surreptitiously towards the shop door again.

'Oh, do pray let us leave,' she implored in an undertone, when she met with surprising resistance, and Sarah continued to examine a length of fine amber silk. 'Didn't you hear how much that gown is costing the customer over there? Why, it's extortionate! I could have at least half a dozen made for that price back home!'

Like her brother, Sarah utterly adored her charming house guest's openness and unaffected manner. The fact that she didn't boggle at plain speaking was also, Sarah considered, very much to her credit, especially on occasions such as these, when only bluntness would serve.

'My dear girl, you cannot possibly go about resembling a country milkmaid here in town if you wish to make any kind of impression.'

'But I don't want to make an impression,' Ruth pointed out.

'Now that's just plain silly,' Sarah didn't hesitate to counter the instant she had fully digested the very interesting reply, which gave her every reason to suppose that searching for a suitable mate really wasn't high on Ruth's agenda at all. 'You're here, are you not, to discover what happened to your late benefactress, and you'll not do so unless you mix with those people who knew her well.'

'Well, I suppose you're right,' Ruth conceded. 'But I do think Hugo would be better at doing that.'

'Of course he wouldn't! It would create a very odd impression if he suddenly began asking questions about a woman he hardly knew, whereas it would be deemed quite natural for you to do so.'

Honesty obliged Ruth to concede that this was possibly true also, before adding, 'But I simply cannot have Hugo presented with such extortionate bills. It was good of him to offer to stand my banker, but I shall not take flagrant advantage of his generosity.'

'My brother is no pauper,' Sarah assured her. 'Not only did he attain sizeable sums of prize money during the Peninsular Campaign, not to mention his share of dear Papa's private fortune, he was left a considerable sum by a wealthy aunt of ours. She favoured him above any other member of the family. But I was not one whit jealous. She very generously left me most all her jewels.'

Ruth couldn't help smiling at this. Although she had grown to like Hugo's sister very much, there was no denying there was a streak of quaint snobbery in her character, much the same as Lady Beatrice had possessed. Money and social position meant a great deal to both ladies. Which wasn't so very surprising when one considered they both sprang from the same social class, Ruth decided.

But she did not, and spending so much money on just one gown seemed outrageously extravagant, not to say downright sinful. She was on the point of attempting to argue further when she was foiled by none other than the proprietress of the establishment herself, who appeared from behind a curtain and immediately approached Sarah, instantly capturing her attention.

'Lady Lansdown perhaps wishes a further gown for this Season?' she said in a French accent that sounded distinctly false to Ruth's ears.

'I must confess I'm rather taken with this amber silk, Madame Carré. But I'm not come for myself. Miss Harrington, here, has recently arrived in town and is in urgent need of several evening gowns.'

The modiste threw up her hands in an exaggerated Gallic gesture. 'Ah, *madame*! I should be only too happy to oblige, especially to one who has remained a loyal and valued customer for so many years. But, alas, the start of the Season, my busiest time, and so many orders to complete...'

Her words fading, the proprietress turned her attention to Ruth for the first time, casting an expert eye over a trim figure that couldn't fail to do justice to any creation.

'Ha! But wait, *madame*, I beg of you,' she added, when Sarah turned, about to leave. 'I just might be in a position to help, after all... If you and Miss Harrington would care to follow me?'

Clearly better pleased than Ruth with the modiste's unexpected change of heart, Sarah didn't hesitate to follow the famous dressmaker into a small back room, leaving Ruth to bring up the rear. A young assistant was dispatched to a stockroom and duly returned with three dazzling creations carefully draped over her arms.

The modiste then proceeded to display them on a wooden rail, announcing as she did so that, although unsuitable for a young girl embarking on her first Season to wear, they would admirably suit someone with Miss Harrington's colouring.

On this particular issue, Ruth could not fail to agree, after trying on each beautifully made gown in turn, all of which required the merest adjustment to ensure a perfect fit. Although she did consider the low-cut necklines faintly immodest, it was the total cost of the creations that troubled her most of all.

'You must not consider the cost,' Sarah cautioned the instant Ruth attempted to broach the subject. 'Hugo has promised to pay for anything you need.'

'None the less, I've no intention of continuing to take such flagrant advantage of your brother's good nature. I'm hard pressed now to look him in the face, after all the purchases I've made during these past days.'

'A few furbelows, mere trifles!' Sarah returned, with a dismissive wave of one hand.

Having followed this little exchange with interest, the wily modiste decided to intercede before she risked losing a promising sale, not to mention a brand new client who appeared to have already made for herself some influential friends.

'You will have possibly appreciated by now, Mademoiselle Harrington, that these gowns were ordered by another client of mine, whose name I shall not divulge. Suffice it to say I accepted the commission on the strict understanding that all outstanding bills would be settled. This has not occurred and I therefore feel at liberty to sell the garments to another. However, I do appreciate that you did not personally select the garments yourself and I am prepared, therefore, to reduce the price…a little. I also promise to have the gowns adjusted, at no extra cost to yourself, and delivered to you within the next few days. Now, what could be fairer than that?'

Nothing as far as Sarah was concerned, and before Ruth could even begin to query the extent of the reduction, she was being whisked from the premises with unseemly haste, experiencing the distinct feeling that the sooner she focused on the business which had brought her to town, the better it would be for her peace of mind.

Chapter Seven

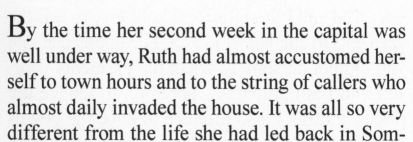

By the time her second week in the capital was well under way, Ruth had almost accustomed herself to town hours and to the string of callers who almost daily invaded the house. It was all so very different from the life she had led back in Somerset, where it was unusual to receive more than half-a-dozen visitors a week!

In many ways she enjoyed all the hustle and bustle of town life. It was all so new and exciting. Although she had yet to attend any formal gatherings, she had received several invitations to accompany Sarah out, when that lively matron had called to see friends in the afternoons. Ruth's days had also been occupied by viewing many popular sites, which had also proved to be enjoyably interesting. What hadn't pleased her so much was the fact that Hugo had never once offered to accompany her. It had always been either her personal maid or Sarah.

As the days had passed, she had seemed to see less and less of him. He was always out in the evenings, meeting up with his wide circle of friends, a great many of whom, apparently, he hadn't seen for several years. She knew she ought not to feel aggrieved. After all, she had absolutely no right to expect him to dance attendance upon her. He had already done more than enough for someone who was neither a long-standing friend, nor a family member, by escorting her to London, not to mention ensuring her continued safety by placing her in the care of his sister. The trouble was she found herself missing him more and more when he wasn't there. Worse, still, she couldn't rid herself of the lowering feeling that he just might be deliberately avoiding her and was possibly already regretting his altruism towards a virtual stranger.

Consequently, she couldn't conceal her delight when, midway through the second week, he strolled into the breakfast parlour and instantly banished all those foolish notions about a possible thawing of pleasure in her company by casually asking her to accompany him out a little later in a curricle.

This instantly captured his sister's attention. 'When did you purchase a sporting carriage, Hugo?' Sarah asked, after listening to her house guest's enthusiastic response.

'I haven't, although I expect I shall in the near future. No, Kingsley's in town for a few days on business. Ran in to him last night at my club and he kindly said I might avail myself of his as often as I wish, as he himself doesn't expect to be staying too long, or doing much socialising, either.'

'What a pity! I don't suppose Briony has accompanied him… Oh, how foolish of me!' Sarah exclaimed in the next breath. 'I was forgetting she's increasing again. Hoping for a girl this time, I shouldn't wonder.'

'I don't think Luke minds either way,' Hugo enlightened her from behind the folds of the *Morning Post*. 'But I expect Briony would like a daughter, after having given birth to two healthy sons.'

'Ah, what a devoted couple they are, to be sure!' Sarah remarked to no one in particular. 'Much like dear Lansdown and me. Did you know Hugo purchased the Kingsleys' property in Dorset, Ruth, shortly after he retired from the army?'

'Yes, he did mention it. But I'm not acquainted with either the Viscount or his wife.'

'In which case we shall remedy that before too long,' Hugo announced, folding up the journal and rising to his feet. 'But not today. I shall go and collect the curricle and be back in an hour.'

Unlike so many of her sex, Ruth was unfailingly punctual, a trait in her character that Hugo very much admired. He strongly suspected she must have been on the lookout for him in the front parlour and had spotted him tooling the sporting carriage along the street, for no sooner had he brought his friend's prime horses to a halt before the house than the front door opened and she came running lightly down the steps to meet him.

Another quality he much admired in her was a superb taste in dress. Which was most surprising when he came to consider the matter, he decided. By her own admission until recently she had not been in a position to spend vast sums on her attire. Yet, she knew precisely what suited her and nothing he had witnessed her wearing thus far had given him any reason to suppose that she had been in any way influenced by Sarah's occasional peculiar taste in fashion.

'What an utterly charming bonnet!' he announced, leaning down to assist her up on to the seat beside him. He was surprised to discover the compliment hadn't appeared to please her very much. If anything, she looked distinctly mortified.

'Oh, Hugo, don't!' she implored, thereby confirming his suspicion. 'It was wickedly expensive. I'm afraid I've been shockingly weak-willed since I arrived in London. I've permitted your sister to persuade me to purchase such an array of new things, most of which I'll not have occasion to wear once I've left town. And what makes it so unforgivable is that I haven't heard a word from Mr Pearce. Heaven alone knows when I'll be in a position to refund you.'

She peered up at him through her long, dark lashes—yet another of those endearing characteristics that never failed to evoke tender feelings. She put him in mind of nothing so much as a child seeking approval. Which, too, was most strange, for she could be quite determined when she chose, knowing her own mind. Perhaps it was just that she would much rather win his approbation than do without it. Which boded well for a future life spent together, he mused.

'Do not fear, m'dear, I shall certainly call a halt to your spending spree long before you have a chance to ruin me.'

She gurgled in response, then was content to sit quietly, studying the expert way he tooled the curricle through the busy London streets. It wasn't until they had left the familiar, fashionable thoroughfares behind and were travelling along roads in a much less affluent part of town that it occurred to her to ask where they were bound.

'In an attempt to keep myself out of dun territory, I thought it was time to turn your thoughts from acquiring fashionable falderals and focusing your mind on the main reason for visiting the metropolis.'

Although he had spoken lightly enough, Ruth wasn't one hundred per cent certain the remark hadn't contained the merest trace of criticism over her behaviour.

'I can assure you, Hugo, it has never been far from my thoughts, no matter what impression I might have given. I wasn't quite sure just how to set about things, that's all, and was waiting for an opportunity to consult with you. Sadly, I've seen so little of you of late and I just never seemed to get a chance to discuss matters with you alone.'

She trusted the response would vindicate her and looked at him, hoping to receive some confirmation of this, only to catch what looked suspiciously like a smugly satisfied grin fading from about his mouth. She couldn't imagine what had pleased him so much, but felt sure something must have done.

'In that case you'll no doubt be relieved to discover I know precisely how to proceed and that is why you find yourself in this part of town,' he revealed, sounding smugly satisfied, too.

'You mean you've located the whereabouts of one of those travellers, Hugo?'

'I was armed with their precise directions before leaving Dunsterford Hall,' he enlightened her. 'I don't know...' He shrugged. 'For some reason I just hung on to them. Perhaps it was fate.'

'Perhaps it was,' she reluctantly conceded, frowning suspiciously. 'But that doesn't explain why you didn't enlighten the Justice of the Peace at the time.'

'No, you're quite right, it doesn't,' he agreed. 'I dare say I must have had a reason. It just escapes me for the present, my angel.'

She was even more suspicious now. 'Don't you try to flummery me, Hugo Prentiss! I've never known anyone with a more acute mem— Oh! What did you call me?'

'Sorry, just slipped out.' In Ruth's opinion no one could have looked less apologetic. Not only were his eyes alight with devilment, he was grinning from ear to ear, too! 'Cannot get your given name out of my head, for some reason. And, as you've strictly forbidden me to use it, that's the closest abbreviation I can come up with,' he added, drawing the curricle to a halt outside the premises of Messrs Blunt, Blunt & Caldecott, Notaries & Commissioners for Oaths.

It was a timely arrival, as far as Hugo was concerned, for it immediately turned her thoughts away from what she had evidently considered an outrageously improper endearment. 'Do you intend to go inside?' she asked.

This only served to add to his amusement. 'What…and leave you with the horses? My friend Kingsley would have my liver and lights if I were even to contemplate anything so reckless. No, we'll save that meeting with Mr Henry Blunt for another time. Besides which, I think it might arouse suspicion if we were to be seen together, so we'd best not tarry,' he continued, once again giving the horses their office to start. 'We'll save locating the homes of the good doctor and his sister and Mrs Adams for another time, too, and return to the house to put our heads together to decide how best to proceed.'

Any thought of planning future action was temporarily set aside when they returned to find Sarah in a positive fervour of excitement. Not only had all three of Ruth's new evening gowns arrived at the house and were now taking pride of place in the wardrobe, Sarah had also been active on their behalf and had paid an impromptu call on Lady Constance Styne, the once-close friend and confidante of the late Lady Beatrice Lindley.

'And when she discovered you were staying at my house, Ruth, she insisted I bring you to see her and invited us all to attend the informal dinner party she's holding tomorrow evening in an attempt to ease her granddaughter gently into polite society.' All at once Sarah's brow was marred by lines of perplexity. 'It was most odd, my dear, really, it was. But she seems to know so much about you already. In fact, I would go so far as to say she knows a deal more about you than I do myself.'

Smiling faintly, Hugo moved towards the door. 'Might I suggest that, even though Lady Beatrice chose to spend her last years living the life of a recluse, she did maintain contact with her closest friends by letter.'

'That must surely be the explanation,' Ruth agreed. 'Writing letters remained her chief occupation during the years I resided with her.'

Sarah gave vent to an unexpected gurgle of mirth. 'Although she's a grandmother, there's absolutely nothing wrong with Lady Constance's understanding. She's delighted her friend Beatrice didn't leave any of her money to her sisters. Vicious tabbies is how she refers to them!'

'At the risk of appearing rude, ladies, I believe I shall leave you alone to discuss the visit and whether you wish to accept Lady Constance's invitation. I must return the curricle to Kingsley's residence in Berkeley Square.'

'The verbal invitation included you, Hugo,' Sarah assured him, thereby arresting his immediate departure.

His expression betrayed neither delight nor dismay as he announced he would be happy to escort them if they chose to accept. Then he left the room without further ado and Ruth with the return of that uncomfortable feeling that he might have felt duty-bound to accompany her.

She didn't attempt to conceal her unease. 'It would be perfectly in order for us to go alone, would it not? Hugo need not accompany us, if he truly doesn't wish to?'

'Oh, yes, perfectly in order,' Sarah assured her. 'But it will do my brother good to bestir himself and go about into society more,' she continued, clearly not experiencing the pangs of conscience that were afflicting Ruth. 'He's becoming far too set in his ways. All he's done since his arrival is visit his club and pay calls on his male friends. That's all he's ever done for years when visiting London. Which, I might add, has been rare!'

'But might there not be a very good reason for his seemingly unsociable behaviour?' Ruth suggested hollowly, a clear and highly disturbing memory returning now with painful clarity. 'I—I've been led to understand that he suffered a tragic loss in his youth. Maybe he still hasn't fully recovered from it and has no desire to form a further attachment.'

Sarah appeared taken aback. 'Oh, so you know all about Alicia, do you? Was it Hugo himself, perchance, who told you about her?'

Ruth shook her head, deciding to be perfectly frank in the hope of discovering a deal more about Hugo's lost love. 'No, he's never so much as mentioned her name within my hearing. It was Lady Beatrice, as it happens. She touched upon their relationship briefly when Hugo sought shelter at Dunsterford Hall last year.'

Although Sarah was now looking decidedly ill at ease, Ruth didn't allow this to deter her from discovering everything she could, even if it meant the knowledge would bring little comfort and, worse, destroy all those hopeful dreams that had been steadily growing since embarking upon this visit to London. 'How did she die, Sarah?'

For several moments she thought she was destined to remain in ignorance, then Sarah said softly, leaning her head back against the comfort of the upholstery, 'No one seemed to know, not really. It was all so unexpected. That was perhaps why Hugo found it so hard to accept—a simple fall from a horse, little more than a sprained ankle.'

'But no one dies from a sprain!' Ruth, incredulous, pointed out.

'Quite!' Sarah agreed. 'The doctor was called. Alicia was ordered to bed for several days, during which time she succumbed to a slight chill, which settled on her chest. She rapidly worsened, developed a high fever and was dead within days.'

'And the doctor could do nothing?' Ruth contemplated the arrangement of flowers on the low table close to her elbow for a moment, as memory stirred. 'That might well account for your brother's poor opinion of those engaged in the medical profession.'

She hadn't realised she'd spoken her thoughts aloud until Sarah revealed that he swore the surgeons in the Peninsula killed more soldiers than they saved and that he wouldn't have one near him whenever he had been injured in battle. 'Always relied on Finn to care for him whenever he was wounded.'

This came as no surprise to Ruth. She had witnessed often enough during the journey to the capital that special rapport that existed between Hugo and his groom. It went far beyond that of master and servant. It was much the same as her own relationship with Agatha, a bond based on trust and mutual respect.

In the circumstances, though, Hugo's attitude towards the medical profession, and his scathing remarks about Dr Dent in particular, were faintly troubling. An alarming possibility had already begun to occur to her, but she decided not to dwell on it for the present, as his relationship with Alicia was very much at the forefront of her mind.

'They were engaged, were they not?'

'Unofficially, yes,' Sarah surprisingly revealed. 'Papa thought Hugo too young to be contemplating wedlock, even though he, like the rest of the family, simply adored Alicia and thought they were admirably well suited. But Hugo had just turned three-and-twenty and he was willing to fall in with Papa's wishes and wait a couple of years.'

'And Alicia...? Was she happy to delay their union?'

Sarah frowned. 'Where Alicia was concerned

it was sometimes difficult to know what she was thinking and feeling. She certainly never voiced any objection to the delay, at least not within my hearing.'

'You appear to have known her well, too?' Ruth ventured and received immediate confirmation of this.

'The Thorndykes were our nearest neighbours. We grew up together. Initially, she was more my friend than Hugo's. But all that quickly changed when she developed a taste for outdoor pursuits. She was, I suppose, a bit of a tomboy. She loved nothing more than a day's hunting, or fishing, or careering about on horseback with Hugo, not caring what state she was in when she arrived home. Which, I suspect, was part of the reason why Hugo adored her so much. She wasn't forever concerning herself over the state of her appearance. At the same time, though, she could be so gracefully feminine when she chose.' Sarah chuckled suddenly. 'She was exactly my height, yet she always made me feel so awkward and clumsy. Had she not been my very best friend, I think I could quite easily have hated her for being so graceful!'

Ruth could well understand that sentiment and was finding it difficult to quell a growing resentment towards the dead girl. She knew it was wrong, almost childishly spiteful, but she simply couldn't help it. How could any normal female compete with the memory of a girl who had not only shone in a ballroom, but had also been superb on the hunting field? Hugo's continued bachelor state suggested strongly that he had yet to meet Alicia's equal.

'And in all these years he never found anyone to replace her,' Ruth remarked hollowly, echoing her depressing thoughts. 'It's hardly surprising, really, is it?'

'It wasn't through lack of effort on my part,' Sarah assured her. 'Down the years I've introduced him to a score of suitable young ladies, all of whom shared Alicia's passion for outdoor pursuits. And some remarkably pretty ones, too! He was always unfailingly kind to them all, but never betrayed the least sign of wishing to further the acquaintance.' Sarah frowned as she cast a considering look in Ruth's direction. 'I believe, now, I shouldn't have attempted to interfere, that it was a complete waste of my time and effort, and that I should have permitted him to—'

A servant entered, immediately capturing Sarah's attention by reminding her that she had promised to go over the menu for her forthcoming party with Cook.

Knowing how much the event meant to Sarah, Ruth didn't attempt to detain her further by seeking more information about Hugo's lost love. In truth, what she had learned already had depressed her more than she cared to admit. So she sought immediate refuge in her allotted bedchamber, where even the sight of those three beautiful new evening gowns hanging in the wardrobe quite failed to lift her spirits.

Seating herself on the window sill to stare blindly down at the assortment of vehicles making their way along the busy street, where the hustle and bustle never entirely ceased, not even in the dead of night, Ruth could only wonder at herself. Ashamed though she was to admit to it, she was experiencing definite pangs of jealousy, now, towards a female whom she had never met... could never meet. How could she compete with an ideal...at least Hugo's ideal of the perfect mate?

Honesty obliged her to own that she possessed no obvious weapons in her armoury to assist her even to attempt to win his deepest affections. Had she been blessed to have a brother, she just might have learned how to fish. Had her mother not been so stubbornly determined to make her own way in the world and had accepted financial assistance from her father-in-law, there might have been money enough to have kept a horse for riding. And as for hunting…? The poor Reverend Mr Stephens would have suffered an apoplexy had he ever caught her with a firearm in her hands! No, there was no avoiding the fact that her life at the rectory had been vastly different from Miss Alicia Thorndyke's privileged upbringing.

Of course she might well be able to compete on the dance floor, she continued to reflect, achieving a modicum of satisfaction. More than one person had remarked on her gracefulness. She was accounted better than average on the pianoforte, too, and could certainly carry a tune, even though she did say so herself. Those accomplishments, commendable though they might be, hardly set her apart from other young women, something which Alicia evidently had been. And, from what she had learned today, Hugo had yet to meet anyone to compare with the girl who had played such a vital part in his youth.

Well, she couldn't say she hadn't been warned, she reminded herself, recalling once again words uttered months before with agonising clarity. Lady Beatrice had suggested strongly that Hugo Prentiss's heart had been buried along with his childhood sweetheart all those years ago; the fact that, having attained the age of five-and-thirty, he remained a bachelor, rather seemed to substantiate this, surely?

And yet, never once had he betrayed by so much as a look, word or gesture that he was anything other than heart-whole, Ruth continued to reflect, after recalling vividly numerous recent occasions when they had been alone together. She would have been the first to admit that her experience of the opposite sex was more limited than most females of her age. After all, she'd had no father, brothers or uncles in her life with whom she could draw comparisons. Yet, rather than a world-weary soul, Hugo had always seemed to her an educated and well-adjusted person who had been blessed with a charming personality and strong values, not to mention a wonderful sense of humour.

His character rather than his looks had attracted her from the first. Foolishly, perhaps, she had swiftly grown increasingly fond of her self-appointed protector, and now there was absolutely nothing she would ever wish to change about him. There was little point in denying the fact that she had already lost her heart to the big man. Yet, thankfully, she had succeeded thus far in maintaining a sense of perspective.

Although he had never once taken advantage of the situation by attempting to seduce her, or being overly familiar in any way, she was now convinced, after their carriage ride that morning, and the sweet endearment he had used to address her—for she hadn't doubted for a moment that that was precisely what it had been—that he, too, was not indifferent to her. No one could take such tender care of another human being, as he had her, and remain completely detached. The truth might be, of course, that he had reached a time in his life when he had come to the conclusion that if he didn't marry soon and raise a family, perhaps the opportunity would pass him by.

Maybe he thought they rubbed along so well together that he would be content to spend the rest of his life with her.

For her part she could think of nothing she could desire more than to become Hugo's wife, mother of his children. What had persuaded her to maintain a tight rein on her own feelings thus far, keeping them well hidden, was one soul-destroying doubt that had increased so rapidly in recent days and now refused to be quelled. Would she really be happy married to someone who would possibly always privately think of her as second best, a mere substitute for the woman he had really wanted? Until she could face that demon, and, should he ever ask her, be willing to take Hugo on his terms, then she must continue to keep her emotions well hidden, offer no encouragement and continue to treat him like a surrogate brother, if not for his sake, then certainly for her own.

The following evening Ruth entered the parlour to discover only Hugo, dressed formally in evening attire, ready to leave for the dinner party. Although she secretly preferred to see him more casually attired in top-boots and buckskins, there was no denying that, for a tall man, he cut an impressive figure no matter what he wore.

Dressed in the least revealing of her evening gowns, and with one of her new and shockingly expensive silk shawls draped becomingly about her shoulders, she felt she, also, looked very well. Consequently, she was somewhat surprised, and slightly aggrieved, too, to discover a slight frown creasing Hugo's brow, after his eyes had slowly appraised her from head to toe and then back again.

'Clearly I do not meet with your approval,' she said, striving not to appear offended. 'But I flatly refuse to buy anything else until I've heard from my man of business.'

'In that case it behoves me to purchase something for you. I've seen you wearing that locket on numerous occasions. Seemingly, it's the only necklace you've brought with you.'

She slanted a mocking glance. 'When I set out from Dunsterford Hall, Hugo, I never imagined for a moment I would be residing in the capital before the month was out. I brought sufficient clothing for several days, but few other possessions. Which just goes to prove what a goose I am for not having considered more carefully before embarking on the journey here. What I should have done, of course, was to return to Somerset first and then set out for London, carrying sufficient funds and jewels for my entire stay...no matter how protracted it was destined to turn out to be.'

When he offered no comment she regarded him thoughtfully, silently debating again that troubling possibility that had first occurred to her the day before. 'Hugo, you don't suppose all this effort on our part might turn out to be a complete waste of time...that we might in the end come to the conclusion that Lady Beatrice did, in fact, die of natural causes?'

Hugo glanced at her keenly before taking up a stance by the hearth. Leaning one arm along the mantelshelf, he gave the distinct impression of being completely unperturbed at the prospect, even before he said, 'At the outset I did suggest this could turn out to be very much the case. There remains many unanswered questions surrounding Lady Bea's death—many aspects of it that are distinctly suspicious. That said, it might well be that she did die of natural causes, but if not...' His regard became searching once more.

'But if not, have you considered what action you might consider taking?'

Ruth immediately shook her head, honest enough to admit she hadn't wished to dwell on this unpleasant possibility. She didn't even wish to contemplate it now and sought a way of avoiding the issue. 'My initial suspicions might have been borne of a guilty conscience and yours of a possible mistrust of the medical profession as a whole,' she suggested. 'We might yet be obliged to acknowledge that Dr Dent's assessment was an accurate one.'

If his regard had been searching at the outset, it had grown positively probing now, making her feel totally exposed. 'Now, why should you suppose I have a negative view of the medical profession as a whole, I wonder...? Aha!' He raised one finger in a triumphant gesture, which matched perfectly the set of his smile. 'Sarah, of course!'

Very slowly he went over to the window and stared out on to the street, his back towards her. 'If you take my advice, Ruth, you'll not pay too much heed to what my sister tells you, most especially when she reveals—er—personal details about me,' he advised softly. 'She's not entirely hen-witted, far from it, but she does have a tendency to be excessively blinkered on occasions, viewing matters entirely from her own standpoint. I do not consider all doctors a disgrace to their profession. I hope I haven't become such a bigot.'

Although his tone had remained velvety smooth and level, she sensed he was annoyed over something. It might well have been her show of uncertainty over Lady Beatrice's death that had given rise to irritation. And she could hardly blame him if this turned out to be the case, she decided, striving to be fair. She wouldn't be best pleased if she'd taken the trouble to escort someone all the way to London, only to be told, once there, that the reason for embarking on the journey in the first place was now in question. Somehow, though, she didn't think this lay at the root of his displeasure.

A moment later she began to question her own reading of his mood. Sarah entered and instantly his whole demeanour changed, suggesting at a stroke that he bore his sister no ill will for discussing his private concerns with a virtual stranger.

He came forward, assuring her that she looked particularly handsome that evening, a compliment which clearly pleased her. 'But I would never have supposed you to be so mean spirited, Sal, as not to lend your house guest an item or two from your trinket box, knowing as you do that she has left most all her jewellery back in Somerset.'

It would have been difficult to say who appeared more taken aback: Ruth could only gape in disbelief as the crimson hue worked its heated way up her neck and into her cheeks; while poor Sarah suddenly appeared awkwardly shamefaced, like a reprimanded child that had been caught red-handed being deliberately spiteful to a less privileged friend by not sharing her toys.

'Pay him no heed!' Ruth implored, finding her voice first. 'He's being wickedly provoking this evening. I shouldn't dream of borrowing any of your necklaces, Sarah. Besides which, it might show me in a very poor light if I were to go be-jewelled this evening,' she continued, after a moment's consideration. 'Lady Constance might applaud the fact that her friend disposed of her wealth outside her immediate family, but I doubt very much she would consider it anything other than a vulgar display if the recipient of such generosity were to go about town flaunting the fact.

And it's of vital importance that I make a favourable impression on that particular lady.'

'You couldn't fail to do otherwise,' Hugo assured her gently.

'I wish I had your confidence,' Ruth returned abruptly, while secretly pleased by the compliment. 'You see, I have the distinct feeling that that particular matron just might hold the key which could eventually unlock the mystery surrounding Lady Beatrice's death. And if she doesn't possess it, she just might know who does.'

Chapter Eight

All Ruth's reservations about meeting her late employer's closest friend vanished the instant she set foot inside the fashionable town residence, and none other than the Dowager Lady Constance Styne herself came forward to greet her personally, with a genuine warmth that instantly put her at ease.

The dinner which followed, consisting of numerous side dishes, was the most sumptuous Ruth had ever tasted in her life. So, to show her appreciation, she was only too happy, after the delicious meal was over, to accept the kindly hostess's invitation to take a turn on the fine instrument in the corner of the drawing room.

Although she would never have boasted about her abilities, she had been complimented enough times during her adult life to be sure that she was considered most accomplished on the pianoforte. She performed her chosen piece with confidence, and a skill borne of natural ability, rather than hours spent practising scales. The fulsome applause that greeted the end of her recital was very pleasing to hear. What she found most gratifying of all, however, was the look of combined surprise and pride she chanced to glimpse on Hugo's face as she surrendered her place at the instrument to another female guest.

'That was utterly charming, my dear!' the Dowager enthused, the first to come forward to compliment her personally. 'But I knew well enough how gifted you were. Beatrice frequently praised your abilities in her letters to me.' Her smile could not have been more kindly. 'No doubt you made my dear friend's last years so very happy. Did she, I wonder, come to look upon you as the daughter she'd never been blessed to have?'

Ruth was instantly conscience-stricken and had no intention of repaying the lady's kindness towards her thus far with a mouthful of lies. 'I wish I could confirm the truth of that, ma'am. Sadly, I cannot. I do not know what Lady Beatrice was like when young, but during the time I spent with her she maintained an air of detachment, betraying little emotion, at least nothing that could be interpreted as deep, genuine affection towards me.'

'No,' the Dowager responded gravely. 'I'd hoped it might have been otherwise, of course, but I cannot say I'm unduly surprised to hear you say that. And I appreciate your honesty.' She took a moment to look about her before guiding Ruth across to a door leading to a small ante-room. 'I think my guests are quite capable of entertaining themselves for a short while. There's something I should like you to see.'

Before following her into the room, Ruth instinctively glanced across in Hugo's direction once more to discover him on the point of disengaging himself from a small group of gentlemen. Evidently he had already guessed their hostess's objective and was determined the opportunity shouldn't be wasted. He wasn't to know it, of course, but Ruth had no intention of doing so! That said, she couldn't deny she was fast coming to rely on his support and sincerely hoped his aim was to join them.

She was obliged to delay her questioning while the Dowager began rummaging through a drawer.

The lady quickly located a gilt-framed miniature, a likeness of a young woman with large bright eyes and a mass of soft brown ringlets, which she promptly handed over.

Ruth was immediately aware that there was something familiar about the innocent young face that smiled shyly back at her from the oval frame. 'Heavens above! This was never a likeness of Lady Bea, surely?'

The Dowager nodded solemnly. 'Hard to believe, I know, Miss Harrington. None the less, I can assure you it is Beatrice, painted some few years before her marriage, when she was an innocent girl, full of romantic dreams.'

The slight click of the door instantly captured the Dowager's attention. Unlike Ruth, she was surprised by the interruption. Hugo, however, with his customary aplomb, easily excused his unexpected appearance by solicitously enquiring after Ruth's health. 'I saw you slip in here, and couldn't help wondering…'

'I'm fine, Hugo,' she assured him, with only the faintest betraying tremor and quite forgetting to be more formal now that they were in public.

Hugo, of course, didn't miss the slight solecism.

More importantly, he noticed that the Dowager hadn't either, when she began to look at them both with renewed interest. He raised a questioning brow.

'Forgive me, but I was under the impression that Miss Harrington was a guest and friend of your sister's, sir.'

'Indeed, she is, ma'am…now,' Hugo concurred, before cunningly divulging just when and where he and Ruth had first become acquainted.

'Oh, I see! So you were there at the time of Beatrice's death.' She transferred her gaze to the young woman who appeared remarkably at ease in the tall Colonel's company. 'It must have been a terrible time for you, my dear. No doubt you found having a gentleman present of great comfort.'

Hugo once again took it upon himself to intercede, especially as he had detected the faint yet unmistakable choking sound from the female beside him. Seemingly she was having considerable difficulty containing her mirth. And little wonder! No doubt she was recalling that, at the time, it had foolishly crossed his mind to suppose that she just might be a murderess!

'I offered what assistance I could, ma'am.

Which was little enough,' he divulged, after he and Ruth had accepted the Dowager's invitation to seat themselves together on the sofa. 'I'm happy to say that in recent weeks I've fared rather better, persuading Miss Harrington to remain as a guest of my sister for, this, her first stay in the capital.'

When the Dowager made no comment and continued to regard them both with what could best be described as a quizzical little smile, Ruth took the opportunity to show Hugo the miniature of her former employer in the hope that he could take full advantage of this private little interlude.

He didn't disappoint her. 'I would be the first to admit, ma'am, that I wasn't well acquainted with Lady Beatrice. In fact, I cannot recall ever having conversed with her at all, until I was obliged to seek refuge with her last autumn. But my one clear recollection of years ago was of a very sociable creature. What do you suppose turned her into a virtual recluse?'

It had been the perfect opening gambit and won an immediate response from the Dowager, who gave vent to an unladylike snort. 'I suspect there were many reasons. But the main one, I suppose, was her disastrous choice of a husband. You may perhaps just remember Lindley, sir, though he died some years ago. Not to put too fine a point on it, the man was nothing more than an unfeeling monster, a debauched womaniser and gamester, past praying for long before he had attained the age of thirty.'

Lady Constance shook her head solemnly, clearly plagued by unhappy memories. 'Perhaps, though, poor Bea had only herself to blame. Several of us tried to warn her against him. From a young age Lindley never attempted to curb or conceal his scandalous exploits—his many vices were common knowledge.'

'Little wonder she had scant regard for the male sex as a whole and no respect at all for the marriage state,' Ruth murmured, after digesting all this. 'I believe that is one of the reasons why she left me her fortune…so that I need never wed.'

'If that is so, then it was very wrong of her!' Lady Constance declared staunchly, after watching Hugo lower his eyes to stare solemnly down at a certain portion of the floor. 'I wouldn't for a moment attempt to suggest that most all unions result in marital bliss, because they do not. Even so, I should like to think that a great majority turn out to be very tolerable, with husbands and wives rubbing along together in harmony for the most part. Sadly, there are those that seem doomed from the start. Poor Bea's union fell very much into this category.'

Ruth deliberately refrained from enquiring too deeply into certain aspects of the disastrous marriage. She, too, was not oblivious to the fact that Hugo had grown quiet all of a sudden and couldn't help wondering whether he felt uncomfortable discussing the unsavoury character of a member of his own sex in mixed company. Besides which, she didn't suppose, either, the Dowager would choose to reveal all she knew, so she merely asked why Lady Beatrice had remained with her husband for so long.

'Surely, ma'am, she could have sought refuge from his cruelty with a member of her family?'

The Dowager's expression grew distinctly cold. 'I know for a fact that, early in the marriage, she approached both her sisters, but neither would offer sanctuary.' She shook her head sadly. 'I suppose in a way I can understand their refusing.

Both were keen to maintain their social positions and so shied away from any type of scandal.'

She paused for a moment before adding, and encompassing both her listeners in her steady gaze, 'You must remember, also, that when a woman marries, under the law, she becomes her husband's property. Everything she owns becomes his. She is to all intents and purposes at his mercy. Furthermore, her late brother-in-law was a formidable and powerful man. His kind have had influence enough to make the laws of the land and power enough to enforce them.

'In the Duke's defence, though, it must be said, that Beatrice owed the comfort of her widowhood, her later life, entirely to his generosity. He bought his brother and bride a fine country mansion soon after their marriage. Naturally enough, the house retained no happy memories, so Beatrice sold the place within a twelvemonth of her husband's demise and removed to Somerset. I believe I'm right in saying the late Duke also ensured that she was to be paid a handsome quarterly allowance for her lifetime.'

Memory stirred and Ruth vaguely recalled Lady Beatrice's man of business remarking on this, and on the fact that her quiet lifestyle had enabled her to save a goodly portion of this allowance over the years; more than enough to ensure that Ruth herself would want for nothing throughout her life, providing she did not foolishly spend to excess time and again.

All at once those pangs of guilt over Lady Beatrice's demise returned with a vengeance. Her future comfort had been assured only through another's bitter unhappiness.

'Poor Lady Bea,' she found herself murmuring aloud. 'If only someone could have helped.'

Surprisingly enough Lady Constance betrayed scant sympathy, swiftly reiterating, 'As I've mentioned before, child, she was warned against marrying that man. Moreover, she could have fled the house at any time had she truly wished to do so and I don't suppose for a moment her husband would have forced her return.'

Again she shook her head. 'I do not doubt she suffered during her fifteen-year marriage at that brute's hands. But the fact remains she chose to stay locked in the loveless union… And one cannot help but ask oneself why?'

'One can only suppose that life with Lord Charles

Lindley seemed preferable to an existence of near poverty and obscurity in some hidden corner of the land,' Hugo announced, breaking his long silence and proving at a stroke that he had been concentrating on everything that had been said.

'And there you have it, Colonel!' Lady Constance agreed wholeheartedly. 'You may remember, sir, that Lady Beatrice was the daughter of an earl. Like her two younger sisters, she had grown accustomed to social position and luxury. It's my honest belief that she was prepared to put up with her husband's bouts of drunken brutality, which it must be said became increasingly less frequent as the years passed, in preference to a life of obscurity.

'Oh, I must seem quite unfeeling!' the Dowager declared, when both her listeners continued to sit quietly digesting everything they were hearing. 'And it would be wrong to think me so. I did attempt to help in my own small way. Unlike poor Beatrice, who sadly never bore a child, I produced four offspring in my first five years of marriage. As a result my dear husband bought a most charming little house at a small coastal town not too far distant from Brighton, where I would stay yearly in the summer, enjoying the benefits of sea air and walks along the cliffs. I thought Beatrice would benefit from the change of air. She sometimes stayed at my little retreat on the coast, in preference to remaining in the country, once the Season was over. Her husband never accompanied her. So I'm sure she attained some solace, though it must be said she never remained for more than a few weeks at a time. Beatrice, I'm afraid, had one thing in common with that husband of hers—both were social creatures.'

Something the Dowager had revealed had succeeded in touching a chord of memory, but it was the last comment made that remained at the forefront of Ruth's mind.

'If that was, indeed, the case, ma'am,' she returned, puzzled, 'what on earth, do you suppose, prompted her to up and leave London for the tranquillity of Somerset to live the life of a virtual recluse? As Colonel Prentiss remarked earlier, it just doesn't make sense. Lady Beatrice had endured years trapped in a loveless union. She was free of the chains of matrimony. Why on earth didn't she remain in the capital with her friends and enjoy her widowhood?'

Lady Constance smiled wryly. 'Ah, my dear, I suspect there were several reasons, none of which redound to the credit of shallow society… And in that I suppose I must include myself, I'm ashamed to say.'

'I'm sorry, ma'am, I do not perfectly understand,' Ruth prompted, determined still to discover all she could, even at the risk of embarrassing her kindly hostess.

'For all Lord Charles Lindley was a blackguard of the highest order, he did, right up until his death, retain some influential friends and few doors were ever closed to him. He left a mountain of debts, which resulted in his widow becoming wholly dependent on his brother's generosity. Poor Beatrice soon discovered that even the wife of a dissolute lord wielded more prestige than that of a respectable, if sadly faded, widow. Invitations to those prestigious parties she had once enjoyed no longer came her way. A few close friends retained contact and stood by her, but her life was a mere shadow of what it had once been and so she removed to the country, well away from shallow society. And I for one never blamed her for doing that.'

* * *

And neither could Ruth, a fact she made clear to her companions, later, during the carriage ride back to the Lansdowns' town house. 'It's little wonder she grew so bitterly resentful. She must have felt that society as a whole was slowly abandoning her. And that, after years of enduring a dreadfully unhappy marriage. I'm beginning to appreciate just why she was so keen for me never to take the matrimonial plunge,' she added. 'Women have few rights under the law, and fewer, it would seem, after they wed.'

As she had turned her head to stare meditatively out of the window, Ruth quite failed to see the troubled glance Sarah shot at her brother's impassive countenance, before asking, 'Did you happen to discover anything that might shed light upon Lady Beatrice's demise?'

Ruth shook her head. 'And to be perfectly honest I thought she might become suspicious if, on so brief an acquaintance, I attempted to delve too deeply into certain aspects of her friend's past.'

'On the contrary, my dear,' Hugo corrected, with the faintest edge of disapproval in his voice. 'Evidently, you were paying far too much attention to comments made on the evils of matrimony to absorb the very interesting fact Lady Constance disclosed about a property situated on the coast that offered long cliff walks and solace to a tortured soul.'

Ruth sat bolt upright, accepting the mild rebuke with a good grace, as he had spoken no less than the truth. She had paid more heed to the perils in store for any woman should her judgement prove faulty when it came to choosing a future mate.

'Yes, you're right, Hugo! I had almost forgotten that very interesting detail.' Narrow-eyed, Ruth fixed her gaze on the intricate folds of his cravat. 'So Lady Constance once owned a small house on the coast, or rather her husband did. And Lady Beatrice stayed there on several occasions without her husband. And, if I remember correctly, it was while enjoying a coastal cliff walk that she witnessed an altercation between two persons, later to discover that one had been found at the foot of the cliffs.'

'It would certainly be beneficial to discover the identity of the poor unfortunate who met his death that day,' Hugo commented, after his sister, at a complete loss, had demanded an explanation and had been regaled with the few details known. 'From something that was said, I'm fairly certain the deceased was a man, but I cannot recall any mention of the year he died.'

Ruth shook her head, confirming this. 'All we do know is that the incident took place some time during Lady Bea's marriage. She married Lord Lindley in 1786, and the marriage lasted fifteen years.'

Ruth paused to consider for a moment. 'The person who might know, of course, is the abigail Lady Beatrice employed during the last years of her marriage. It stands to reason she would have accompanied her mistress on those trips to the coast.' She sighed. 'Sadly, though, she left Lady Bea's employ shortly after the removal to Somerset, before I went to live at Dunsterford Hall, and I've no notion of where she might have gone. Or even if she's still alive, come to that.'

'Oh!' Sarah gave a visible start, instantly capturing both her companions' attention. 'I just might be able to help you there.'

'Do you mean you know what became of the wench?' Hugo asked, thinking it a stroke of great good fortune if it turned out to be the case.

'I'm fairly certain my good friend Marjorie Gilmorton mentioned to me once that she'd employed Lady Beatrice's maid. Said how very efficient the woman was…though whether she's still in my friend's employ, I couldn't say.'

'Should be easy enough to find out,' her brother suggested. 'Is she spending the Season in town this year?' After receiving a confirming nod, Hugo added, staring at them both, 'Then pay a call on her tomorrow, if possible. And it might be worthwhile taking Aggie along with you.'

'What a capital notion, Hugo!' Ruth agreed. 'Aggie knew her, briefly. It would be quite natural for her to raise the subject of Lady Beatrice, as they were both employed by her.' She looked across at him hopefully. 'Will you be accompanying us?'

Disappointing her, he shook his head. 'No, I think my time would be better spent paying a visit to a particular firm of lawyers. I'm certain some believable reason for making an impromptu call will have occurred to me before morning.'

Although Hugo left the house promptly after breaking his fast the following day, he did so with distinctly mixed feeling, and a decidedly heavy heart. Only his conscience had forced him to continue helping solve the mystery of the widow's demise. He had given his word and had no intention of breaking it, even though he was brutally aware that once the mystery was solved, there was nothing to keep Ruth in London and any hope of them forming a serious attachment would be gone.

As he turned his head to stare sightlessly out of the grimy window, he couldn't help wondering whether something more meaningful between them was a forlorn hope. Poor Ruth hadn't had what one would call a normal upbringing. Furthermore, for the last ten years she had lived with an out-and-out man-hater. It would be something marvellous, indeed, if she'd remained impervious to all that vitriolic loathing. And, it didn't help, of course, when she was being continually reminded of the perils of contracting an unsuitable alliance!

He hadn't missed that look of doubt, of fear, almost, when Lady Constance had touched upon her late friend's disastrous union. Yet, he wouldn't have said that Ruth betrayed the least dislike of his sex. In fact, he'd go as far as to say she at least enjoyed his company.

He wasn't oblivious to the way her face lit up whenever he walked into a room: an indication, had he needed one, that she was always pleased to see him; that she was, perhaps, growing more than just fond of him. Yet, she had never once, either by word or gesture, offered him the least encouragement to further their relationship. It was almost as if she was constantly attempting to remain just that tiny bit aloof, friendly, but no more. His eyes narrowed. Was that because she was so terrified of contracting a disastrous union? Or was there some other underlying reason for that faint air of reserve in her?

When the hackney carriage drew to a halt outside the premises of Messrs Blunt, Blunt & Caldecott, Hugo was obliged to consign the conundrum to the back of his mind to ponder over on another occasion, as he wasted no time in seeking out his particular quarry. As luck would have it Mr Henry Blunt was available to see him at once and Hugo was immediately shown into a small and somewhat grimy back office.

'I see you remember me,' he remarked, as the little lawyer, not attempting to conceal his surprised recognition, rose from behind his desk to take Hugo's outstretched hand.

'But, of course I remember you, sir! If you'll pardon my saying so, you're not the sort of gentleman one easily forgets,' he admitted, after watching Hugo lower his much taller-than-average frame on to a chair. 'I shan't attempt to deny I'm somewhat surprised to see you here in town. I seem to recall your remarking on the fact that you seldom visit the capital nowadays.'

'Your memory serves you well, Mr Blunt. But I'm hopeful that in the future I'll have reason to make the trip more often. You see, I'm seriously considering acquiring a property here in the not-too-distant future, if not this year, then possibly next, and was wondering whether you might be interested in dealing with any legal aspects on my behalf?'

'I'd be delighted to do so, of course!' Mr Blunt assured him, before offering a glass of port. This was precisely the companionable reaction for which Hugo had hoped, for it granted him the opportunity to turn the little lawyer's thoughts to their first encounter and the sad event that overshadowed it.

For a moment or two the lawyer appeared genuinely bewildered, then raised one finger. 'Indeed, yes! Unlike you, though, sir, I'd never encountered the lady before.'

'It was business, was it not, that took you to that part of the world?' Hugo remarked in a light, conversational way.

'Indeed, it was.'

'And does your profession oblige you to travel about the land a good deal?'

The lawyer shook his head. 'No, sir, most all the firm's business is conducted, here, in the capital, I'm pleased to say. I'm not too fond of travel myself. Too many—er—imponderables involved, so to speak. Although roads are much improved, at least some of them, travel remains a risky business, not to mention a tiresome one.'

After nodding in agreement, Hugo paused to sample his port, while continuing to assess the little man on the opposite side of the desk. 'So you're not one to desert the capital to sample the fresh sea air, as some of the professional classes are inclined to do during the summer? Spa towns used to be the favourite visiting places, but I believe their popularity has been diminishing in recent years. Sea air, not to mention a spot of sea bathing, is all the rage nowadays, or so I'm reliably informed.'

Although he fell short of a grimace, there was no doubting the prospect of such activity didn't appeal to Mr Blunt. 'Oh, no, sir. I'm more than content to remain in London throughout the year. Being a confirmed bachelor, I've only myself to consider.' He appeared to ponder for a moment. 'Would you believe, until that trip I made last year, I'd never glimpsed the sea in my entire life, though I did once travel very close to the mouth of the Thames... But I don't suppose that really counts as visiting the coast, does it?'

'I think we might agree it does not,' Hugo responded, well satisfied with the outcome of his visit, as he'd discovered precisely what he wished to know and could cross the lawyer's name off the list of suspects.

Ruth was equally satisfied with her visit to Sarah's friend. If possible, Mrs Marjorie Gilmorton turned out to be even more easygoing than Sarah. Once the subject of personal maids had been raised and it was confirmed that she had engaged the abigail previously employed in the Lindley household, the lively matron was only too happy to allow Agatha to take tea with the maid Dwight in the small parlour at the rear of the house so that they might be private together to chat over old times.

Although Ruth found Mrs Gilmorton to be a most likeable matron, she could hardly wait for the visit to end so that she might learn what, if anything, Agatha had managed to discover from the bird-like little woman who had remained with her former mistress throughout those last unhappy years of marriage.

She was destined not to be disappointed, either. The instant they had returned to Sarah's fashionable town carriage, Agatha confirmed that Edith Dwight had, indeed, accompanied her former mistress to the coast on several occasions. She had also remembered very clearly a certain Sir George Hilliard having been discovered one morning among the jagged rocks at the foot of the cliffs, though she was quite unable to confirm whether his demise had occurred when she and Lady Beatrice had been staying at the coastal retreat.

'Sir George Hilliard...?' Ruth echoed. Of course, the name meant absolutely nothing to her, so she cast a hopeful glance in Sarah's direction.

'Oh, yes...yes, I do now recall the incident, vaguely,' Sarah confirmed after a moment's thought. 'It must have been fifteen, maybe sixteen, years ago. It happened during my very first Season, if my memory serves me correctly. There was some mystery surrounding his death, I seem to remember. His wife couldn't understand why he should have been at that coastal town, when he was supposed to be staying with friends in Brighton. It was strongly rumoured at the time that he might well have been kidnapped and murdered. By all accounts he had made cuckolds of several gentlemen, so there was no shortage of suspects. But no charges were ever brought against anyone.'

Were all husbands unfaithful to their wives? Ruth couldn't help wondering, before she concentrated her thoughts, once again, on solving the mystery that had brought her to the metropolis in the first place.

'Are you, perchance, acquainted with the family, or the widow?' she asked hopefully, but was destined to be disappointed.

'Sadly, no. Lady Hilliard retired permanently to the country, after her husband's death, to bring up her children. I believe her only son visits the capital from time to time, though I'm not acquainted with him, personally. Whether he's in town at present, I really couldn't say. Hugo, I think, is better placed to discover more. I dare say the late baronet is remembered by some. Perhaps he might learn a thing or two about him at his club.'

That evening Hugo, accompanied by his good friend Viscount Kingsley, entered White's and quickly found a secluded corner table. Although the Viscount intended to return to his country estate the following day, he was willing to assist his friend in the matter of discovering more about the late, if not lamented, Sir George Hilliard.

'As I've already mentioned, old friend, I was more than happy to accompany you here tonight, as you're not a member,' his lordship began,' but I'm damned if I know what else I can do to help. Sir George's death was a bit before my time. I wasn't precisely a scrubby schoolboy when it happened, but I hadn't embarked on the social scene either.'

His lordship remained silent while a waiter deposited a bottle and glasses on the table. 'I must confess I'm somewhat surprised to find you're continuing with this, Hugo,' he went on, the instant the waiter had moved away. His smile was distinctly crooked. 'You say you're certain Miss Harrington had no hand in the lady's demise. I would have imagined you'd have had far more important and—er—personal matters occupying your thoughts at the present time.'

Hugo was in no doubt where his friend's conversation was leading and his smile in response, though equally crooked, was distinctly rueful. 'If I were to tell you that Ruth's never long or very far from my thoughts nowadays, you might appreciate the state of my own mind and feelings in the matter now. I no longer harbour any doubts,' he revealed. 'But it isn't so simple, Luke. There are certain—er—unforeseen complications developing, so I've yet to declare myself.'

'Away with you!' his lordship exclaimed disparagingly. 'Faint heart…etcetera. You'll never get anywhere if you don't let the girl know your affections are engaged. What's needed is action, not all this fiddle-faddling around! How's the girl supposed to know how you feel if you don't tell her outright that you're smitten?'

'Upon my word!' Hugo returned in a flash. 'That's mighty rich coming from you, I must say! Here sits the man who took almost six months to consummate his own marriage to one of the loveliest women who ever drew breath! If that's not dragging one's feet—if one might describe it so—then I don't know what is!'

The Viscount glanced about him in some alarm. 'For pity's sake, man, keep your voice down! You don't know who might be listening. I revealed that in the strictest confidence. There were…unusual circumstances, as well you know.'

'Just as there are in my own relationship with Ruth. And I don't intend to do anything to jeopardise our blossoming…friendship, not yet a while.'

Hugo ran a hand through his hair, not attempting to conceal his puzzlement and deep concern. 'You don't realise, Luke, the isolated life she was obliged to endure, when what she should have been doing was socialising, going to parties… meeting prospective husbands. And I know I ought to grant her that opportunity. Apart from that, the time isn't right for a declaration. There's something troubling her, troubling her about me... I sense it. Yet I'm not yet sure just what her concerns might be, or where they've sprung from. It might be that she's just wary about taking the matrimonial plunge. Which is understandable in the circumstances.' His frown deepened. 'Yet, I just sense there's something...'

'Well, all I can say is I hope your patience holds out,' the Viscount returned bluntly. 'Mine wouldn't, that I do know, not a second time.'

His lordship's attention was then caught by a new arrival, a confirmed old bachelor who had resided in town for a great many years. He beckoned the worthy over, convinced he might be of help in Hugo's endeavours.

'Carlisle, old fellow, good to see you!' his lordship declared, as the elderly gentleman joined them at the table. 'I don't know whether you're acquainted with my friend here, Colonel Prentiss?'

A myopic gaze was then fixed in Hugo's direction. 'Prentiss...? Not one of the Hampshire Prentisses, are you, m'boy? Oh, in that case I knew your father well,' the new arrival revealed, after Hugo's nod in response. 'Fine man! One of the best. And you've a great look of him, if I may say so.'

Hugo didn't object in the least. What he didn't wish to do, however, was dwell on his own lineage if he could possibly avoid it. The Viscount would not have caught the elderly bachelor's attention without good reason. Seemingly his lordship supposed Lord Carlisle just might be able to shed some light on the mystery surrounding the death of a certain notorious baronet.

'As you say, sir, my sire was a fine man. And one who, moreover, was blessed, if one may describe it so, to die in his own bed, and of natural causes, unlike so many others in recent years,' Hugo began artfully, in the hope of steering the conversation in more profitable lines. 'Of course his lordship and I saw many friends killed on the battlefields in recent years. One expects that in time of war. But it's surprising how many lose their lives in decidedly suspicious circumstances.'

His frown of puzzlement was masterly. 'Now, who was it, Luke, we were talking about only the other day—the fellow found dead on a beach somewhere, when he should have been visiting friends?'

His lordship's thoughtful pose was no less convincing. 'Yes, who the deuce was it…? My uncle knew him, said something about him being on the Sussex coast, not too far from Brighton…Hilliard, George Hilliard.'

'By Jove, you're right!' Lord Carlisle confirmed, much to Hugo's intense satisfaction. 'I knew the fellow, too. Devil for the ladies, so he was. Well, we've all dabbled in our time, I suppose, but most of us know where to draw the line. No woman was safe around old George. He was reputed to have ruined more than one poor girl's reputation—servants, society hostesses—all the same to old George.'

Hugo exchanged a glance with the Viscount. 'More than likely his death wasn't an accident,' he suggested. 'Must have made a few enemies in his time, most especially among those whose wives had fallen victim to his charm.'

'Seem to remember that's what was rumoured at the time. But I'm not so certain,' Lord Carlisle countered. 'He was a likeable rogue for all his philandering ways. Things might have been different if he'd married one of his own class. But he married a wealthy cit's daughter who didn't know the rules. Most women of our class know to turn a blind eye to a husband's extramarital affairs.'

'Not all of us are inclined to stray,' the Viscount pointed out drily.

'Oh, no, dear boy! Wasn't for a moment suggesting you'd do such a thing,' the older man returned apologetically. 'Happily married, I'm sure. Not that I'd know much about it myself, you understand, being a confirmed old bachelor. But it was generally believed that George only behaved the way he did to spite his father-in-law, who it was strongly rumoured kept a firm grasp on the purse-strings, so to speak. If George had been allowed to keep a mistress openly, he maybe wouldn't have conducted so many liaisons behind his wife's back. It was a commonly held belief at the time that he did keep a mistress at that place where he was found dead. What other reason could there have been for him going there, I ask you!'

'What, indeed?' Hugo agreed, feeling there had to have been some very good reason for the baronet to visit that coastal town.

Chapter Nine

Although Ruth had been most interested to hear what Hugo had discovered at that famous gentlemen's club in St. James's and, like himself, felt it had opened up several avenues not hitherto considered, she managed to thrust Sir George Hilliard's decidedly suspicious demise to the back of her mind in order to concentrate all her efforts in assisting with Sarah's forthcoming party.

The arrival of the master of the house provided a welcome respite from all the frantic activity, at least for a day or two. Lord Merrell Lansdown, known to all his friends as Merry, was a larger-than-life character. Although having been built very much on the same lines as Hugo, tall and well muscled, Merry, sadly, had weakened and succumbed to the finer things of life a good many years before and, as a direct result, had become increasingly portly with the advent of middle age. None the less, Ruth liked him from the first and was pleasantly relieved to discover that, contrary to many unions contracted between members of the *ton*, the Lansdowns' marriage seemed a happy one, wherein both parties betrayed a genuine affection for the other.

Although Sarah's behaviour towards her husband might have been viewed in certain quarters as somewhat unorthodox, there was absolutely nothing irregular about her attitude to holding social gatherings. She oversaw everything with meticulous attention to detail in an attempt to ensure that her party, although not to compare with the most lavish held during the Season, would be universally remembered as one of the most enjoyable events in the social calendar.

Naturally, Ruth couldn't match Sarah's expertise in organising such an affair; moreover, she wouldn't have attempted to interfere even if this hadn't been the case. In one aspect, though, she knew she could be of immeasurable help and didn't hesitate to offer her services.

It was considered by the late Lady Beatrice Lindley herself that Ruth's skill on the keyboard was matched only by her innate gift for arranging flowers. It was one way she knew she would be able to repay Sarah, at least in part for all the kindness she'd shown towards a virtual stranger. Consequently, on the day of the party, she was more than happy to be left to her own devices for several hours in a small back room.

If Sarah had experienced any qualms about designating such an important task to someone whose abilities were totally untested, she certainly never revealed the fact. Quite the contrary—she betrayed confidence by not once entering the parlour to see how things were progressing until late in the afternoon, when she threw wide the door, only to stop dead in her tracks.

'Yes, the scent is somewhat overpowering,' Ruth declared, after glancing over her shoulder in time to catch the almost stunned expression flicker over Sarah's face. 'I've almost finished. Just these final few blooms to place in this last vase.'

'Breathtaking…quite breathtaking!' Sarah at last managed to utter, after she had gazed in wonder at the two dozen-or-so arrangements of varying sizes that had been completed that day. Her eyes were suddenly lit by an impish gleam. 'All my friends will be quite pea-green with envy. I shall gain such delight in teasing them all by saying I went to the expense of hiring a professional arranger. They'll all be begging me to reveal the genius's name. Though that,' she went on, after moving forward to study the creations more closely, 'would be doing a great disservice to you who should receive all the credit.'

'Heavens! I don't crave approbation. As long as you're satisfied, that's all that concerns me,' Ruth assured her, only to be the recipient of a long, considering look.

'Do you know, you and Hugo are much alike. He's always had a tendency to undervalue his abilities and speak lightly of his achievements.'

After placing the last flower in the arrangement, Ruth acknowledged the truth of this. 'No, neither of us is what you'd call boastful by nature.'

'Oh, you have far more in common than just that,' Sarah returned, after having cast a second considering glance. 'You both much prefer the peace and quiet of the country. And speaking of Hugo,' she continued, when she quite failed to elicit a response this time, 'he's just administered the most tremendous scold because I've monopolised you for most of the day. He also reminded me that if you don't hurry to your room you won't be ready in time for the pre-party dinner. I should warn you, he's determined to have you seated beside him at the table.'

This succeeded in capturing Ruth's attention. She knew Hugo had been out of the house for much of the day. 'I wonder whether he's succeeded in discovering more about the late womanising baronet whose death might be in some way linked to Lady Beatrice's.'

'Oh, can you not put that horrid business out of your mind entirely just for one night?' Sarah demanded testily. 'I want you to dance and enjoy the evening. I also want you to look your best. So hurry along now, whilst I arrange for the servants to place these beautiful creations in positions where they'll be most admired.'

Although she didn't delay in seeking her bedchamber, Ruth didn't seem able to summon up the least enthusiasm for the evening ahead. She had spent far too much time on her own that day; she realised that now. Thinking mostly about Hugo, she had allowed those feelings, which she had done her utmost in the past few short weeks to keep well concealed, to come to the fore. How could she adhere to Sarah's advice and forget her purpose in coming to the capital? To do so would leave her exposed to too much heartache, or worse. To do so just might reveal emotions to one very astute gentleman that he might not really wish to see.

Several hours later, the sight of herself dressed in a beautiful gold-coloured creation of lace and silk, and with her hair elaborately arranged in a crown of chestnut curls, quite failed to lift her spirits. How could she gain any pleasure from her reflection when she was continually plagued by the heartrending prospect of a certain pair of blue eyes regarding her while perhaps longing to see quite another lady in her place? She had to face the fact, here and now, that she might always figure in Hugo's heart as second best. Furthermore, she must also face the possibility that she might never be able to swallow her pride sufficiently to accept such a destiny.

A knock on the bedchamber door, quickly followed by the entry of a young maid, brought a welcome distraction. 'Begging your pardon, miss, but I were asked to bring you this.'

Ruth took the square velvet box from the outstretched hand and guessed what it contained, even before she had opened the lid to discover a pair of pearl-drop earrings, accompanied by the most beautiful pearl necklace.

She couldn't fail to feel moved by the kindly gesture and so didn't hesitate to request Agatha to fix the adornment, which had been fashioned to resemble a pendant, about her throat. 'That was most kind of Sarah to lend me these,' she declared, after donning the earrings, and the lovely necklace, the bottommost and largest pearl of which almost touched the swell of her breasts.

Her conscience then smote her and she gave herself a mental shake. The very least she could do to show her appreciation was to do her utmost to appear as if she were enjoying the evening ahead, she decided, leaving her room, only to very nearly collide with none other than the hostess herself making her way along the passage in the direction of the staircase.

'Oh, my dear, you look lovely! Positively captivating!' Sarah declared, before fixing her gaze

on the beautiful adornments. 'And those pearls…
What I wouldn't give to have those about my
throat this evening!'

Ruth, quite naturally, was taken aback. 'Why
on earth did you loan them to me for the evening,
if you wished to wear them yourself?'

It was Sarah's turn now to appear startled. 'But
I didn't. They're not mine.'

'Not yours? Then who…?'

'You've a secret admirer.' Like an excited
schoolgirl, Sarah uttered a squeal of delight. 'Now,
I wonder who that can be? As if I didn't know!'

Unlike Sarah, Ruth began to feel distinctly uneasy. 'You don't suppose Hugo bought them for
me?'

'Well, who else do you suppose! Unless you've
secret admirers strewn across the capital about
whom I know absolutely nothing.'

Ruth's confusion was increasing by leaps and
bounds, along with her doubts and anxieties. Was
the gift a token of his sincere affection? If not,
she couldn't imagine what else it might signify.
'You—you imagine your brother admires me?'

'Well, of course he does! Any fool can see that
you two rub along together famously. I've never

seen him so at ease with anyone for a very long time…not since his youth and his attachment to Alicia. Why, even darling Merry, who isn't given to noticing much as a rule, said that you two would make a remarkably handsome couple.'

The reference to Alicia had been unfortunate to say the least, bringing as it had that most besetting anxiety once again to the forefront of her mind. Not only that, Ruth also felt somewhat shaken by the way events all at once seemed to be over-taking her. Even so, she felt some response was expected. 'Yes, we do get on very well. We—we always have, right from the first, but…'

No one could have mistaken the clear note of misgiving in her voice. 'You do care for my brother, don't you?' Sarah asked, all at once sounding distinctly unsure. 'I was convinced you were not indifferent to him.'

'Oh, no, I'm not indifferent to him.' Ruth smiled wistfully. 'But I think we need more time, both of us do.' A worrying possibility then occurred to her, instantly wiping the half-smile from her face. 'You don't suppose he intends making an announcement this evening, do you?' she added, the beautiful adornment resting against her chest having suddenly acquired a distinctly worrying significance—a betrothal gift perhaps?

Sarah's amazement could not have been feigned. 'What…without discussing the matter with you first? I very much doubt it. My brother might have a string of faults, and be infuriatingly pig-headed on occasions, but he certainly isn't presumptuous.'

'No, of course he isn't.' Ruth silently cursed herself for allowing sheer panic to override common sense. 'I'm just being foolish, worrying too much over this party of yours, and praying the flowers won't wilt in their vases before the evening is over.'

The explanation might have convinced Sarah that all was at it should have been, but the display of feigned gaiety Ruth tried desperately to maintain in order to conceal those heartfelt misgivings didn't fool Sarah's astute brother—no, not for a single second!

With all the inherent skill of a seasoned campaigner Hugo easily prised her away from the other dinner guests, once the meal was over, and guided her towards a secluded corner in the large salon where the party was being held. Once out of earshot he didn't waste any time, either, in discovering what he wished to know.

'Why, there's nothing wrong,' she refuted with all the conviction she could muster. 'Why on earth should you imagine there is?'

'Nice try, my angel!' Hugo returned, totally unconvinced. 'But might I remind you that it is your self-appointed protector you're attempting to convince, the one who has possibly come to know you better than any other in recent weeks, and not some bumpkin newly arrived from the country. So let's have no more prevarication.'

Ruth couldn't help smiling at this. It was perhaps the first genuine curl that had appeared on her lips all evening thus far. Hugo was without doubt the most considerate and most likeable gentleman she'd ever known, was ever likely to know. Yet, there was no denying he was damnably perceptive, and more than capable of being quite dictatorial on occasions. She accepted at once that she would need to reveal at least some of her misgivings without, she fervently hoped, betraying that most heartrending concern. She couldn't bring herself to share that with him, not yet a while.

'Well, for one thing, you haven't allowed me to thank you properly for this beautiful necklace. And I do sincerely thank you, Hugo.' No one could have mistaken the sincerity in her expression or her voice, before she lowered her head to peer down at that lowest gem seductively nestling at the swell of her breasts. 'It's without doubt the most beautiful thing I own and I include all Lady Beatrice's trinkets in that judgement... But you shouldn't have bought it for me.'

'Strictly speaking, I didn't,' he confessed. 'I did purchase the earrings from Rundell & Bridge the other day, when I—er—just happened to be passing. The necklace I inherited from an aunt of mine some years ago. Sarah inherited the bulk of the jewellery, but my aunt left that particular gaud to me. I cannot imagine why. Perhaps she thought I'd find a suitable wearer for it one day.' He paused to study the glowing cluster of chestnut curls crowning her head. 'But that isn't what you mean really, is it, my angel?' he continued, resorting to the endearment he used nowadays with increasing frequency. 'What you're desperately trying to convey to me is that it is perhaps a little too soon...that, unlike me, who now knows perfectly where his future lies…and with whom…you need a little more time.'

This blunt and not particularly romantic expression of his feelings brought her head up as he knew it would. He would have been the first to admit that, given the choice, he would have much preferred to make his declaration in the privacy of some sweetly perfumed rose arbour; to have presented her with the beautiful engagement ring, which he had also purchased from Rundell & Bridge, before taking her into his arms. Sadly, a salon rapidly becoming increasingly crowded with guests was not the ideal setting for such romantic overtures.

All the same, he was well aware that Ruth was no fool. The instant she had realised those pearls had come from him, she would have strongly suspected the overriding significance of his gift— that his interests were well and truly fixed. So, quite naturally, he had experienced heartfelt relief earlier to see her wearing the set, simply because, at the very least, it clearly showed that she wasn't indifferent to his regard. What he glimpsed now, as she at last raised her eyes to his, sent his spirits soaring, for it left him in no doubt whatsoever as to the state of her own feelings.

There was no hint of feigned shock or needless maidenly displays of embarrassment; only the warmth of a sweetly loving smile, accompanied by an expression of real gratitude for his understanding, was all there was to see.

'Very well, my angel,' he said softly, before gently capturing one hand in order to press his lips lightly across the soft skin. He would have much preferred a more ardent display of his passion, but he was prepared to maintain the tight control he'd exerted over himself for a while longer. 'I shall allow you more time… But don't keep me waiting too long…please.'

'I shan't do that,' she promised, before becoming aware of the inordinate number of guests now having arrived for the party. 'Heavens above! I never realised Sarah had invited so many.'

'She'll be greeting one or two more than initially expected. I took it upon myself to invite a couple of people I just happened to run across the other evening when I was out with my friend the Viscount. Most fortuitous!' he declared, sounding very well pleased with himself.

Instantly alert, Ruth scanned the ever-increasing throng for likely candidates, but, apart from one or two exceptions, there was no one she recognised. 'Do I know them, by any chance?'

'One of them you certainly do…a young reprobate by the name of Boothroyd.'

'Heavens above!' she exclaimed again. 'What's he doing in town? I gained the distinct impression last autumn that he hoped to return to Oxford. Or did I completely misunderstand?'

Hugo slanted a mocking glance. 'I think it would be more accurate to suggest his family was hoping he would be allowed to return. Seemingly, young Tristram had other ideas, and is now renting rooms in Curzon Street. I believe you'll find his young companion of far more interest, however.'

She raised her eyes in order to favour him with a questioning glance. 'Shall I?'

'Oh, yes, most definitely! He's a—er—young baronet by the name of Hilliard, Sir Philip Hilliard, to be exact.' He smiled at her astounded expression. 'Yes, most interesting, is it not, my angel? Our young Mr Tristram Boothroyd turns out to be none other than a good friend of the deceased baronet's son. They were at school and at Oxford together for a time, apparently. I wonder how many confidences they exchanged down the years? Yet another of those surprising connections, don't you agree? The plot undoubtedly thickens!'

'I'll own it is intriguing. All the same, I don't quite see why young Tristram should wish to kill Lady Beatrice.'

'Oh, I'm not for a moment suggesting he did. In fact, I'd go a deal further and say I discounted him right from the beginning, mainly because of his age. But his knowing the dead man's son is most fortuitous. You must have appreciated yourself by now that the key to this mystery lies somewhere in Sir George Hilliard's life, and not, as we had first supposed, in Lady Beatrice's. And who better to shed some light on that particular issue than his own son. He just might be able to divulge something of interest. Sadly, he's unlikely to relate any details to me.'

'Why so?' Ruth demanded to know, having considered Hugo just the sort of person in whom one would instinctively confide. He simply oozed an aura of trustworthiness and discretion.

'Because I strongly suspect he was brought up by his mother, without too much masculine interference. I would describe him as a retiring young chap, totally unlike Tristram Boothroyd. Their friendship, unless I much mistake the matter, is a classic example of opposites attracting. It's also my belief the young baronet is much more likely to feel comfortable in the company of women… older women,' he added, with only the faintest betraying twitch about his mouth when brown eyes regarded him suspiciously.

'I see… You believe he'll look upon me as some harmless maidenly aunt who enjoys a good gossip.'

'I wouldn't go as far as to say that, exactly, my angel,' he responded, exerting praiseworthy control over his voice. 'But should you succeed in putting him at his ease, I earnestly believe he'd be far more likely to confide in you than in me.

'Ah! And you shall soon be granted the opportunity to put my theory to the test,' he added, his gaze now fixed on the entrance to the salon, where Sarah, ably supported by her husband, stood greeting the steady stream of new arrivals. 'I think it's time we began circulating before too many more perceive we have a distinct partiality for each other's company, which will ultimately set the gossips' tongues a-wagging, of course. But, have no fear, I shall remain extra-vigilant this evening and bring the young baronet over to you at an opportune moment.'

Ruth didn't attempt to detain him further, for she, too, had begun to notice certain glances being directed at their particular corner of the room. She had noticed, too, the arrival of a lady who had welcomed her so graciously to her home just two short weeks before and didn't hesitate to further their acquaintance.

'Ah, my dear! How lovely it is to see you again,' the Dowager Lady Constance Styne greeted her, with the same degree of warmth as she had shown at their first encounter. 'Do make yourself comfortable beside me. You remember my granddaughter Clara, I'm sure.'

Ruth politely exchanged greetings with the shy young woman on Lady Constance's left before addressing the Dowager directly again. 'Do you happen to be acquainted with the young gentlemen over there, at present in conversation with Colonel Prentiss, ma'am?'

Lady Constance reached for the lorgnette fixed to an elaborate chain about her neck and peered through it in the general direction of the door. 'No, my dear. I cannot say I recognise either of them. Do you happen to know them?'

'The golden-haired young gentleman is a Mr Tristram Boothroyd. You might possibly be acquainted with his great-aunt, Lady Augusta Fitznorton. She resides not too far distant from Dunsterford Hall, as it happens. Lady Beatrice knew the nephew, slightly. She was also acquainted with the father of the dark-haired young man, one Sir George Hilliard. I seem to remember he was found dead at the very coastal town where your husband owned that little house Lady Beatrice sometimes stayed at.'

Although it wasn't strictly true that Lady Beatrice had ever mentioned the name George Hilliard within her hearing, Ruth didn't allow the little white lie to prick her conscience, especially when it produced an immediate result.

'Oh, good gracious! I'd forgotten all about that! Yes, you're perfectly correct, my dear. There was some mystery surrounding it, I seem to remember. Sir George was supposed to be some miles away in Brighton, with a group of friends.' Again she made use of her aid to vision. 'So that's Sir George's boy, is it…? Cannot say he resembles his father overmuch. Devil for the ladies, rumour had it at the time. But charming for all that, and very handsome, of course.'

The Dowager turned the lorgnette on Ruth for a second or two before letting it fall. 'How on earth did you come to hear about that, my dear? I feel sure it all happened years ago, a year, maybe two, before Beatrice moved to Somerset.'

Ruth raised one hand in an airy, dismissive gesture. 'Lady Bea did occasionally talk about her life in London and the people she'd known. She was unlikely to forget that particular incident when she happened to have stayed in the coastal town where the tragedy occurred.'

Seemingly Lady Constance found nothing odd about the response as she immediately went on to reveal, 'I seem to remember Sir George's wife couldn't understand why he was there at all. His death then gave rise to a deal of speculation. The gossips at the time would have it that some hidden mistress held the key to the mystery. Given his reputation where the fair sex was concerned,

I suppose it was understandable. But I cannot recall that anything ever came to light. No one, apparently, came forward offering information and his death was eventually put down to a tragic accident.'

Again she subjected Ruth to a prolonged gaze. 'I must say I'm rather surprised Beatrice ever discussed any aspects of her past with you, my dear. I gained the distinct impression from the many letters we exchanged, after her removal to Somerset, that she wished to forget the life she'd left behind. I gained the distinct impression, too, that she had grown very bitter towards a great many people, including friends. She never asked after anybody. The only time she ever wrote about a person from her past was to scribble something derogatory about the poor soul.'

She shook her head, appearing genuinely saddened. 'I was reading through the correspondence we exchanged only the other day, as it happens. Afterwards, it seemed to me, although I might be quite wrong, that she had changed out of all recognition; that she derived much enjoyment out of other people's misery. Perhaps because she had

suffered so much herself she had grown quite in-
sensitive to other people's feelings.'

'No, ma'am, Over this defect I do not think you're
wrong,' Ruth responded, her mind's eye having
conjured up a clear image of Lady Beatrice's
expression over dinner on that fateful evening so
many months ago. She had resembled nothing
so much as a vicious predator with some hapless
victim within her power. Only on that particular
occasion, of course, the victim of her spite might
well have found the courage to retaliate.

'Although, perhaps, I hadn't been aware of it
during the ten years I was with her,' Ruth admitted, 'I cannot now recall she had a favourable word to say about anyone. Sad though it is
to say, there was a streak of vindictiveness in her
nature...of spite.'

It was at this point that two young gentlemen
guests approached to invite both Ruth and Lady
Constance's granddaughter to join them in a
set of country dances that was forming. To avoid
arousing suspicion, Ruth graciously accepted,
even though she would have much preferred to
remain in the hope of discovering something,

anything, that might shed more light on Lady Beatrice's untimely death.

Unfortunately, by the time the set had come to an end her place at Lady Constance's side had been taken by another. As it would have created a decidedly odd impression were she to boldly return to occupy the granddaughter's position on the lady's other side, she resigned herself to the fact that she was destined to learn nothing further from the informative matron for the time being at least.

So, in an attempt to fulfil the hostess's wishes, Ruth remained on the dance floor, with a succession of partners displaying varying skills, until such time as exertion demanded she quench her thirst. She then made a beeline for the table where the fruit punch was being dispensed and had only just been presented with a refreshing cup when Hugo amazingly appeared from nowhere, with two much younger gentlemen in tow.

Quite skilfully affecting a look of amazement, she allowed Mr Boothroyd to take her hand. 'What a delightful surprise! I never thought to renew our acquaintance. At least though, sir, it is a much happier occasion than when we last spoke.'

His momentary expression of puzzlement only went to reinforce her belief that he, at least, had absolutely nothing to do with Lady Beatrice's death. 'By Jove, yes!' he finally exclaimed, clearly having at last recalled the widow's demise.

He then went on to explain briefly to his silent friend his adventures in the snow the previous autumn, before glancing about the room. 'I must say, sir, this is a jolly party you've invited us to,' he declared, addressing himself to Hugo, while eyeing several of the younger ladies present. 'Who's that dashed pretty girl sitting over there, do you happen to know?'

'Miss Clara Styne. Allow me to make you known to her,' Hugo invited with aplomb, before favouring Ruth with a conspiratorial wink, while demanding she save him the supper dance.

As she was acutely aware of precisely what the wink had meant to convey, she gave little thought to Hugo's personal request and concentrated all her thoughts on attempting to keep the shy baronet with her. She was surprisingly aided by the young man himself, who proved at a stroke that he might be diffident, but he was not ill mannered, when he remained by her side and politely asked if she would care to step out on to the dance floor.

'That is most kind of you, sir. But I rather fancy I should prefer to sit for a while to regain my breath and should consider it a great kindness on your part if you would bear me company for a short time, as I know so few people present this evening.'

This turned out to be the perfect thing to say, for Sir Philip himself then freely admitted to having been a rare visitor to the metropolis; Ruth was then able to engage him in conversation about the joys of living in the country.

'And I believe we have something else in common, sir,' she enlightened him, after they had discussed country pursuits at some length and there was a slight lull developing in the conversation. 'You, so I understand, lost your father when you were very young.'

Ruth had been expecting to see his suddenly startled expression. Although he was a reserved young man, whose shyness was evident in a slight stammer, there was, she had already decided, absolutely nothing wrong with his understanding.

In fact, she would go so far as to say he was, in his own quiet way, refreshingly adroit, quite unlike his friend Mr Boothroyd.

'I'm not in the least surprised you appear shocked, Sir Philip. It was observing your friend on the dance floor a moment ago that suddenly brought it to mind,' she continued without suffering any pangs of conscience, before going on to explain, with a few other slight deviations from the truth, how Lady Beatrice had happened to have stayed at the place where his own father had met his death.

'Of course, I never knew mine. But for you it must have been such a grave shock to have lost him in such an unexpected way.'

Although he appeared distinctly thoughtful, it was a relief to Ruth to detect no real evidence of grief etched in the young face, before he finally admitted, 'Y-yes, I suppose it was a shock, Miss Harrington. B-but, truth to tell, my sisters and I rarely saw much of him. We lived for the most part in the country with Mama, while he stayed mostly in London. On those occasions when Mama did remove us all to the town house, Papa seldom visited the schoolroom…except during that time when my youngest sister was so gravely ill and Mama was constantly occupied with the doctor. It was a very unhappy period, as you can imagine. Our baby sister died and so, too, did Papa not so very long afterwards. And then, of course, Shippie left us, too, about that time.'

'Shippie…?' Ruth echoed gently, sensing the young man had grieved more for the loss of his young sister than he had his father. 'Was she a nurserymaid?'

'Oh, n-no, our governess. And a great gun! Her real name was Shipley, if my memory serves me correctly. M-my sisters and I really liked her.' He frowned. 'I seem to remember, too, she was n-newly arrived from the country when she came to us. She took us out for a great many walks, at any rate. I was s-sorry when she left us so unexpectedly. I was sent away to school not long afterwards and my poor sisters were forced to put up with an old d-dragon of a governess.'

It was at this point that the set of country dances came to an end. Almost immediately afterwards guests were invited to take to the floor for the supper dance. Hugo again miraculously appeared to claim his partner, thereby bringing the conversa-

tion with the baronet to an abrupt end. Even so, as
she watched the young man walk away, Ruth experienced the distinct feeling that she had learned
something of real significance. Unfortunately she
was denied the opportunity to dwell on just what
it might possibly have been, for she found her arm
being entwined possessively round her partner's,
as he escorted her on to the dance floor.

Although conscious of the light pressure on her
waist the instant the musicians struck up a chord,
which immediately resulted in everyone taking up
their positions in readiness for the commencement
of the dance, Ruth was not in the least alarmed by
that gentle hold. Why on earth should she have
been? She was no stranger to Hugo's touch. Why,
he had assisted her in and out of carriages on a
score of occasions, sometimes going so far as to
clasp her waist in his large hands and lift her quite
off her feet with effortless ease, she reminded
herself.

Moreover, she didn't feel in the least concerned
about performing a dance she had never attempted
in public before. After Sarah's careful tuition earlier in the week she felt she was admirably following Hugo's lead without the need to stare down

at her feet. Consequently, she couldn't quite understand why so many pairs of interested eyes appeared to be following their every movement.

'Hugo?'

'Yes, my angel.'

'Why do you suppose people are staring at us? It isn't as if the waltz is still frowned upon, at least not by the vast majority. What's more, I think we're performing the dance rather well together, don't you?'

'Admirably well, my angel. You are a born dancer, naturally graceful. And, as for myself, I believe I waltz tolerably well.'

'Indeed, you do,' she assured him, secretly pleased by his compliment, for it clearly proved he had been watching her earlier in the evening.

'Then, of course, we make a striking couple, even though I do say so myself,' he opined, sounding very well pleased about something. 'Being taller than most, I quite naturally stand out in a crowd. And your innate elegance sets you quite apart from the vast majority of your sex. There are several here present tonight who would do well to attempt to ape your taste and graceful carriage.

I have yet to see you look less than impeccably groomed.'

Ruth could feel herself going quite pink with pleasure. Perhaps because Hugo was not a gentleman given to uttering flowery compliments, his opinion on her appearance was all the more gratifying. Even though she didn't for a moment doubt his sincerity, she felt the need to point out that she hadn't been so elegantly groomed when first they had met.

'Nonsense!' he countered abruptly, clearly having had no difficulty remembering. 'You even managed to wear that sadly outmoded gown you donned for dinner that evening with a dignified air. I doubt there is a modiste in London who wouldn't relish the dressing of you!'

Understandably enough, after that supreme praise, Ruth began to feel somewhat gratified by the attention they were receiving and to a certain extent ceased to notice. Even when the dance came to an end and Hugo found them a secluded table in the adjoining salon, where a superb buffet supper had been laid out, she paid little heed to the whispered asides and knowing looks darted at their corner of the room, so engrossed was she in what Hugo was telling her about his past exploits with his good friend Viscount Kingsley. It was only after she had returned to the main salon and was immediately heralded by Lady Constance that the real reason for the attention she was continuing to receive finally became crystal clear.

'Why, my dear, aren't you the sly little puss!' the Dowager declared, rapping Ruth playfully across the knuckles with her fan the instant she had sat beside her again. 'When am I to wish you happy? Or haven't you settled upon a date quite yet?'

It took every ounce of self-control Ruth possessed not to gape at the matron. 'I—I beg your pardon, ma'am. I do not perfectly understand.'

'Oh, come now, child! I do not think you can keep it secret after tonight. It will be all over town by morning. Of course, I would be telling an untruth if I said I hadn't had my suspicions already. Why, he was most attentive towards you on the evening of my little dinner party, rarely letting you out of his sight. Not only that, Colonel Prentiss seldom comes to London, and has never been known to escort a lady about before. What is more, he's never been known to stand up with a lady. Why, he could not have made it clearer to the world that he considers you his possession already had he had his family's coat of arms embroidered all over that beautiful gown of yours!'

Chapter Ten

The following day Ruth was the last to put in an appearance at the breakfast table. Hugo, always a reasonably early riser, even on those rare occasions when he did visit the capital, had consumed his first meal of the day some little time before. All the same, he had decided to await Ruth's arrival, primarily because he wished to discover if her mood had improved by any significant degree from the night before, when he had received his first ever dagger-look from those large brown eyes of hers. She had chosen, also, to seek her bed fairly smartly once the party had drawn to a close, when it had seemed that it was as much as she could do to issue a distinctly frosty goodnight.

Not that he could blame her, of course. It had been a distinctly underhanded trick for him to have played on the poor unsuspecting girl, he was obliged silently to own. The wonder of it all was that, unless he was very much mistaken, she hadn't had a clue as to what he had been about until that latter conversation with Lady Constance Styne had taken place. Which was most strange now he came to consider the matter. She was a sharp-witted little madam who, generally, didn't require matters explaining to her.

Perhaps, though, he continued to ruminate from behind the folds of the *Morning Post*, she'd never suspected a thing simply because she trusted him implicitly and hadn't considered him capable of such devious stratagems to attain his ends.

But what was a red-blooded male supposed to do? All at once his conscience smote him, yet he couldn't bring himself to regret his actions. He was now firmly convinced that she was as much in love with him as he was with her. Softened by deep affection, her eyes had betrayed the extent of her feelings at the commencement of the party. Something, though, continued to trouble her, preventing her from making that final commitment to be his wife. She needed more time, and he was still prepared to grant her that. What he wasn't prepared to do was sit idly by and watch other men attempting to pay court to her.

She was without doubt a stunningly attractive female who stood out from the mainstream of young women who flooded to town at the start of each Season, hoping to achieve a suitable alliance. He wasn't blind to the fact that she hadn't been without a dancing partner throughout the first part of the evening. It had pleased him to see her dancing, enjoying herself. He had even gained a certain satisfaction knowing that a great many other men found her as appealing as he did—as long as evident admiration of her looks didn't prompt one of them to attempt to further his acquaintance. To that end he had shown the world that, as far as he was concerned, she would now be spending the rest of her life with him.

The door opening interrupted his thoughts and he peered above the folds of the newspaper to see the object of his musings entering the room. One glance at the distinctly frosty expression was sufficient to convince him that she was nowhere near ready yet to forgive him and that he was going to have to work hard to regain her approval.

Then, of course, his sister—curse her!—hadn't

exactly helped matters, he continued to reflect. Throughout the latter part of the previous evening Sarah's mouth had been set in that inane smile of someone smugly satisfied with life in general. She was even smiling broadly now as she asked Ruth if she had recovered her spirits after the rigours of the party. Thankfully, Merry, after helping Ruth to some coffee, succeeded in changing the topic of conversation by suddenly announcing he fancied a day or two at the races.

'Care to accompany me, Hugo? We could stay over and return to town the following day…or, better still, the day after that.'

It suddenly occurred to Hugo then that for the remainder of his life he would not have just himself to consider and automatically turned to discuss the matter with his chosen life's helpmeet.

'I quite fail to see what it has to do with me,' Ruth returned, determined, it seemed, to maintain that icy barrier between them. 'I'm not your keeper, Hugo…just as you are not mine…not yet, at any rate.'

'Quite true, my angel,' he concurred with deliberately provocative affability. 'But might I remind you of the reason we came to London in the first place. I don't think we should lose sight of that initial purpose, at least not for a while.'

Her smile could not have been sweeter as she looked at him directly for the very first time since taking her place at the table. 'I shall take leave to inform you that I've never once lost sight of our objective in coming here,' she assured him. 'But I rather fancy you did last night. I gained the distinct impression during the latter part of the evening that everyone seemed to suppose that you had come up to town for some definite purpose of your own and that congratulations were in order. Now, why was that, do you suppose?'

Not only did Sarah's face disappear behind the folds of the *Ladies' Journal* with lightning speed, there was a distinct choking sound emanating from Merry's end of the table.

Hugo, however, had himself well in hand. He had fought too many military campaigns in recent years to be rattled by what he deemed a slight skirmish. Besides which, he was determined to bring her out of her sulks. The most effective way, of course, would be to get her on her own at the earliest opportunity, as his relatives' evident levity was doing precious little to help the situation.

'My darling girl, I've spent far too little time in the capital even to begin to attempt to comprehend the mental workings of members of the *ton*. Deriving the utmost pleasure from exchanging scurrilous gossip, which more often than not has no basis in fact, they are a law unto themselves.'

He rose to his feet. 'I am in possession, however, of the precise direction of a certain person engaged in the medical profession, and his good sister. So, if you should care to accompany me I shall be back in an hour with my friend the Viscount's curricle.'

'Why don't you ride, Hugo?' Merry suggested, after glancing out of the window at the small garden at the rear of the house, now bathed in bright spring sunshine. 'There's a hack in the stables up to your weight and there's that sweet-natured mare that Sarah seldom rides nowadays. You're both welcome to make use of them if you wish?'

Ruth met Hugo's half-questioning, half-hopeful glance with a suddenly lowering feeling in the pit of her stomach, while at the same time accepting that he was going to find out about her shortcomings sooner or later. Better to admit to it now and get it over and done with, she decided.

'That's kind of you, Merry, but I'm afraid I've no habit with me. As it happens, I've never possessed such a garment in my life, simply because I don't ride.'

'Don't choose to, or cannot?' Hugo put in bluntly, thereby preventing his sister from offering the use of her own garment.

'I was never granted the opportunity to learn,' she admitted, holding her head high, and was amazed to see not the expected look of blatant disenchantment at her evident failings, but an expression of delighted surprise flickering over wholly masculine features.

'How splendid! I shall attain the greatest pleasure in teaching you myself. But not today,' he decided. 'For the present, it would serve us better if we concentrate our efforts on solving that little mystery.'

'I couldn't agree more,' Ruth concurred affably, while rising from the table with a glint in her eyes that suggested strongly that her sweet smile might not have been wholly sincere. 'And I think it would be mutually beneficial if I accompanied you on foot to Berkeley Square, don't you?'

There was the suspicion of a twitch beside

Hugo's mouth. 'But you've hardly eaten any breakfast.'

'Does it really surprise you that I have little appetite this morning?'

'If Aggie is otherwise engaged, I can arrange for one of my maids to accompany you,' Sarah offered in a decidedly unsteady voice, thereby halting Ruth's progress across to the door, and she turned, eyes glinting brighter than ever as she encompassed them all in one sweeping glance.

'Oh, I rather fancy we can dispense with the proprieties now, don't you? After last night few will be surprised to discover me in your brother's sole care.'

The walk to Viscount Kingsley's very fashionable town house would normally have taken Hugo no more than twenty minutes or so. Quite naturally he had been obliged to moderate his pace so that his chosen life's companion had no difficulty in keeping up with him. Moreover, he felt that maintaining a more sedate stroll would grant her more opportunity to give voice to those pent-up emotions she'd done her utmost to suppress thus far.

When, however, Berkeley Square was growing increasingly closer and she had made not the least attempt to remonstrate with him, he decided it behoved him to offer sufficient inducement to vent her spleen.

'You know it does no good whatsoever to keep things bottled up inside, my love. Like as not it will result in a fit of the vapours, followed by a prolonged stay in bed.'

'I'll take leave to inform you—you wretch!—that I've never suffered with nerves in my entire life and have no intention of doing so now because of your dastardly behaviour!'

She shot a sideways glance in time to catch that telltale twitch at the corner of his mouth yet again and knew at once that she had allowed herself to fall victim to a well-baited trap. Which, understandably, only served to fuel her sense of ill usage.

'Hugo, how could you? And after you'd promised me more time, too!' Angry though she was, she refused to screech at him like some belligerent fishwife and maintained beautiful control over her voice. 'How long will it be before the whole of the polite world considers we're betrothed?'

'No confirmation has passed my lips,' he avowed, sounding supremely virtuous. Ruth, however, was decidedly unimpressed.

'Actions speak louder than words,' she countered. 'For a gentleman, who has never once been known to stand up with a female before, to suddenly take to the floor for the first time in his life… Your intentions could not have been made more clear had you placed a note of our betrothal in every journal!'

'Now, loath though I am to do so, I must take issue with you here. I've been seen to dance the waltz on numerous occasions in Paris and later in Vienna, when the Duke asked me to be amongst those who accompanied him there.'

As he rarely alluded to his experiences during his many years in the army, this very interesting revelation instantly diverted her thoughts. 'I didn't know you were so closely connected with Wellington. You've never mentioned anything about it before.'

Hugo considered for a moment. 'Well, I wouldn't go so far as to say we were ever what you'd describe as bosom friends. There were plenty of others much closer to him. But, as we'd known each other a good many years, I suppose I was someone he knew he could trust…but that's beside the point… What I'm trying to tell you is that I've danced on countless occasions in the past. I even waltzed at the Duchess of Richmond's ball on the eve of Waterloo, as it happens.'

She regarded him now with distinct suspicion. 'That might well be so. And I'll go further and say that your execution of that particular dance would suggest you're no novice. But you haven't been known to take to the floor in this country. Refute that, if you dare!'

He didn't attempt to try and, when that smile she found so endearing began flickering about his mouth, she could feel those lingering feelings of resentment ebbing away.

'Well…' He paused to kick at a convenient stone in his path, resembling nothing so much as a mischievous schoolboy caught out indulging in some harmless prank. 'What the deuce was I supposed to do? I'd spent half the evening watching a string of fellows standing up with you, all of whom I suspect were eligible enough. A fine sort of a chap I'd be if I stood by and allowed some flashy marquis's son to steal the girl I want to spend the rest of my life with from right under my nose, without putting up some sort of a fight. Especially as I'd waited such a confounded long time to find her.'

As he was staring steadfastly down at the ground, he quite failed to see her take her bottom lip between her teeth in an attempt to stop it trembling. 'Besides,' he continued, the toe of his boot making contact with another hapless pebble, 'I might not be every female's idea of a handsome knight in shining armour… Well, I don't expect I'm any girl's, really. But at least I'm no dashed fortune-hunter! I don't doubt word's got round by now about your recent inheritance. I'm not suggesting for a moment there won't be plenty of fellows who'll pay court to you just because you're a fine-looking filly. But, inevitably, there'll be those whose intentions aren't so honourable. And the last thing I wish to see is you fall victim to some dashed fortune—'

Not only did Hugo cease speaking, he also stopped dead in his tracks, thereby obliging Ruth to do likewise. 'Good gad! It isn't that, is it? Because I'll tell you plainly I'd take you with only the clothes on your back… Much rather, if I'm honest! I've told you before I'm no pauper, my angel. Don't be concerned that I cannot keep us both in comfort for the rest of our lives.'

As they were now attracting no little attention from passers-by by standing stock-still in the middle of the walkway, Ruth didn't hesitate to entwine her arm round his, encouraging him to move on.

'I don't doubt it, Hugo,' she assured him gently. 'It never crossed my mind for a moment to suppose you wanted me for my money.'

'Well, that's something, at any rate,' he responded, sounding genuinely relieved, while doing little to disguise his lingering puzzlement. 'And if you don't think it's too presumptuous of me, I think it would be no bad thing if you asked that man of business of yours to invest your money for any daughters we might be blessed to have. That way they'll have a decent dowry to offer any future husband, should they choose to marry, and if not they could at least live a life of relative comfort in some small house of their own.'

'What a splendid notion!' Ruth agreed, knowing that her late benefactress would have wholeheartedly approved of that at least.

'Good, that's settled then!' Hugo responded,

now looking very well pleased. 'So, I can send a notice to various journals without delay officially announcing our engagement.'

'I never said that,' Ruth countered, only to witness a look of acute disappointment instantly wiping away his smile and automatically placed a reassuring hand over the large one gently resting on her arm. 'Have those couple of days away at the races with Merry,' she urged softly, 'and when you return we'll discuss matters further, then maybe announce our betrothal to the polite world.'

If she had doubted his honest desire to make her his wife his sudden shout of pure joy would have vanquished it in an instant. No, she didn't doubt for a moment that he truly desired to marry her. She didn't believe, deep down, she ever had. It was her own niggling little demons that still needed to be vanquished. And, God willing, their short time apart might enable her to do precisely that!

A few minutes later they had arrived at their highly fashionable destination. Hugo wasted no time in escorting her straight round to the mews, where he discovered the young groom whom his friend the Viscount left in sole charge of the stables at his London residence, when he and his family were in the country.

The lad wasn't precisely overworked, of course, for his master left only a pair of carriage horses and a decent hack behind whenever he returned to the estate in Kent. The lad seemed genuinely pleased to see Hugo, and only too happy to harness the high-stepping greys to his master's curricle, and accompany them out.

Ruth, on the other hand, wasn't so enthusiastic about having the groom along, as she felt it would naturally inhibit conversation, and voiced her disappointment in an undertone before the groom had had a chance to take up his position on the perch behind.

'Although it's hugely gratifying to learn that you'd prefer having me all to yourself, I must bring the lad along to look after his master's horses, should we be fortunate enough to find the good doctor and his sister at home. As I've mentioned before, my angel, Kingsley would be furious, understandably so, if I were negligent enough to leave his cattle in the care of some street urchin.

And I value his friendship too highly to risk his displeasure. Besides which, it adds a certain respectability having a groom along.'

She didn't pretend to misunderstand. 'It didn't seem to concern you overmuch during our walk not having a maid along,' she reminded him.

'It wouldn't do for you to make a habit of it,' he warned. 'At least not until after we've tied the knot,' he added, thereby giving the impression that he had accepted this as a foregone conclusion.

She hadn't the heart to disabuse him and merely voiced her eagerness to return to the country before too long. 'The restrictions placed on females here in the capital are nothing short of ludicrous!' she declared with feeling. 'And don't try to persuade me that it's significantly better for married women, because from what I've witnessed these past few weeks I consider it isn't. How many married ladies do you see walking about the streets alone—precious few,' she answered for him. 'Oh, how I miss those long, solitary walks in the country!'

Hugo didn't like the sound of this—no, not at all! It had to be said that, in general, the country was a deal safer than the capital, but even so accidents could and did sometimes happen even in the remotest spots. 'Accustomed to taking long walks by yourself, are you? Well, you'll not have much time for that, my angel, after we're married.' He experienced a deal of satisfaction in enlightening her. 'You'll be far too busy running the house, not to mention learning how to ride. But I suppose there will be time, too, for us to go out walking together, should you wish to.'

Either she didn't quite appreciate his gently phrased opposition to her going about on her own, or she was too interested in her surroundings to pay much heed to his objection, for she made no attempt to respond.

She continued to sit quietly, observing what was going on about her, until they had arrived at their destination. 'Good heavens!' she exclaimed, genuinely surprised at the overall shabby appearance of the small house before which Hugo had drawn the team to a halt. 'Don't tell me Dr Dent and his sister live here. From what I can remember of him he attempted to give the impression of a gentleman successful in his chosen profession.'

'It's always a mistake to judge by appearances. First impressions, too, more often than not turn out to be grossly inaccurate,' Hugo warned, before jumping nimbly down from the curricle, the instant the groom had moved to the horses' heads.

'I cannot say how long we'll be, lad, so you'd best walk the horses. Or better still take a turn round the streets from time to time,' Hugo added, after helping Ruth to alight, then placing his hand gently in the small of her back in readiness to assist should she miss her footing on the slightly overgrown path leading to the front entrance. Yet another of those spontaneous thoughtful acts that proved to her what a considerate and caring spouse he would make.

A somewhat tarnished brass plaque, fixed to the front wall of the house and bearing the doctor's name, suggested that they had arrived at the correct address. Moments later a young maid readily confirmed the fact when she opened the door in answer to their summons.

'I'm afraid the master be out at the moment, sir,' she revealed in answer to Hugo's request to see the doctor. 'But Mistress be home, if you'd care to wait in the parlour?'

Clearly the girl had been well trained. All the same, Ruth could detect at a glance that she lacked the overall neatness and that certain air of efficiency found in maidservants working in more affluent homes in the capital. She was instantly struck, too, by the shabby gentility of the front parlour. The curtains, though clearly of good quality, were now faded and, although no effort had been spared to give the appearance of comfort, even the beautifully embroidered cushions could not disguise the fact that the furniture upholstery was sadly threadbare in places.

Yet there were suggestions here and there of prosperity, too. There were several fine porcelain ornaments dotted about the room and a beautiful silver rose bowl taking pride of place on an occasional table; indications, surely, that the good doctor and his sister had experienced more prosperous times.

The door opening instantly captured her attention and she watched the neat and diminutive figure of Miss Dent sweep into the room, Hugo's gilt-edged calling card still clasped in one hand.

Ruth had quite forgotten just how tiny the woman was. Surely far too fragile a creature ever to contemplate attempting murder, she decided, suddenly wondering how on earth they were going to explain their joint presence in her front parlour.

She need not have concerned herself. Smiling, Hugo came forward to take the little woman's outstretched hand briefly in his own, while announcing with consummate ease that they were in the area and felt they could not pass so close without calling to see how Miss Dent and her brother went on.

'Why, that is most thoughtful of you, Colonel Prentiss!' Miss Dent declared, while darting a puzzled glance in Ruth's direction, which clearly conveyed that, although gratified by the unexpected visit, she couldn't quite understand why they were together. 'It is always agreeable to meet up with former acquaintances, brief though our association was,' she added, before offering refreshments.

Ruth politely refused and was very glad she had when she saw Hugo's grimace, only partially disguised, after taking his first sip of wine. 'Although it is many months now since we all met for the first time,' Ruth began, in an attempt to fill the slightly awkward silence after they had been invited to sit down, 'I have frequently thought of

you all and wondered how you fared with the remainder of your journey back to London.'

'Oh, it was quite uneventful,' the spinster revealed. 'Tediously tiring, of course, but uneventful. Quite unlike the tragic occurrence at
Dunsterford Hall! That was dreadful! I have often
thought of you, too, my dear.'

Frowning, she stared at Ruth for a moment before transferring her puzzled gaze to Hugo. 'You
must forgive me, sir, but I didn't realise that you
and Miss Harrington were so well acquainted.
For some reason I seemed to suppose we were all
strangers, thrown together as it were by unforeseen circumstances.'

'You were not in error, ma'am,' Hugo assured
her, before bravely tossing the remainder of the
wine down his throat in one swallow and setting
the glass aside. 'Miss Harrington is at present
staying in town as a guest of my sister.' His lips
twitched only ever so slightly as he reached for
one of Ruth's hands. 'I'm sure Miss Harrington
will not object to my divulging that, although
nothing official has been announced as yet, we
hope to be married in the not-too-distant future.'

Although Ruth had already accepted that some

explanation for their being together would be required and a future alliance between them was the most natural reason in the world for them being seen together, she could still quite cheerfully have boxed Hugo's ears, mainly because he seemed to derive such amusement from the fact that she could hardly refute the explanation.

'How lovely!' Miss Dent enthused, clapping her hands together joyfully. 'So something good did come of that terrible time.' Smile fading, she looked directly at Ruth. 'We all felt very sorry to leave you like that, Miss Harrington. But, sadly, we all needed to return to London. My brother, of course, has his practice to run. A doctor's reputation can so easily suffer if he neglects his patients for too long.'

'And you were in the West Country to attend a relative's funeral, if my memory serves me correctly,' Hugo prompted when the spinster, for some reason, continued to stare silently down into her glass of ratafia.

Clearly her mind had been wandering somewhere, for she gave a visible start. 'Oh, no...well, not initially. We had planned a short visit to a maiden aunt of ours who we'd discovered had been unwell. She kept house for our father for a number of years before his death. Sadly, she passed away the day before we arrived, so we remained for the funeral and to deal with legal matters regarding the disposal of her property.'

'Mrs Adams, too, attended a funeral, I believe,' Ruth reminded her, while finally becoming aware that Hugo retained her hand. She attempted to remove it, only to feel those strong fingers fractionally tighten their grasp. Was this a show of possession? If so, for whose benefit—hers or the female seated opposite?

'Yes, that is correct. It was her father's funeral, I believe.'

'And do you enjoy travel, Miss Dent? Do you find you need to travel a great deal?'

'Oh, no, Colonel Prentiss,' she answered in a trice. 'Quite the contrary! I came to London more than twenty years ago to keep house for my brother. My journey to the West Country last year was the first occasion I'd left the capital in all that time. My brother, of course, has travelled about a good deal more than I have, while I have been quite happy to remain in my home.'

'You've lived in this house a very long time,

Miss Dent,' Ruth remarked, striving to focus on the reason for their visit and not Hugo's possessive hold. 'Clearly you both prefer life in the town.'

'Oh, we haven't always lived here, Miss Harrington,' the spinster enlightened them, an almost wistful expression flickering over her pinched features. She then went on to name an address in a much more affluent part of the metropolis, where properties had been bought and sold for increasing sums in recent years. 'Unfortunately, because of—er—unforeseen circumstances, my poor brother was obliged to sell our beautiful home and set up a practice here.

'But we cannot complain,' she continued, after staring with scant enthusiasm at her surroundings. 'My brother's services are called upon reasonably frequently, so we go along quite well.'

Ruth couldn't help wondering what exactly had obliged them to relocate. She could only suppose the move must have been somewhat forced upon them. No one in his right mind would have chosen to reside at this address in preference to their former fashionably located property.

Seemingly a similar thought must have been crossing Hugo's mind, because he said, 'It must have caused you great distress to leave your former home, Miss Dent. It's a truly charming part of town, especially those properties overlooking the park. I should like to own a house there myself.'

'It was lovely, sir! It gave me such joy to invite people into the drawing room. My brother had his own little consulting room across the hall, overlooking the park. More than one titled person crossed our threshold in those days.'

'You must, indeed, have been very sorry to leave, Miss Dent.'

'I was, Colonel, I truly was,' she freely admitted. 'Even after all these years I still cannot help feeling a trifle resentful. Such wicked lies were spread abroad about poor Samuel. It doesn't take long before a doctor's reputation begins to suffer. Most all his wealthier patients deserted him and went elsewhere, once the wicked rumours had begun circulating. Then, inevitably, the bills started mounting up and he was forced to leave, and buy this smaller property in order to settle his debts.'

Narrow-eyed, Hugo gazed across at the spinster. 'The medical profession can be both a lucrative and a very precarious one,' he remarked sagely. 'It only takes one—er—unfortunate death attributed to negligence to destroy a practitioner's good name.'

Ruth could see at once that Hugo, astute demon that he was, had hit the mark, when the sister drew out a piece of fine lawn and commenced to dab at the corners of her eyes.

'It is a sad fact of life that most infants succumb to a variety of ailments during childhood and many do not survive. That particular child had, apparently, been sickly from birth, always falling prey to some contagion or other. Poor Samuel did his best to save her, but the child's father insisted Samuel had been negligent and should have recognised the symptoms of the more serious condition earlier. He held my poor brother entirely to blame for the death of his daughter and wasn't slow to spread such wicked lies abroad, ruining poor Samuel's reputation. And just because he happened to be a titled gentleman he was allowed to get away with it!'

'You're very quiet, my angel,' Hugo remarked a short while later, as they headed in a westerly direction, without having seen, according to the loyal sibling, the much-maligned Dr Dent. 'You didn't object, I hope, to my revealing our future plans to the—er—good doctor's sister?'

This succeeded in interrupting Ruth's clear recollection of a conversation she'd had the evening before with a young baronet. She then darted Hugo an exasperated glance. 'I don't suppose it would trouble you overmuch if I had objected. You seem intent on divulging the fact.'

His shoulders shook. 'Only because it seemed the most natural reason for us to be about together. And you must admit, she didn't seem in any way suspicious about our visit after that.'

'That's true enough,' Ruth was obliged to concede. 'Furthermore, we did learn something of great interest—the doctor's reputation was ruined because of the death of a titled gentleman's daughter.' She regarded the strong line of his jaw as he continued to keep his eyes on the road ahead. 'It just so happens that Sir Philip Hilliard mentioned the death of his youngest sister last night. And I think, unless I'm much mistaken, it would have occurred about that time.'

'Interesting,' Hugo responded.

'Yes, isn't it, just,' she agreed. 'Of course it

might be pure speculation, but if Dr Dent happened to have been the practitioner attending the child during the time of this illness, which sadly proved fatal, then it does give him a motive for murder. Miss Dent clearly blames the titled gentleman for her brother's damaged reputation, and their current much-less-affluent lifestyle. If the good doctor was of a similar mind, then he might have sought revenge on that cliff top, overlooking the sea.'

'He could, of course,' Hugo agreed, but not sounding wholly convinced. 'But why go to the trouble of killing him there? And how on earth did he manage to lure Sir George to the coast? Why not just kill him here in town?'

He shook his head, clearly sceptical. 'No, it's no good speculating, my angel. We must discover, first, whether Dr Dent was the Hilliard family's practitioner at the time of the girl's demise, and then, maybe, take things further from there.'

Chapter Eleven

The following morning, after being informed the gentlemen were on the point of departure for the races, Ruth went down to the front parlour to discover only Hugo present.

He was an imposing figure by any standard, but there, within the confines of the small parlour, dressed for the journey ahead in top-boots and a many-caped travelling cloak, he seemed much larger somehow, made an even more impressive figure than usual. Even so, she'd never once felt daunted by his obvious strength or breadth of shoulder, not the least intimidated by his superior height. Yet, perversely, as she went to stand beside him and slipped her hand shyly into his, she could feel the unexpected surge of colour heating her cheeks as those bronzed fingers wrapped themselves round hers in immediate response.

She could only put her shyness down to the fact that it had been the first time ever that she herself had instigated any physical contact between them.

If he was aware of this fact he certainly gave no indication as he remarked almost casually, 'Occasionally my sister displays an amazing degree of sensitivity, my angel, as now, by allowing us these few precious moments alone together.'

Ruth smiled. Since her arrival in London she had more than once heard him make some derogatory remark about his sister. Yet, it must have been obvious to anyone with a ha'p'orth of intelligence that, even though he made few outward displays, he held Sarah in great affection.

'How did you know it was I and not Sarah?' she asked, when he continued to stare resolutely out of the window.

'Because I recognised your footfall. You have a much lighter tread, besides having far daintier hands.'

He did no more than capture the other in order to hold them both imprisoned against his chest, as he turned to look down at her for the first time. Ruth returned his gaze, instantly noting the unmistakable gentleness in his eyes, while wishing fervently that she was more adept at reading his expressions.

As Lady Beatrice had remarked all those many months before, Hugo Prentiss gave little of himself away. He was just too skilled at concealment, only ever revealing what he wanted people to see. Oh, yes, she knew beyond a shadow of a doubt that he was fond of her… No, she amended silently, he was deeply, deeply fond of her. She didn't doubt either that he sincerely wished her to be his wife. Sadly, it did not automatically follow that he had, finally, fallen in love with her. After all, that taunting little voice in her head was only too quick to remind her, he had never once admitted as much, and it wasn't as if he hadn't been granted numerous opportunities to do so had he so desired. Was it simply that he was too honourable a man to tell her a barefaced lie?

She was given scant opportunity to ponder this most poignant issue, for a moment later he had slipped his hands possessively about her, drawing her ever closer as he claimed her mouth.

So unexpected, the embrace had taken her completely by surprise. His displays of affection thus far had been tempered by gentlemanly restraint, limited to mere reassuring or protective grasps of her hand, or a chaste salute on her wrist. But there was nothing restrained in this demonstration of masculine desire.

Betraying remarkable dexterity, he succeeded in moulding her mouth to his, parting her lips with a gently demanding pressure, while his hands worked a heated, arousing course down the length of her spine and round to grasp her hips in that possessive hold he was increasingly adopting.

She was powerless to break free, even had she wished to do so. Yet there was nothing remotely intimidating in his touch; nothing that made her fear placing her future in this man's hands. Quite the contrary! She sensed his capacity for loving tenderness; instinctively felt he would own, guide and protect by love, not force, by gentle persuasion, not brutal intimidation. Yes, any woman could safely place her future well-being in this man's hands.

The conviction acted like a palliative, and in those wonderfully reassuring moments, before the sound of Sarah's tactfully raised voice in the hall reached their ears, all doubts about a future together were blessedly forgotten. Freed from lingering anxieties Ruth was conscious only of a sensual, persuasive touch that instantly evoked sensations in her, and she found it so very easy to believe that she had miraculously become the centre of this man's world; that his heart now truly belonged to her, unconditionally.

It was only later as she stood staring down from her bedchamber window at the very spot from where the Lansdowns' light travelling carriage had departed a mere thirty minutes before that those heartrending misgivings returned with a vengeance to torment her.

While she had been held very willingly captive, she'd been oblivious to everything save that gently awakening contact that had promised so much pleasurable shared satisfaction in a future bound together. Any lingering doubts of how deeply fond of her he was had been vanquished completely. Any slight concerns about the type of husband he would make had been eradicated, too. In her heart of hearts she knew that Hugo would be the antithesis of the late Lady Lindley's choice of mate. No, she had never doubted that for a moment. What continued to torment her was that heartbreaking fear that in his mind's eye Hugo might have been imagining quite a different girl in his arms when he had kissed and caressed her, and that he always would. Was she doomed always to be the understudy, good enough to take on the part of leading lady in his life, but not his first choice for that privileged role?

An involuntary sigh escaped her. The truth of the matter was that, even after these weeks in London, she still lacked the experience to judge. Maybe, too, she was a coward, afraid of knowing the truth. Doing her level best to avoid stark reality by having her worst fears confirmed, she had steadfastly avoided even mentioning Alicia's name within his hearing, for how could she go through life knowing that in Hugo's eyes she would always continue to figure as just the best replacement for the one with whom he had truly wanted to share his life, no matter how faithful a wife or how good a mother she turned out to be. She shook her head, accepting that her choice was woefully limited. Either from somewhere she found the courage to face those twin demons by conquering both jealousy and pride, and accept what affection Hugo was capable of offering, or risk losing perhaps the only man she would ever truly love.

'Don't know why you didn't accompany Lady Lansdown out to pay some morning calls, miss, instead of staying up here all by yourself, moping.'

So wrapped up in her own private misery had she been that Ruth had completely forgotten she hadn't been alone in the room; that Agatha had been busily putting away freshly laundered clothes.

'I'll have you know I haven't been moping,' she countered as convincingly as she could. 'I've been considering something Colonel Prentiss revealed over breakfast earlier.'

She salved her conscience by reminding herself that at least part of the response had been truthful. Hugo had, the night before at his club, discovered that it was indeed none other than Dr Samuel Dent who had been in attendance when the youngest of Sir George Hilliard's children had died.

Which, of course, gave the doctor a strong motive for murder, as Hilliard had taken revenge by ruining the doctor's reputation, Ruth reminded herself, desperately striving to turn her thoughts away from her own painful concerns and concentrate on something else.

Furthermore, Dr Dent had seemed most eager to quit Dunsterford Hall that morning. But then, she recalled quite clearly, so had all the others. And Hugo was right, of course—why go to all the trouble of killing Hilliard on a coastal pathway, when it would have been so much simpler to lie in wait for him somewhere here in the capital?

Unable to come up with any obvious explanation, and quickly accepting that, in her present mood of heartfelt despondency over her own troubles, she was unlikely to come up with any plausible reasons for the cliff-walk murder, she decided it might be advisable to get away from the house for a while in the hope it would clear her head.

'If you must know, I didn't accompany Lady Lansdown out simply because I didn't relish spending the next couple of hours or so listening to the latest tittle-tattle going round the capital. All the same, I could do with some fresh air, so I think I'll pay a visit to Julia Adams. You remember—that nice woman who stayed at Dunsterford Hall last October,' Ruth reminded her maid. 'I rather liked her. And she's the only one Colonel Prentiss and I haven't yet seen.'

An hour later Ruth stepped down from a hackney carriage before a large redbrick house. The street wasn't so very dissimilar to the one in which Dr Dent and his sister resided, both being lined with trees, now majestically in full leaf and looking their best. The area, though, was generally thought to be very respectable, if not on a par with the fashionable thoroughfares further west. Moreover, Mrs Adams's property was much larger than the Dents', not to mention a great deal better maintained.

A girl of about fifteen or, maybe, sixteen came in response to the summons. Ruth was instantly struck by a similarity she bore to someone she'd met quite recently, certainly since her arrival in London. Yet, for the life of her she couldn't immediately bring to mind who it might possibly have been as she asked to see the mistress of the house.

'I'm afraid Mama is not home at present. She's out doing the marketing, but she shouldn't be too much longer, should you care to step inside and wait?'

After requesting Agatha to pay off the jarvey, Ruth crossed the threshold into a small and spotlessly clean hall and introduced herself. 'Your mama and I met last autumn when she was obliged to seek refuge at my home during a snowstorm,' she went on to explain. 'She might possibly have told you all about it.'

Ruth could tell at a glance from the girl's expression that she had known nothing about the incident, even before she admitted as much. It momentarily crossed her mind as being slightly odd that Julia Adams hadn't confided in her daughter. Even so, she put it from her thoughts as she was shown into a charmingly furnished, sunny front parlour.

'What a delightful room!' Ruth announced, echoing her thoughts, as she accepted the offer of a seat.

'Oh, Mama likes this room, and likes it kept "just so" as it is her private sitting room,' the girl revealed ingenuously. 'She believes no respectable person would wish to rent rooms in a property where standards are allowed to fall.' She looked Ruth over from head to toe, possibly in an attempt to assess her station in life. 'Was it perhaps rooms you were wishing to rent, Miss Harrington? We do have two vacant on the first floor, facing front.'

'No, not at the moment, Miss Adams. This is merely a social call.'

It was at this point the door opened and Ruth turned to see a middle-aged woman, dressed in sombre black, and with her greying locks neatly confined in a chignon, enter the room. The slight resemblance she instantly perceived to the younger and far more attractive owner of the house gave her a pretty shrewd idea of who the woman must surely be.

'I thought I heard the door-knocker and dis-covered a maidservant sitting on the chair in the hall. You should have informed me at once, Alice, that we had a visitor. Your mama would consider it very remiss of me if I didn't welcome possible future boarders to the house on her behalf.'

Although it had clearly been a reprimand, it had been gently delivered by the older woman, who gave every appearance of suffering from a surfeit of nerves. Furthermore, Alice didn't seem unduly troubled by the mild rebuke as she revealed that Ruth had called to see her mother.

'It's a social call, Aunt Ship. Miss Harrington

very kindly offered Mama shelter last year when there was a snowstorm. It must have happened after Mama had visited you in Devon and had remained for Grandpapa's funeral.'

'No doubt you recall that most unseasonably early cold snap we suffered at the beginning of October, ma'am,' Ruth reminded her, when the aunt, too, appeared slightly puzzled. 'Fortunately it didn't linger very long. A mere twenty-four-hour wonder, one might have described it. Your sister was able to be on her way the following day.'

'Oh, yes, I do now recall,' she at last responded. 'Thankfully, over Lynmouth way we had only a fine dusting, hardly anything to speak of at all. I do remember hearing that it was far worse to the east, over the moor.' She frowned. 'But I never knew poor Julia had been stranded in it. She never said anything to me...merely wrote to say the journey had been quite tedious.

'And I must say, I found the journey to London very tiring myself earlier this year, when I removed here,' she went on to reveal in the next breath. 'But, then, I've never been accustomed to travelling, unlike dear Julia.'

Memory stirred and Ruth recalled Mrs Adams

mentioning something about her sister remaining in the country to keep house for their father, whilst she had been obliged to seek employment away from home.

The spinster sister readily confirmed this. 'Yes, Julia was always far more outgoing. I was always a timid little mouse in comparison. Naturally, dear Papa didn't like her moving away. But, as things turned out, she did very well for herself, so perhaps it was all for the best.'

'Would I be correct in thinking she moved away from home to take up a position as governess?' Ruth asked, as memory stirred once again, and received an immediate nod in confirmation.

'Yes, she was very young, but she was always so capable. She attained a position with a good family and lived in Hampshire for a while. A few weeks later she wrote to say that she was travelling with the family to London. Then the next thing we knew she had upped and married Mr Adams and had moved away from the capital.'

Ruth was suddenly reminded of how a tall gentleman had entered her world and how it had changed overnight, but for a rather different reason. 'One can never be sure what life holds in store. One can continue doing the same things week in, week out; year in, year out. Then, quite suddenly, a chance meeting with someone can alter one's life so swiftly.'

'How very true! It certainly happened that way for Julia,' the sister confirmed, before releasing her breath in a sigh. 'Sadly, though, my brother-in-law, some few years older than her, did not enjoy good health and was destined not to live very long after the marriage had taken place. He wasn't even strong enough to make the journey to meet Papa and me, and died even before dear little Alice was born.'

Ruth's gaze strayed towards the girl sitting quietly beside her aunt on the sofa. She didn't seem in the least disturbed by the topic of conversation. But then why should she? Ruth reflected. Like herself, the girl had never known her father.

'You and I have something in common, Miss Adams,' she revealed softly. 'I never knew my father. Naturally, I wish I had. But it's hard to grieve for a parent one has never known. Of course, when I lost my mother I was about your age and it was an entirely different matter.'

The girl's expression changed dramatically. She

appeared to lose every vestige of colour in a matter of seconds. 'Oh, I couldn't bear to lose Mama! No one could ever take her place! She's always been there to take care of me.'

'And has done so very well,' Ruth returned, after staring about her. A further memory then stirred. 'But I believe I'm right in thinking that you haven't always lived here, Miss Adams,' she added in an attempt to turn the girl's thoughts in a new direction and restore that youthful bloom.

'No, for several years we lived in a much smaller house, Papa's own house, where he grew up, about a mile or so from here.'

'But you were born by the sea,' her aunt reminded her, 'not that you'd remember anything about that. You were still a babe in arms when your mother brought you back to live in the capital.'

'No, I don't remember, Aunt Ship,' the girl confirmed. 'Mama never talks about it, either.' She shrugged. 'But then it's perhaps understandable why she chooses not to do so. She and Papa were married for such a short time.'

'Ship...?' Ruth echoed, gazing questioningly at

the aunt. 'Would I be correct in thinking that is a pet name your niece has for you, ma'am?'

'Indeed, it is. Naughty puss! My name is Shipley…Cecily Shipley.'

Ruth could feel herself growing colder as those names, Ship…Shippie…Shipley, echoed over and over in her head, until she had finally recalled just where she had first heard the surname and precisely who had uttered it. She then studied the girl seated opposite more closely, noting the dark hair and eyes, and the faintly aquiline nose. As far as she could remember she bore little resemblance to her mother, who was blonde haired and blue eyed. But she certainly bore a keen resemblance to someone she had met quite recently—a half-brother, perhaps, by name of Sir Philip Hilliard.

Oh God! Ruth inwardly groaned. That poor, poor girl!

Suddenly conscious that she was guilty of rudely staring, she said, 'Forgive me, Miss Adams, for looking at you so keenly. From memory, I do not think you resemble your mother overmuch.'

'No, she doesn't resemble my sister Julia in the least,' Miss Shipley agreed, thereby denying her niece the opportunity to answer. 'Julia assures me that dear Alice is the very image of her late father.'

And I, for one, do not doubt the truth of it! Ruth mused. She didn't doubt either who had been the girl's natural father. 'Did I infer correctly, ma'am, that you were never acquainted with your brother-in-law?'

'No, sadly, neither Papa nor I ever met John Adams,' she readily confirmed. 'We never re-alised that Julia had given up her position as governess, and had moved away from London, until after she had written from her new home by the sea to inform us of her marriage to Mr Adams.'

She drew her wispy brows together in a frown. 'Papa and I did consider the marriage had taken place in unseemly haste. Julia never so much as mentioned his name in any of her previous letters. But when we learned that he had sadly died a matter of weeks only after their wedding, Papa and I quite understood. Poor Julia must have known how very ill he was and didn't wish to delay. Then little Alice was born several weeks before her time.' The frown was vanquished by a rather simpering smile. 'But blessedly she survived and

Julia returned to London to reside in the home her late husband had left her, here, in the capital.'

Ruth listened to all this with increasing interest, placing her own interpretation on certain salient points. 'No doubt the sea air was beneficial and aided your survival, Alice,' she suggested, striving desperately not to reveal the scepticism she was experiencing concerning the girl's birth.

'I have always felt it must have been so, Miss Harrington,' the aunt agreed. 'Alice wasn't born in a fashionable place like Brighton, of course, but in a little town situated not too far distant, I believe. I just cannot recall the name of it now, but no matter. I don't suppose you've heard of it, in any case.'

On the contrary, Miss Shipley, I very much suspect I have, Ruth responded under her breath.

Yes, she certainly had heard of it; had heard, too, more than enough to convince her that to remain longer might prove a grave mistake. She needed time to think what to do, how to proceed. Moreover, she wasn't anywhere near adept enough at concealing her thoughts and feelings from anyone with a degree of discernment. Her close association with Hugo had proved that beyond doubt!

The last thing she needed now was to come face to face with a possible murderess!

She reached for the kidskin gloves that she had earlier placed on the seat beside her and proceeded to put them back on. 'Well, ladies, I mustn't take up any more of your time. It was good of you to welcome a stranger into your home. But a further appointment obliges me to leave without seeing Mrs Adams.'

'Oh, but we haven't offered you any refreshment as yet!' Miss Shipley glanced reproachfully at her niece. 'It was very remiss of you, Alice, not to have done so.'

'Another time, perhaps,' Ruth put in before the spinster aunt could reprimand the girl further. She then rose resolutely to her feet. 'Please be good enough to inform your sister that I called…and shall be in touch in the very near future.'

Once back in the safety of the Lansdowns' town house, Ruth didn't waste time in seeking the privacy of her allotted bedchamber. Fortunately Sarah had not returned from her round of daily visits and so Ruth had leisure to contemplate on what action, if any, to take.

There was no doubt in her mind now that Lady Beatrice Lindley had seen Julia Adams on the cliff walk that day. And after making the acquaintance of young Alice Adams, there was little doubt in her mind either, now, of just why her mother had been in that small seaside town, well away from the capital.

An unconscionable womaniser, Sir George Hilliard had made his young governess his mistress and had very likely housed her in that out-of-the-way spot, well away from the watchful eye of the *ton*, but close enough for him to visit frequently. Perhaps, when he had discovered Julia was carrying his child, he had wished to terminate their liaison, thereby providing poor abandoned Julia with a strong motive for murder. Then, years later, Julia had crossed the path of the only witness to that fateful cliff-top meeting with her former lover, forcing her to act promptly once again. Yes, everything discovered that day strongly suggested Julia had done precisely that, and yet...

An image of the woman, when last Ruth had seen her, on that eventful morning at Dunsterford Hall flashed before her mind's eye. Either Julia Adams was the most accomplished actress who ever drew a breath, or she had been genuinely concerned when she had offered to remain to assist in any way she could. Not only that, she had also appeared shocked to see Lady Beatrice, cold and lifeless, in her bed.

Of course, her real motive for offering to remain might have been to ensure that no finger of suspicion would ever be levelled at her; to ensure that no evidence could ever link her to Lady Beatrice's untimely death, either. Somehow, though, Ruth didn't think this had been the case.

But then, Ruth reminded herself, Julia Adams hadn't come to Dunsterford Hall with the intention of committing murder. That course of action had been somewhat forced upon her after the discussion that had taken place over dinner. No, she hadn't arrived at Dunsterford Hall with malice aforethought; Ruth felt certain of that much at least. If Julia did murder Lady Beatrice, then her actions, surely, had been the result of blind panic, borne of strong desire for self-preservation? She was not a cold, heartless killer. She was a woman who had worked and struggled hard to raise her child in a positive cloak of respectability.

Turning away from the window, Ruth sat herself at the small desk in one corner of the room and drew out a sheet of paper. Serious though the situation was, she found herself unable to suppress a wry smile. Any right-minded person, of course, wouldn't think twice about penning a letter to the authorities, revealing all she knew. Evidently there was a serious defect in her character, she decided, for she simply couldn't bring herself to consider that form of action, at least not yet, not until she knew the whole story—everything. And there was only one way she could achieve that objective!

After taking time to compose the missive, she signed her name before sealing the letter carefully with a wafer and then going over to the bell pull. While waiting for a response to her summons she began to pen another missive, one that she found far more difficult to write. She was still engrossed in the task when her personal maid entered the room.

'We're going out again, Aggie,' she told her, much to the maid's surprise. 'Go and collect your bonnet and send the footman to me. I have an urgent letter here I wish him to deliver by hand.'

A little over an hour later, Ruth re-entered the house for the second time that day. She had hoped to return before its mistress, but sadly had failed by some twenty minutes or so, and felt she must seek Sarah out at once. Not to do so might easily give rise to speculation. And that must be avoided at all cost, she told herself. She must at least attempt to appear normal, even though she was about to embark on the most dangerous subterfuge she'd possibly ever undertake in her life!

Running her quarry to earth in the front parlour, she found it no difficult matter to greet her warmly and indulge in a few minutes' inconsequential chatter. 'It certainly sounds as though you spent an enjoyable morning with friends,' she remarked, when Sarah had related in detail all the latest scurrilous gossip she'd discovered from various sources. 'And it just so happens that I, quite by chance, bumped into an acquaintance of mine whom I haven't seen for many years. That is why I was a little late in returning to the house.'

She hated repaying Sarah's many kindnesses

towards her with a mouthful of lies. But what choice had she? She didn't wish anyone to be concerned for her welfare. Moreover, she had no intention of putting anyone else's life at risk. What she intended to do was entirely her own decision, and she felt, therefore, she had to do it alone. More importantly, her meeting with Julia Adams must of necessity take place away from London, where her close association with the Lansdowns, and more importantly Hugo, could be more easily concealed. Not for the world would she endanger his life.

'It just so happens my friend is leaving the capital tomorrow,' she continued to explain, wondering how she could lie so easily. 'Her family home is situated a few miles only outside the capital and she has kindly invited me to return with her on the morrow. Apparently there's to be a large party at the family home tomorrow evening. She was so eager for me to return with her, I simply hadn't the heart to refuse. I shall be away only for the night and shall have returned long before Hugo and Merry, with luck.'

'Well, of course, you must go if you wish to do so, my dear,' Sarah agreed affably. 'It will be a pity you won't number among the little party I've arranged to go to the theatre tomorrow night, but I shall make your excuses. I'm sure my friends will quite understand. But what about the soirée this evening? Shall you wish to forgo that, too?'

'I think I had better do so, Sarah. I've an early start in the morning, so I'll want to be up bright and early. Aggie, of course, will accompany me as far as the hotel where my friend is putting up.'

This did bring a slight furrow to Sarah's brow. 'Do I infer correctly from that that you do not intend to take her with you?'

'No, there's no need. My friend is adequately chaperoned by her own servants, not to mention a maiden aunt. Apart from which, there will be a number of guests staying overnight, so space at the house will be at a premium, and my friend has kindly offered me the services of her own personal maid. Not only that, I'm more than capable of fending for myself. I've been doing so for years, remember?'

Sarah might have accepted this decision to go travelling alone, but Agatha was not so easily placated, especially as she was very well aware that no meeting with a friend had ever taken place.

'I might not know what you're really about, miss, but I'm very sure it isn't proper for you to go jaunting off on your own,' she warned that evening, after being ordered to pack an overnight bag for her mistress in readiness for the early start the following morning. 'Heaven alone knows what the Colonel will say when he gets wind of your comings and goings!'

'Might I remind you, Aggie, that he isn't your master yet. You take your orders from me and I shall come and go as I please.' She shrugged. 'Besides, with luck, I shall have returned before he's due back, so he'll know nothing about it.'

Agatha's expression betrayed her scepticism. 'Oh, he'll find out. You mark my words,' she warned. 'Not much ever escapes that gentleman, as well you know.' Her expression then grew markedly more disturbed, as she added, 'Besides, I just don't like lying to people, miss, most especially the Colonel.'

'No, I know you don't, Aggie.' Ruth went over to place an arm lovingly around the maid's shoulders. 'And neither do I. I hated lying to Lady Lansdown earlier. Sarah has been good to me. She's treated me like a sister almost from the first.'

This briefly erased the deep lines of concern from the maid's forehead. 'Well, miss, you'd have needed to be a complete simpleton not to have seen that you and the Colonel were made for each other. He's always taken the greatest care of you. Even all those months back, when he turned up at Dunsterford Hall that day, he showed the kind of man he was by his little considerate acts, especially towards you. Oh, can't you wait until he returns, miss? I'd feel a deal happier if the Colonel were with you. I'd know then you'd come to no harm.'

But he might, and I won't risk that, Ruth thought, but said determinedly, 'No, Aggie, I can't. I must do this alone. I truly do not believe I shall be in any danger. I don't believe I could be so wrong in my judgement about someone.'

After hearing this Agatha appeared, if anything, a deal more concerned. 'I really don't know what you're about, miss. And maybe it's better that way. But one thing I do know—you're too kind-hearted by half at times. You tend to think more highly of some folk than they deserve. Look how you always made excuses for Lady Bea's behaviour. You know different now, of course!'

Honesty obliged Ruth to acknowledge the truth of this. 'Yes, I must admit I've not always been the best judge of character, though there have been exceptions—you and Colonel Prentiss being prime examples. And I believe I'm right about this… other person. But I'd be foolish not to accept that there is a very real possibility that I might be quite wrong. That is why I'm not prepared to risk anyone else's life, and must do this alone, and meet this person away from the capital, where my connection to this household is unlikely to be discovered. Besides, more than one life might be ruined if matters aren't handled…discreetly. And I'll not have that on my conscience, either.'

After collecting the now sealed letter from the desk, she handed it to the maid. 'I cannot tell you more, Aggie. And maybe, as you've admitted, it's better that you don't know, then you won't be forced to tell more lies than you need. As I've mentioned before, I intend to remain away one night only. With luck, I should arrive back here Friday afternoon. Should I fail to return, then I wish you to place this letter in the Colonel's hand only…and no other.

'You may go now, and I shall see you first thing in the morning, when you'll accompany me on the first stage of my journey.

'Goodnight, Aggie.'

Chapter Twelve

Hugo smiled lazily across at his travelling companion, as Lord Lansdown apologised for the umpteenth time since setting off on their return journey earlier that morning. Hugo had been obliged to agree that the racing hadn't been up to the standard expected, with many of the favourites not running for various reasons. Even so, he was under no illusion about just why Merry had wished to return to town a day earlier than originally planned.

Poor Merry had caught a slight chill and was feeling distinctly sorry for himself. He was craving his creature comforts and the pampering attention he'd be sure to receive in his own home from a doting wife and loyal servants.

'Not that I suppose you're in the least sorry to be returning early,' his lordship ventured, as his travelling carriage continued along the bustling streets of the metropolis. His blue eyes twinkled suggestively. 'I don't doubt for a moment you're longing to be reunited with the delightful Miss Harrington.'

Again Hugo chose not to be drawn and continued smiling to himself.

Unlike Sarah, his brother-in-law had never once attempted to interfere in his private concerns. Merry had never been party to one of Sarah's harebrained schemes to find him a suitable wife and Hugo had always been grateful to him for that. All the same, Merry had casually slipped Ruth's name into several conversations since they had been away, hoping, no doubt, to hear that an official engagement was imminent. Nothing would have made Hugo happier than to have confirmed this, but he had no intention of uttering an outright lie, for the truth of the matter was, even now, he was far from certain that an official engagement would ever take place.

'I've said it before, and I'll say it again, you've found yourself a sweet little filly there, old fellow. She's a very restful young woman, not the type to fall victim to the vapours too often, if at all.

Mind,' Merry continued, after blowing his nose on a square of fine lawn, 'she doesn't lack spirit, not if I'm any judge. And she's not afraid to stand up to you, as big as you are!'

'No, she doesn't want for courage,' Hugo agreed softly, then shook his head, not attempting to hide his misgivings. 'Yet, she's wary of something, that I do know. She's yet to consent to an official engagement. Which, I'll admit, I find disturbing.'

'Oh, come now!' Merry scoffed. 'Any fool can see the gel thinks the world of you.'

'Yes, I believe she does,' Hugo agreed. 'But she's troubled about something…something is holding her back from making that final commitment.'

He recognised at a glance his brother-in-law's distinctly sceptical expression. 'You forget, Merry, the life she's been obliged to live during the past years, living day in, day out with an out-and-out man-hater,' he reminded him, repeating almost word for word the conversation he'd had with his friend the Viscount a couple of weeks before. 'It would be wonderful, indeed, if she'd remained impervious to all that negativity concerning our sex.'

He shook his head, still not wholly convinced

in his own mind that this was the reason for the reluctance on her part. 'The first opportunity I get, I mean to have a long talk with that young woman, because I'm determined to get to the bottom of her concerns,' he vowed as the carriage finally drew to a halt outside the front of the house.

Alighting first, Hugo led the way into the hall and was informed the mistress was indeed at home and alone in the front parlour. Although understandably surprised, Sarah betrayed sufficient wifely concern when she discovered the reason behind the early return, providing her husband with a glass of brandy before tucking a rug about his knees.

Hugo looked on with some amusement, wondering whether he would appear so smugly contented as his brother-in-law now did if he was to receive the same cosseting in the years to come when suffering from some trifling ailment.

As if by a natural progression of thought, he then asked if Ruth was in the house and didn't attempt to hide his surprise when he learnt she had left the capital early that morning and wouldn't be returning until the morrow.

'Quite by chance she ran across some friend or

other and was invited to a party, and to spend the night,' Sarah then went on to explain, which resulted in Hugo pausing momentarily before raising the glass of burgundy he'd been given the rest of the way to his lips.

He recalled with distinct clarity several conversations he'd had with Ruth during the past few weeks, where she had divulged many aspects of her upbringing. He had gained the distinct impression that during her childhood at the rectory she had enjoyed the company of a wide circle of friends. She still retained contact with many of them by letter. It was not inconceivable, of course, that one of those friends, together with her family, had come to live close to the capital, but it wasn't the norm for people to move far from the area of their birth, at least not those who didn't belong to the privileged class. And by Ruth's own admission, until quite recently, she had known precious few on the highest rungs of the social ladder.

'There's nothing wrong, is there, old fellow?' Merry asked, as he detected the telltale lines of concern etched across his brother-in-law's high forehead. 'Surely you don't object to the gel staying overnight with a friend?'

'I wouldn't be in the least troubled if it wasn't for the fact that I was unaware she had any friends in this part of the country,' he told them both. 'As I remarked earlier, Merry, I don't think either of you quite appreciate the relatively solitary existence she was obliged to live during the past decade. As far as I'm aware her only friends, her only acquaintances, prior to staying here, are all either living in Somerset or the place where she grew up.'

'No, there you must be wrong, Hugo,' Sarah countered. 'I distinctly recall her informing me that this particular friend resides with her family a few miles outside London. I didn't think to ask for names. Although,' she added, after a moment's thought, 'her maid might know.'

At this Hugo looked at his sister sharply, his unease having soared to new heights in seconds. 'Do you mean to tell me she didn't take Aggie with her?'

'Why, no,' Sarah confirmed. 'Said something about her friend being adequately chaperoned, so she wouldn't require the services of a maid.

'And it's no earthly good you glowering at me in that odious fashion, Hugo,' she continued, when he began to regard her sternly, much as he had been wont to do when she had done something to annoy him during their childhood. 'Might I remind you I'm not Ruth's keeper. I'm sure she wouldn't take kindly to me ordering her about, attempting to dictate what she may and may not do. She's a woman grown and is more than capable of making her own decisions.'

Whipping out a piece of lace, Sarah proceeded to dab at her eyes, an action that had always proved worthwhile when confronted by her husband's displeasure, but which had little effect on her brother. 'I must say, Hugo, you will make an odious husband if you set up such a fuss just because she wishes to spend time with friends. I shall feel quite sorry for Ruth should she ever be foolish enough to marry you!'

For answer he strode over to the bell pull, and gave it an impatient tug. 'Is Aggie in the house?'

'As far as I'm aware she is,' Sarah returned petulantly. 'You forget, though, she isn't my servant.'

'Merry, be good enough to allow me the privacy of your library in order to question the woman. I'll get more out of her, I'm sure, if I speak with her alone.'

'Of course, be my guest,' he cordially invited. 'You suspect something's very much amiss, don't you, old fellow?'

Tossing the burgundy down his throat, Hugo placed the empty vessel on the mantelshelf behind him, before nodding his head. 'All I can say at present is that I've the distinctly uncomfortable feeling that something's not quite right.'

The footman arrived in answer to the summons and was dispatched forthwith to locate Agatha's whereabouts, leaving Hugo having only to cross the hall to await her arrival in the book-lined room.

Perching on the edge of the desk, he browsed through the previous day's edition of the *Morning Post*, which had obviously been saved for the master of the house to peruse. A quick scan of the printed pages revealed that nothing particularly momentous had occurred during his absence, at least nothing that would have sent Ruth hotfoot from the capital. But something most definitely had!

One glance at Agatha's decidedly sheepish expression, as she crept into the room a few moments later, only substantiated his belief that something had definitely occurred during his twenty-four-hour absence.

'Yes, come in and close the door, Aggie. You and I are going to have a little talk.' He waited for his command to be obeyed. 'I see by your expression that my early return has overset you somewhat.'

'Yes, Colonel, you m-might say that,' Agatha, ever truthful, admitted.

'Mmm, yes, I can imagine,' Hugo purred silkily. 'So let us not waste time on needless pleasantries or prevarication... Where is she?'

'I don't know, sir.' At his combined look of annoyance and disbelief, Agatha held out a pleading hand. 'Truly I don't, sir. Mistress said she wouldn't tell me, then I wouldn't need to lie.'

'Said that, did she? I see.' Hugo no longer disbelieved her. 'But there was no chance meeting with an old friend, was there, Aggie?'

'Not that I witnessed, sir, no.'

'No, I thought not,' he returned before requesting the maid to sit down. 'Now, Aggie, I want you to relate, in detail, all your mistress's movements during my absence.'

She shrugged. 'Nothing very much to tell, sir,

not really. About an hour after you'd left, she decides to visit the lady that stayed with us during the snowstorm, that Mrs Adams. Mistress just said she liked her above all the others and wished to pay a social visit. Oh,' she added, twin flags of colour now flying in her cheeks, 'of course I don't mean to include you in that, sir. She thinks the world of you.'

Deeply concerned though he was, Hugo couldn't help smiling to himself at this ingenuous revelation. 'I'm relieved to hear it! Now, to return to yesterday. What happened during the visit to Julia Adams?'

Again Agatha shrugged. 'Why, nothing, sir, as far as I'm aware. I awaited my mistress in the hall. She stayed about twenty minutes or so and then returned here, without seeing the lady.'

'Seems odd,' Hugo said, more to himself. 'As she'd taken the trouble to pay her a visit, why didn't she await Mrs Adams's return? She had no other pressing engagements, by any chance?'

'Not that I was aware. And, as I said, we came straight back here.'

Hugo considered for a moment before asking,

'And how did she seem on the return—troubled in any way?'

'I'd say more thoughtful than anything. In a world of her own, you might say.'

'Then what did she do?'

'Lady Lansdown hadn't returned, so she went straight upstairs to her room. Then, about half an hour later, she sent for me again. She gave a letter to the footman to deliver by hand and then we went out once more to some big coaching inn. I don't know London very well, sir. But I did overhear a little of the conversation Mistress had with the jarvey. Heard him mentioning Holborn, so I expect that inn is there, sir.'

'Go on,' Hugo prompted when the maid again fell silent.

'Well, Mistress goes into the inn, leaving me in the hackney carriage, and returns about ten minutes later and tells me she's leaving London in the morning, and won't be back until the next day.'

Again she held out one hand in a faintly imploring gesture and there was no mistaking the genuine anguish in her voice as she said, 'I begged her not to go, sir, and to await your return, but Miss Ruth would have none of it. She'd made up her mind. Said something about having to go alone, having to decide what to do by herself, and that she had to consider carefully, as more than one life might be ruined, or some such. She admitted it could be dangerous, but at the same time she didn't seem at all concerned.'

All at once Hugo felt himself in the grip of an icy-cold fear far stronger than anything he'd ever experienced in all the years he'd been in the army, as he suddenly recollected with terrifying clarity the most popular destination of those coaches setting out from a certain part of Holborn.

'Very well, Aggie, if there's nothing else you can tell me, you may go.'

'There's just one other thing, sir,' she revealed, turning again as she reached the door. 'If Miss Ruth fails to return tomorrow, I'm to give you the letter she wrote you before she left. Said I wasn't to give it to you unless she didn't return and I can't go against her wishes, sir.' All at once there was a distinctly artful gleam in her eyes. 'But there's nothing to stop you from taking it, now is there, sir? The letter isn't hidden in my room. It's there on the top of the chest of drawers for anyone to see.'

Hugo cast her a look of gratitude. 'Thank you, Aggie. Be good enough now to send James to me.'

The footman only confirmed what Hugo had already begun to suspect—that Ruth had written to Julia Adams directly on her return to the house the previous day.

'Was there any reply, James?'

'No, sir. And I was instructed not to wait for one. Miss Harrington was most particular about that. Gave me the money for a hackney carriage, sir. Told me to hand over the letter and to leave at once, without revealing where I'd come from or where I was bound. So I handed the letter over to a girl and just left.'

'I see,' Hugo murmured grimly, before dismissing the footman, and making his way up the two flights of stairs to the servants' quarters. His conscience smote him, but he didn't allow this to stop him discovering all the facts. Ruth's life might depend upon intelligent and decisive action. The one thing he shouldn't do now was allow his deep-seated fear for her safety prompt him into ill-considered behaviour.

He reached for what he supposed might be that

all-important confirmation of his worst fears and broke the seal. *My darling Hugo*, he read—an endearment that at any other time would have sent his heart soaring with untold delight, but which now was like sweet torment, increasing his anxiety fourfold.

He was no stranger to the pain of loss, but the raw anguish that gripped him in those following moments was like nothing he'd ever experienced before as he forced himself to read.

The fact that you are perusing this missive suggests that I have failed to return by the appointed time. None the less, I would still beg you not to act hastily, for there might be some perfectly reasonable explanation for my delay. My experiences of travelling about the land during these past weeks have taught me that a broken trace or wheel, or the loss of a horse's shoe, can delay one by several hours. There is, however, a further possible reason for my non-appearance.

She then went on to explain precisely what she had learned during his absence. The explanation was not embellished with any suppositions on her part, or flights of fancy, just the plain facts, which did little to ease the piercing anxiety. By the time he had finished reading her short, but detailed, account of the interview with both the sister and daughter of Julia Adams, he felt certain she had foolishly put herself in the gravest danger by arranging a private meeting with a possible murderess.

But Ruth herself clearly did not agree with him, as her last paragraph proved beyond doubt.

You once remarked upon the possibility that I might come to regret attempting to discover the truth and honesty obliges me to admit you might well be proved correct. That is why I felt compelled to see Julia Adams alone. I wanted to hear her version of events. I do not doubt that she was Sir George Hilliard's mistress, but even so I cannot bring myself to believe she is a cold-blooded killer. The rearing of her child strongly suggests a totally different character, one full of love and compassion.

I might be wrong, of course, and that is why I've arranged the meeting away from London, where it is much less likely that my association with you and your family will be discovered.

My only concern is for your safety, not my own, and would ask only one thing of you, Hugo—please do not act until you have discovered precisely what has become of me. More than one future might be irreparably damaged by foolish actions.

I rely on your sound judgement in this matter.
My love always
Ruth

'You may rely on my sound judgement, my darling girl. But you cannot expect me to sit back and do nothing when the girl who has become my whole reason for living might be in danger,' Hugo muttered, striding from the room, before proceeding to bound down the two flights of stairs, with an agility and speed quite remarkable in a man of his size.

He strode into the parlour, announcing that he would be leaving the house again within the hour, and quite uncaring that he had rudely interrupted an intimate tête-à-tête between a doting husband

and his wife. Not that either of them appeared unduly put out by the intrusion. If anything, both exchanged concerned glances after noting Hugo's grim expression.

Sarah was the first to find her voice. 'What's amiss, Hugo? Do you know where she's gone?'

'She isn't with a friend,' he assured her. 'But she might well be with a murderer. She's on her way to the south coast. And I must attempt to catch up with her, even though I'm well aware she has a several-hour start on me and is likely to be there now, or very close. I can only pray this meeting she's arranged doesn't take place until tomorrow.'

He turned to his brother-in-law, who continued to sit thoughtfully in his chair. 'Merry, I would beg the use of your carriage, but I won't risk your horses. They've travelled far enough this day. So, it behoves me to hire a post-chaise without delay. I'm sure you'll both excuse me if my farewells are not protracted.'

'Don't give us another thought, dear fellow!' Merry urged him. 'Quite understand. But bear with me a moment. I believe I'm correct in thinking this place she's heading for is not so far distant from Brighton?'

'Well…what of it?' Hugo demanded impatiently, desperate to be on his way.

'In my reprehensible youth, my friends and I used to ride to Brighton on horseback for a wager. Much faster than post-chaise. I have a number of friends living still along the old run. My old lad in the stables here is up to your weight and will see you easily on your first leg, and from there…well, you can call on my friends for fresh mounts. You go and do what needs to be done to make ready for your departure and I'll write a few brief letters. You'll easily reach the gel before nightfall!'

The following morning Ruth was obliged to break her fast in her bedchamber, as the inn at which she was staying had no private parlour. This had come as no very real surprise. The little seaside town had yet to achieve the popularity of such coastal resorts as Brighton. Added to which, the inn was not located on one of the main post roads and, as a result, did not attract too much custom other than local patronage. All the same, mine host, and his good lady wife, kept a clean house and had done their utmost to be obliging and to make her feel welcome.

As she placed the breakfast tray to one side and set about getting herself ready for the day ahead, she couldn't help reflecting on how different her recent journey had been compared to the one she had embarked upon several weeks before.

She had missed not having Hugo with her more than she could ever have supposed possible. In a few short weeks he had come to mean everything to her. Finally, she realised just how empty her life would be without him. Surely swallowing her pride was a small price to pay to be with someone who cared deeply for her, wanted her for his wife, even though she wasn't his ideal mate, the great love of his life?

Not only had she missed Hugo's tender attentions, she had missed not having Agatha with her, too! That, she reflected, as she seated herself before the mirror at the dressing table, had been a gross error of judgement on her part. Had she to make the choice again, she would still forgo Hugo's company, but she wasn't so very certain she'd willingly forgo Agatha's. Travelling for miles with absolutely no one to talk with to pass the time had definitely added to the tedium of the journey. Not only that, she had no one to help her dress, or arrange her hair!

She shook her head, while silently taking herself to task. Really, she had become quite spoilt since coming into all that money! Why, she was almost incapable of doing anything for herself nowadays, she decided, after taking three attempts to arrange her hair in a simple chignon.

Although not wholly satisfied with her final effort, she decided not to waste more time in trying to improve on it. In her letter she had proposed to meet Mrs Adams on the hour; and although it could not be taken for granted that Julia would concern herself to make the journey to the coast, Ruth had no intention of not being on the start of that cliff walk at the appointed time.

Thankfully, the donning of her bonnet instantly concealed her woefully inadequate attempt at dressing her own hair. Reasonably satisfied with her appearance, she picked up her parasol and repaired to the floor below, which was now empty of those noisy revellers who had kept her awake the night before. Not even mine host was anywhere to be seen, a circumstance which pleased her. The fewer people to witness her movements, the better she would like it. Of course, much still depended on what Julia had to say. None the less, if her instincts were proved correct, she had already decided what action she intended to take and a clandestine meeting would suit her purpose far better.

Feeling smugly satisfied, she slipped silently out of the inn, little realising that a pair of distinctly troubled blue eyes had been watching her every move since the moment she had left her bedchamber. In blissful ignorance she crossed the road that separated the row of buildings from the seashore. On she walked to where the shingle beach gave way to an area of sand dunes and the shoreline then began to rise. Beyond the dunes lay a rocky outcrop that, in turn, gave way to a steeply sloping grassy walk up to the summit of the cliffs.

Ruth paused to catch her breath and to look out across the sea, enjoying the freshness of the sea air. It was little wonder that those who could well afford to do so travelled to the coast for relaxation and a change of air. It was so clean and calming here, away from the bustle and unpleasant odours of the capital.

No sooner had the thought entered her head than

a shot rang out, forcing her back to the present with a start. She swung round in an attempt to locate from where the pistol had been discharged, only to discover none other than Julia Adams standing directly behind her, hand outstretched, blue eyes cold, completely lacking any obvious emotion. All concerns about the pistol shot then faded from Ruth's thoughts when, a moment later, fingers grasped her arm and she found herself being hauled back from the edge of the upward-sloping path.

That one simple action told Ruth most everything she needed to know. She had been blissfully unaware of Julia's close proximity. The woman could so easily have pushed her over on to the rocky shoreline a few feet below and there didn't seem to be a soul about who might have witnessed such an encounter.

'It's dangerous to stand so close to the edge, Miss Harrington. One could so easily lose one's footing. More than one has met his maker along this stretch of coastline.'

'Is that how Sir George Hilliard met his?' she asked bluntly and received a twisted smile in response.

Surprisingly she wasn't alarmed by it. The moment she'd discovered her companion's guilty secret she had felt that arranging the meeting here might prove worthwhile; that here Julia would be more likely to relive more keenly those events that were to drastically change the course of her life; that here, above anywhere, Julia would find it difficult to conceal the truth.

What Ruth saw now in her companion's expression only went to substantiate this. Certainly, there was a trace of wry amusement, but no hint of malevolence as Julia said, 'If that is a polite way of asking me whether I pushed him over the edge, then the answer is no. Shall we walk back towards the town, Miss Harrington?' she added and proceeded to do so, without waiting for a response. 'As you can possibly imagine, this location doesn't hold too many happy memories for me.'

'No, I suppose not,' Ruth responded, having automatically complied with her companion's request. 'Might I be permitted to know how it happened?'

Again the widow smiled crookedly. 'I should imagine you've already pieced together the terrible mistake I made when I foolishly knew no better and the consequences of that mistake.' The twisted smile was there again. 'Although I do not regret that. My daughter means everything to me, Miss Harrington. I would do almost…anything to protect her.'

A rough wooden bench provided a welcome place to sit and rest themselves while they stared out across the sea, until finally the silence between them was broken by Julia who admitted, 'I was such a naïve young fool back then, reared as I was by an impoverished, widower clergyman. But circumstances obliged me to spread my wings.'

'So you applied and obtained a position as governess in the household of Sir George Hilliard,' Ruth prompted when the silence again threatened to lengthen between them.

'It was Lady Hilliard who engaged me,' she revealed, 'not her husband. I didn't meet him for several weeks. Then, one day Lady Hilliard decides to leave the country house and join her husband in the capital. At the time I was given no explanation for the move. I assumed that the mistress was merely missing her husband. I had no notion that she was quite accustomed to his philandering ways and frequently joined him in the capital without prior warning in order to keep a watchful eye on him. Poor woman, she certainly played into his hands on that occasion.'

The twisted smile this time was clearly self-deprecating. 'I told you I was a naïve little fool. I believed it was love at first sight for both him and me. I felt flattered when the handsome master of the house began to pay daily visits to the schoolroom. I believed him when he visited my room at nights and told me he loved me. It was a relatively easy thing for us to be together, his wife having moved into a separate apartment, caring for her youngest child who had come down with a fever.'

A thought suddenly occurred to Ruth. 'Did you know the doctor in attendance at the time was none other than Dr Dent?'

The look of astonishment was so spontaneous that Ruth didn't doubt the reaction was genuine. 'Great heavens! I never knew that,' Julia confessed. 'It's a small world, indeed! As I mentioned before, Lady Hilliard, with her youngest daughter, kept to a suite of rooms, well away from the other children. Philip, and his two older sisters, stayed mostly with me, on the floor above in the schoolroom. Whenever we went out we used the back staircase, so I never saw the daily comings and goings, or saw anyone who visited the house. The only contact I had, apart from the children and servants, was with the master of the house.'

She closed her eyes, as though to obliterate a painful image. 'I retained at least a modicum of decency, though. I insisted our affair could not continue under the roof where his wife was fully occupied caring for her youngest daughter, so he arranged for me to come down here, well away from his family and dangers of exposure.'

She turned and pointed. 'It was that house, there, the one at the end of the terrace. Such a little simpleton was I, I even supposed my lover had purchased it for me and intended to join me permanently once his child had regained her health.' Her shout of laughter was distinctly mirthless. 'I discovered that foolish mistake later, after his visits had become increasingly less frequent. Foolishly, I imagined it was concern over his youngest child that kept him in London. I never supposed he was already grooming my replacement. I went two months without seeing him, during which time I realised I was with child. I imagined he would be pleased. How wrong I was!'

Ruth studied Julia as she turned her head to stare up at the steeply sloping path that ran perilously close to the cliff edge in certain parts, and thought she could detect a touch of sadness in those blue depths.

'You were out walking the cliff path when you told him, were you not?'

Julia nodded as she glanced again at the steeply upward-sloping path. 'We were about halfway up when I broke the news to him. I hoped it might in some way ease the pain of losing his youngest child, knowing that he had created a new life. There was a cruel, twisted smile on his lips as he uttered those words I shall never forget, "How very careless of you, m'dear! What possible use are you to me now? What use are you to any man now, carrying a gentleman's by-blow?" I shall not sully your ears with any of his several other cruel taunts. Suffice it to say I was left in no doubt about his true character, or his true feelings for me. I believe I did lash out at him. He merely stepped back a pace or two, laughing in a heartless way at my pathetic attempt to inflict pain. Through the haze of my shame and anger, I seem to remember I was aware that he had moved closer to the cliff edge. He had been drinking heavily that day and throughout our walk continued to reduce the contents of the hip flask he carried. Strangely enough it was the recovery of that engraved silver flask that helped identify him. I remember him swaying...I remember him losing his footing... And, yes, perhaps I might have saved him had I attempted to grasp at the folds of his cloak. But I did not push him over the edge, Miss Harrington, though I made not the least attempt to steady him. Something in me died that day, I think. I didn't even trouble to discover if he was still alive. I merely turned and walked back towards the town.'

'Little wonder you paid scant attention to others walking the cliffs that day,' Ruth remarked when once again Julia fell silent, no doubt locked in those heartrending reflections.

'I remember no one, Miss Harrington,' she confirmed. 'I was left totally numbed by Hilliard's cruel rejection and it took quite some time for me even to begin to recover. I did attain a great deal of solace and pleasure in raising my daughter. Alice quickly became everything to me. I wasn't going to allow her life to be ruined because of my foolish mistake, not if I could do anything to avoid it. I knew Lady Lindley was referring to me at the dinner table that evening. I also knew she was no threat to me, personally. My conscience was clear—she couldn't possibly have accused me of any crime, least of all murder. But she could harm Alice, if it became known I was once one of Hilliard's many mistresses.'

Ruth understood perfectly. 'Yes, I can fully appreciate why you've never told her the truth. I cannot imagine she would benefit from knowing her natural father was a heartless philanderer. Had I been in your position I would have wanted my daughter to remain in ignorance. And Lady Beatrice, of course, was a real threat... But did you kill her to ensure her silence?'

After several long moments Julia parted her lips to say, without a trace of emotion, 'If you want the absolute truth…then, yes. I suppose I must have done.'

Oh, dear God no! Ruth turned her head to look

out across the Channel once more. The one thing she had never wished to hear…

Now what was she supposed to do?

Chapter Thirteen

An hour later, after strolling back to the inn with Julia, and seeing her safely on her way in the gig hired from a Brighton hostelry, Ruth didn't wish to delay in making ready for her own departure and was surprised to discover her overnight bag already packed and awaiting her in one corner of the taproom.

Although slightly taken aback, she wasn't unduly troubled and assumed the landlady, having been aware of her patron's desire to be away as early as possible, had perhaps kindly taken it upon herself to do the packing when she had gone to the chamber in order to collect the breakfast tray.

The landlord didn't leave her labouring under this misconception for very long. 'No, 'twern't the wife packed for you, miss. Wouldn't do that, not without you giving 'er leave to do so first.

No, 'twere the gentleman, the one that arrived an hour or so after you did, miss, that packed your bag and paid your shot.'

'Settled my bill…?' For a moment or two Ruth thought she must surely have misunderstood. 'Gentleman…? What gentleman? I know no gentlemen hereabouts.'

'Oh, yes, you do, my girl,' a beloved deep voice countered from the general direction of the entrance porch and Ruth swung round to discover that much taller-than-average frame leaning against the doorjamb.

Uncaring that his stern expression was proof enough that he was not altogether pleased, she made her own feelings abundantly clear. Her heart having finally won the battle over those twin evils of pride and jealousy, she uttered a spontaneous squeal of delight before very nearly launching herself into his arms. He seemed to accept her willingly enough, holding her gently captive while she stood on tiptoe to place a chaste salute at one corner of his mouth.

His lips twitched slightly as he stared down into dark eyes that were aglow now with undisguised delight at seeing him. 'You'll need to do a deal better than that, my girl, if you're to stand the remotest chance of getting back into my good books.'

He put her from him most reluctantly. 'And before you scandalise the landlord further by your immodest displays, we'd best be on our way. The carriage awaits us and my gear is already stashed aboard', and so saying Hugo swept up the overnight bag and escorted her outside to the post-chaise.

Disposed though he might have been to play the irate suitor a while longer, while leaving her in no doubt about what he thought of her downright dangerous escapade, he found he wasn't proof against a sweetly loving smile, or the small hand that stole into his a moment after he had closed the carriage door and had seated himself beside her. Nor was he able to delay further in finding an outlet for those numerous emotions he'd managed successfully to suppress during the past twenty-four hours.

That she was a willing recipient of these, his more ardent displays of masculine passion, boded very well for their future life together. Eventually, though, he reluctantly set her from him a little, while he retained a semblance of control over his rapidly increasing ardour.

'Oh, God! If anything had happened to you,' he murmured huskily into the soft chestnut curls. 'You must promise me never again to take such a foolish risk.'

Although she smiled, Ruth was moved by his evident fears for her safety and promptly set about attempting to placate him by explaining the reasons for her actions, and revealing, too, in part, what she had discovered that morning.

Easing herself a little away, she gazed up in to his anxious face. 'I've already appreciated, as you're here, that you must have returned earlier than planned from the races and read the note I left for you, so you're aware of what I discovered when I visited Julia's home—that she was once employed as governess in the Hilliard household.'

He nodded. 'And the daughter bears a marked resemblance to Sir Philip Hilliard, you say.'

'Yes, she does,' Ruth confirmed, before smiling wryly. 'I'm afraid I did poor Julia an injustice by supposing her widowed state merely assumed in order to maintain respectability. She did, in fact, legally marry a Mr John Adams. He was a retired notary and in poor health. He came here for a few weeks during that summer Julia was here. He hoped the sea air would improve his consumptive condition. They met one day while out walking. He quickly became aware of Julia's unfortunate— er—predicament and offered a solution to all her woes. In exchange for taking care of him during the last months of his life, he would not only give her the protection of his name, but would leave her everything he owned to enable her to raise her child in moderate comfort. He died before Alice was born, but the girl has always believed him to be her father.'

'And you say you don't believe Julia killed her daughter's natural father?'

Ruth didn't hesitate even for a moment before shaking her head. There was no doubt in her mind whatsoever of Julia's innocence. 'She didn't attempt to deny they did exchange harsh words, but she didn't push him to his death, though she freely admitted she made no attempt to prevent him falling.'

'And what about Lady Beatrice…? Did she murder her?'

'She attempted to, yes,' Ruth revealed after a moment.

'Good gad!' Hugo exclaimed, visibly paling. 'I'm not sorry now that I did follow you from the inn, or fired that warning shot. Not that I suppose you'd have sustained more than a bruise or two had she pushed you over the edge from where you were standing. The drop couldn't have been more than a few feet. I could, I suppose, have made my presence known by shouting a warning, but I did appreciate that you wished to meet Julia on your own.'

Memory stirred. 'So it was you who fired that shot.' She smiled lovingly up at him. 'You needn't have worried. Julia never had any intention of attempting to harm me.'

'I realised that myself when I saw her draw you away from the path's edge. I watched for a little longer, then feeling confident you were in no danger I returned to the inn to ensure my presence wouldn't be discovered. But I must confess I began to be concerned again. You were away a long time.'

After taking a moment to position herself more comfortably in the crook of his arm, Ruth decided to reveal everything she'd learned that morning, and began by reminding him of how they had discovered Julia lurking in the passageway at Dunsterford Hall all those months ago. 'She had been attempting to locate Lady Bea's bedchamber, in the hope of speaking with her in private, and pleading with her not to divulge what she'd witnessed on that cliff walk all those years before.

'It wasn't a guilty conscience she was suffering from,' Ruth assured him, 'at least not in respect of murdering Hilliard. But she was desperately concerned about her daughter, and what effect it would have on Alice if she were ever to discover she was not the legitimate offspring of John Adams.'

'Well, that's understandable,' Hugo remarked fair-mindedly. 'After all, the girl had been brought up to believe her birth was entirely respectable.'

'Precisely!' Ruth sighed. 'But what happened next Julia herself can only put down as having been in the grip of insane desperation. It was only as she saw the hot toddy I'd made for Lady Beatrice that the idea all at once occurred to her. On the pretext of requiring a nightdress, she succeeded in getting rid of me for those few precious minutes necessary to slip back into her own room to locate a bottle of laudanum. She was sharing a chamber with Miss Dent, you may remember. And Miss Dent always carried a small case containing various nostrums her brother considered indispensable when travelling about the land. As Miss Dent was already sound asleep, it was a simple matter for Julia to extract the bottle she was looking for.'

'Ah, yes!' he said, raising a triumphant finger. 'I distinctly recall detecting laudanum in the remains of that toddy you made.'

'But unlike you,' she reminded him, 'Lady Bea never supposed for a moment that I'd attempted to drug her.'

She raised her eyes to cast him a brief, accusing look. His attempt at appearing shamefaced was belied somewhat by a wicked glint in his eyes. 'Furthermore,' she continued, after quickly deciding little would be achieved by remonstrating with him, 'Lady Beatrice had vast experience in the use of opiates and, according to what Julia told me earlier, Lady Bea took one sip and tossed most of what had remained out of the window, leaving just a little in the bottom so as to give the impression she had drunk it. And that is precisely what Julia had assumed when she went into the bed-chamber later, via my room.'

'It's a wonder she didn't wake you, my darling,' Hugo remarked, while absently twisting one shining chestnut lock round his finger.

'Something did rouse me and I do recall detecting a flickering light beneath the communicating door, but I quickly went back to sleep. I was feeling tired after the long day I'd had. I certainly didn't hear anything of what subsequently took place within the adjoining chamber.'

'And what did take place?' Hugo prompted when Ruth fell silent, attempting to recall, verbatim, Julia's confession. 'She entered the room to discover a lighted candle on the bedside table. Lady Beatrice, though, appeared in the throes of a drug-induced sleep. She then slid one of the pillows from beneath her head, and placed it over Lady Bea's face.'

'So, she did attempt to murder her?'

'Oh, yes, Hugo, she did. But the instant Lady Bea began to struggle, clawing at the pillow, Julia, according to her own admission, regained her senses. She dropped the pillow on to the floor, appalled at what she had just attempted to do.

'What happened next I can only piece together from what I've been told. Julia then attempted to reason with Lady Bea, assuring her that she hadn't murdered Sir George Hilliard and pleading with her not to spread the encounter she had witnessed on the cliff walk that day abroad, as her daughter would be the one to suffer, not her. According to Julia, Lady Bea said she would consider the matter further and discuss it again in the morning.'

'And you believed her, believed she left Lady Bea alive and well in her bed?' Hugo prompted when Ruth again fell silent, collecting her thoughts.

'Alive, certainly. And, yes, I did believe her, and for various reasons. Firstly, Julia said when she left the room Lady Bea was propped against her pillows, smiling. It was not a pleasant smile—twisted, almost smugly satisfied, Julia described it. And I can well believe it because I'd witnessed that selfsame smile on numerous occasions during those years I'd spent at Dunsterford Hall. Sadly, Lady Bea attained some perverse pleasure out of other people's misery. One might almost say there was a sadistic flaw in her character. She would have enjoyed leaving Julia on tenterhooks until the morning.

'Secondly, someone must have picked up that pillow and blown out that candle. The candle had not guttered and someone had replaced that pillow. And the most intriguing fact of all is that Julia, for fear of rousing me, returned to her bedchamber by way of the door leading to the landing, not through my chamber again. So who relocked it? Julia couldn't have done so. The key remained on the inside.'

Ruth then shrugged, ever the realist. 'She could have lied, of course, and left using my room. But I don't think so. When she visited the bedchamber the following morning, I swear her shock at seeing Lady Beatrice lying there wasn't feigned, simply because the last time she'd seen her she'd been very much alive. No, I believe Lady Bea relocked the door herself and replaced the pillow. Then, sometime before morning, she suffered some kind of seizure. In her last throes she must have clawed at the bedcover, and in so doing clasped again that piece of lace she had torn from the pillow earlier.' She shrugged. 'Who can say?'

'So what do you intend to do now?' Hugo asked, even though he suspected he already knew the answer.

She confirmed it a moment later. 'Why, nothing! Why should I? I don't believe Julia murdered anyone. And I certainly cannot find it within me to blame her for attempting to protect her daughter. Whether she was directly responsible for causing the seizure that subsequently killed Lady Beatrice we can only speculate. But that is something she herself must live with. What I flatly refuse to do is ruin young Alice's life. I shan't be the one to deprive her of a mother who loves her and has done her utmost to protect her and raise her decently. And it will definitely not improve her lot to discover that she wasn't a respectable notary's daughter, but the by-blow of a rakehell!'

At this blunt choice of language, Hugo turned his head away in order to conceal his twitching smile and by so doing drew Ruth's attention for the first time since setting out to the view beyond the window.

She frowned. 'Are we going back a different way? I cannot recall passing through such a densely wooded area prior to arriving at the inn yesterday.'

'We are not returning to London, my darling,' Hugo apprised her, determinedly, 'at least, not for a week or so. You may not be sure where your future lies, but I most certainly do. So, we're now heading towards the border with Kent, where we shall stay with my good friend the Viscount and his charming lady wife for a week or two. I fully intend to obtain a special licence as soon as may be, so that when we do return to the capital to enjoy the remainder of the Season together, we do so as man and wife, and we'll not take up so much room in my brother-in-law's home, as we shall be sharing one bedchamber.'

The prospect clearly pleased him as he was looking quite smugly satisfied with himself. And, in truth, Ruth couldn't find it within herself to object to these almost cavalier arrangements he was making for her future, as her heart continued to remain firmly in charge of her head. Only one typically feminine objection instantly sprang to mind.

'It might possibly have escaped your notice, but I brought with me only the barest essentials and sufficient clothing for an overnight stay, not a so-journ at a country mansion.'

'Fear not, my angel, all has been arranged,' he assured her. 'Aggie, accompanied by my man Finn, left the capital yesterday afternoon for Kent, taking most all our belongings and carrying a letter to my friend the Viscount, apprising him of our intention to be his guests for the following couple of weeks.'

Ruth couldn't help smiling at this piece of down-right impertinence. Really, it was the outside of enough to inflict himself, not to mention a complete stranger, on the Kingsleys without receiving an invitation to do so first! 'Well, let's hope they haven't made other plans and are away from home.'

'Oh, they'll be there, right enough,' Hugo assured her blithely, thereby betraying his supreme unconcern. 'Luke told me himself they were spending the rest of spring and summer quietly at Kingsley Hall. They'll not be travelling any great distances until Briony's had the baby. And before you raise her condition as a reason not to inflict ourselves upon them,' he added, reading her thoughts with unerring accuracy, 'I can tell you now they would both be grievously disappointed were they ever to discover we used that as an excuse not to visit them, as they employ an army of servants.'

'Well, let us hope we don't scandalise them both by the improper mode of our arrival.' She regarded him accusingly. 'Who was it who told me that no gently nurtured female would consider travelling alone with a gentleman in a closed carriage?'

A wickedly smug and satisfied smile played about his mouth. 'Yes, that was rather well done of me, even though I say so myself. Ruined in the eyes of the world, your only option now, my angel, is to accept the protection of my name, especially as there's no guarantee we'll arrive at Kingsley Hall before nightfall. We might be obliged to put up at an inn somewhere and complete the journey in the morning.'

'You needn't have resorted to such extremes,' she assured him, before resting her head against his shoulder once more, 'as I had already decided I should very much like to spend the rest of my life with you. And I promise you, Hugo, I shall do everything within my power to make you happy.'

It wasn't so much the assurance itself that gave him pause for thought as the hint of determination he couldn't fail to detect in the soft voice. Placing his fingers beneath her chin, he easily raised her eyes to his.

'And why should you suppose there's a possibility you might not do so?' he demanded to know, thereby revealing the sagacity for which he was famed.

Although by dint of lowering her lids she easily achieved breaking the hold of that fiercely direct gaze, Ruth knew well enough that he was far too perceptive to be deceived by some trifling response. Besides which, it couldn't hurt, surely, for him to know that she perfectly understood her position in his affections?

'Because I know I wasn't your first choice for a wife,' she said, doing her level best to sound quite matter of fact. 'I'm well aware you've been in love before, and that if cruel fate had not intervened you would have married long ago.'

She wasn't quite sure what reaction she might obtain. Never in her wildest imaginings did she expect to see him clap an impatient hand across his eyes, while giving vent to a low, threatening growl.

'I'll ring my interfering sister's blasted neck when we get back to London!' he vowed, sounding as though he'd relish the exercise.

Placing both hands on her shoulders, he held her away, the better to search every endearing contour of the face he had swiftly grown to adore. 'What maudlin nonsense has she been spouting in your ears since you've been staying with her, my darling? No, don't tell me!' he ordered in the next breath. 'I can guess. Told you some sentimental rubbish about me wearing the willow for a girl called Alicia Thorndyke, I'll wager!'

'Well, I—er…' Although somewhat confused, there was no doubt in Ruth's mind that she might well have been labouring under a huge misconception during these past weeks, not to say months. Naturally, her spirits soared at the mere thought that she might have been grossly misinformed, while at the same time she felt she ought to do her utmost to protect the woman who was shortly to become her sister.

'Oh, Hugo, you mustn't blame Sarah,' she implored. 'Lady Beatrice told me months ago that you were once engaged to be married and hadn't so much as looked at another woman since the death of your fiancée.'

'Heaven spare me! I would have supposed that you, my angel, would have had more sense than to believe such twaddle!' he told her with thinly veiled impatience. 'What was I doing during the past ten years or so? Answer me that! I was carving out a career for myself in the army, that's what,' he continued without granting her the opportunity to edge in a word. Not that she minded, of course. His every contradiction of what she had foolishly supposed to be true was acting like a powerful restorative, sending her spirits soaring to giddy new heights of delight.

'Half that period was spent fighting the French,' he continued meditatively. 'A fine sort of a fellow I'd have been had I taken a wife, when there was every chance I might not return home to her. And as for those other years…well, they were spent enjoying my bachelor state, not pining for a lost love.

'Now, I'm not denying that I wasn't damnably cut up over Alicia's death, because I was. And, maybe, had she lived, we would one day have married. But I wasn't in the least opposed to waiting a year or two before announcing anything official. Looking back, I appreciate now that my father had been right. We were too young, at least I was. I appreciate, also, now how a fellow's preferences can change.

'And just to set the record straight I've never done this before', and so saying he delved into the pocket of his jacket to draw out a small square box, which he deftly opened in order to slide its contents on to the third finger of her left hand.

He raised his hands to cup a face that was staring in awestruck silence at the sparkling diamond now nestling on her finger. 'I've never searched for a replacement for Alicia. Nor have I consciously been on the lookout for a wife. I just chanced upon the perfect girl for me one early October afternoon, when I was obliged to put up at an unprepossessing pile during a snowstorm. I might not have realised then, but I certainly do now… You are the only girl I want.'

No further explanations were necessary as far as Ruth was concerned. She was now firmly convinced that her future husband was every bit as much in love with her as she was with him, and they would achieve true happiness only by spending the future together.

* * * * *

MILLS & BOON®

Why shop at millsandboon.co.uk?

Each year, thousands of romance readers find their perfect read at millsandboon.co.uk. That's because we're passionate about bringing you the very best romantic fiction. Here are some of the advantages of shopping at www.millsandboon.co.uk:

* **Get new books first**—you'll be able to buy your favourite books one month before they hit the shops

* **Get exclusive discounts**—you'll also be able to buy our specially created monthly collections, with up to 50% off the RRP

* **Find your favourite authors**—latest news, interviews and new releases for all your favourite authors and series on our website, plus ideas for what to try next

* **Join in**—once you've bought your favourite books, don't forget to register with us to rate, review and join in the discussions

Visit **www.millsandboon.co.uk**
for all this and more today!